P9-CLW-526

HATE
NOTES

OTHER TITLES BY VI KEELAND AND PENELOPE WARD

Other Titles by Vi Keeland

HATE
NOTES

VI KEELAND
PENELOPE WARD

Montlake
Romance

This is a work of fiction. Names, characters, organizations, places, events, and incidents are either products of the author's imagination or are used fictitiously.

Text copyright © 2018 by Vi Keeland and Penelope Ward
All rights reserved.

No part of this book may be reproduced, or stored in a retrieval system, or transmitted in any form or by any means, electronic, mechanical, photocopying, recording, or otherwise, without express written permission of the publisher.

Published by Montlake Romance, Seattle

www.apub.com

Amazon, the Amazon logo, and Montlake Romance are trademarks of Amazon.com, Inc., or its affiliates.

ISBN-13: 9781503904484
ISBN-10: 1503904482

Cover design by Eileen Carey

Printed in the United States of America

To Kimberly, for finding Reed and Charlotte the right home.

CHAPTER 1

CHARLOTTE

I wouldn't have been caught dead in here a year ago. Don't take that the wrong way—I'm not a snob. Growing up, my mom and I spent hours combing the racks at the secondhand store. And that was back when secondhand was called Goodwill, and the stores were predominantly in blue-collar neighborhoods. These days, used is called vintage and sold on the Upper East Side for a small fortune.

I sported "gently worn" before the gentrification of Brooklyn.

Secondhand was not my issue. My problem with used wedding dresses was the stories I imagined they carried with them.

Why are they here?

I pulled a Vera Wang sweetheart ball gown with a crisscross bodice and cascading tulle skirt from the rack. *Fairy-tale expectations. Divorced after six months,* I decided. A delicate lace Monique Lhuillier mermaid dress—*the groom died in a horrific car accident.* The devastated bride-to-never-be donated it to the church for its annual tag sale. A savvy shopper picked it up for a steal and tripled the return on her investment by reselling it.

Every used dress had a story, and mine belonged on the *He turned out to be a cheating son of a bitch* rack. I sighed and returned to the two women bickering at the front desk in Russian.

"It's from next year's collection, yes?" the taller woman with bizarre, unevenly drawn eyebrows asked.

I tried not to stare at them, but failed. "Yes. It's from the Marchesa spring collection."

The women had been flipping through catalogs, even though I'd told them twenty minutes ago when I walked in that the dress was from an unpublished future collection. I assumed they wanted to get an idea of the designer's original prices.

"I don't think you'll find it in there yet. My future mother-in-law—" I corrected myself. "My *ex*–future mother-in-law is related to one of the designers or something."

The women stared at me for a moment and then resumed bickering.

Okay, then. "I guess you need more time," I mumbled.

Toward the back of the store, I found a rack labeled CUSTUM MADE. I smiled. Todd's mother would've had a heart attack if I'd taken her to a place where the signs were misspelled. She'd been appalled when I went to look at a dress in a shop that didn't serve her champagne while I was in the fitting room. God, I'd really been drunk on the Roth Kool-Aid and had nearly turned into one of those snooty bitches.

Running my fingertips along the custom-made gowns, I sighed. These dresses probably had even more interesting stories behind them. Eclectic brides too free-spirited for their boring boyfriends or husbands. These were strong-minded women who went against the grain, women who marched at political rallies, women who knew what they wanted.

I stopped at an A-line white dress embellished with bloodred roses. The corset bodice had red piping running along the bones. *Left her banker boyfriend for the French artist next door, and this was the dress she wore when she married Pierre.*

No designer dress could have possibly worked for these women, because they knew exactly what they wanted and weren't afraid to say it. They went after their hearts' desires. I envied them. I used to *be* one of them.

Deep down, I was a custum girl—misspelling intended. When had I lost my way and become a conformist? I hadn't had the balls to admit my feelings to Todd's mother, which was how I ended up with the fancy, boring wedding dress to begin with.

When I got to the last dress on the Custum rack, I had to stop for a moment.

Feathers!

They were the most beautiful feathers I'd ever seen. And this dress wasn't white; it was blush. This dress was *everything*. It was exactly what I would have picked if I could have *custum*-designed a dress. This wasn't just any dress. This was THE dress. The top was strapless with a slight curve. Smaller, wispy feathers peeked out of the neckline. Lace overlay covered the entire bodice, which led to a beautiful trumpet-style skirt. And the bottom was a crescendo of feathers. This dress *sang*. It was magical.

One of the women up front saw me eyeing it.

"Can I try this on?"

She nodded, leading me to a dressing room in the back.

I undressed and carefully slid the dress up. Unfortunately, my dream dress was a size too small. All the stress eating I'd been doing lately had caught up with me.

So I left the back unzipped and marveled at myself in the mirror. *This.* This did not look like a twenty-seven-year-old who'd just dumped her cheating fiancé. This did not look like someone who needed to sell her wedding dress to be able to eat something other than ramen noodles for two meals each day.

This dress made me feel like someone who hadn't a care in the world. I didn't want to take it off. But honestly, I was sweating and didn't want to ruin it.

Before I removed it, I looked at myself in the mirror one last time and introduced myself to the imaginary person admiring the new me.

Standing confidently with my hands on my hips, I said, "Hello, I'm Charlotte Darling." I laughed, because I sort of sounded like a news reporter.

After I slipped off the dress, a patch of blue on the inside caught my eye. It was a piece of stationery stitched into the inside lining.

Something borrowed, something blue, something old, something new. That's how it went, right? Or was it the other way around?

It occurred to me that perhaps this was supposed to be the "something blue."

Lifting the material closer, I squinted to read the note. At the top, *From the desk of Reed Eastwood* was embossed. I ran my finger over each letter as I read.

> *To Allison—*
> *"She said, 'Forgive me for being a dreamer,' and he took*
> *her by the hand and replied, 'Forgive me for not being*
> *here sooner to dream with you.'"—J. Iron Word*
> *Thank you for making all of my dreams come true.*
> *Your love,*
> *Reed*

My heart pounded. That had to be the most romantic thing I'd ever read. I couldn't begin to imagine how this dress ended up here. How could any woman in her right mind give such a powerful sentiment away? If I'd thought this dress was everything before . . . now, it was definitely *everything.*

Reed Eastwood had loved her. *Oh no.* I hoped Allison hadn't died. Because a man who writes those words to someone doesn't just fall out of love.

The attendant called out to me. "Everything okay?"

I pulled the curtain back to face her. "Yes . . . yes. I seem to have fallen in love with this dress, actually. Have you figured out how much I can get back for my Marchesa?"

She shook her head. "We don't give money. You get store credit."

Shit.

I really needed the cash.

I pointed to the blush-feather dress. "How much would this dress cost?"

"We can give even exchange."

It was tempting. The dress was my spirit animal, and I felt like the note could have been written for me by my imaginary perfect fiancé. I didn't want to guess the story behind this one. I wanted to *live* it, create my own story for this dress. Maybe not today, but someday in the future. I wanted a man who appreciated me, who wanted to share in my dreams, and who loved me unconditionally. I wanted a man who would leave me a note like this.

This dress needed to hang in my closet as a daily reminder that true love can exist.

I said the words before I could change my mind. "I'll take it."

CHAPTER 2

CHARLOTTE

Two months later

My résumé needed a makeover. After two hours online searching the help-wanted ads, I'd realized I was going to have to embellish my skills a bit.

The crappy temp job I'd finished today could spruce up my administrative experience. At least it would look good on paper. I called up my sad excuse for a résumé in Word and added my latest position as a legal assistant.

Worman and Associates. Now there's a name that fits. David *Worm*an, the attorney I'd just finished a thirty-day temp gig for, was indeed half worm, half man. After I typed in the dates and address, I sat back in my seat and thought about what I could list as experience gained working for that jackass.

Let's see. I tapped my finger to my chin. *What did I do for the worm man this week? Hmm . . .* Yesterday, I'd removed his hand from my ass while threatening to file a complaint with the EEOC. Yes, that needed to be on there. I typed:

Adept at multitasking in a high-pressure environment.

On Tuesday, the worm had taught me how to backdate the postage-stamp machine so the IRS would think his late tax check was timely and wouldn't charge him a penalty. *Good stuff.* That needed to be added, too.

Thrives within deadline-driven conditions.

Last week, he sent me to La Perla to pick up two gifts—something nice for his wife's birthday, and something sexy for a "special friend." I might have added a little something for myself on the jerk's bill. Lord knows I couldn't afford a thirty-eight-dollar thong these days.

Demonstrates superb work ethic and commitment to special projects.

After adding a few more bullshit, buzzword-phrased accomplishments, I sent my résumé off to a dozen new temp agencies and rewarded myself with a full-to-the-brim glass of wine.

What an exciting life I led. *Twenty-seven and single in New York City on a Friday night, and I'm sporting sweats and a T-shirt at barely eight o'clock.* But I had no desire to go out. No desire to sip sixteen-dollar martinis at fancy bars where men like Todd wore expensive suits to hide their inner wolf. So instead, I clicked on Facebook and decided to check out the lives everyone else had—at least the ones they put on display.

My newsfeed was full of typical Friday-night posts—happy-hour smiles, pictures of food, and the babies some of my friends were already starting to have. I scrolled mindlessly for a while as I sipped my wine . . . until I came to a photo that made my swiping finger freeze. Todd had shared a photo posted by someone else. It was of him and a woman arm in arm—a woman who looked a lot like me. She could've passed for my sister. Blonde hair, big blue eyes, fair skin, full lips, and the foolishly adoring look I'd once had for Todd as well. The way they were dressed, I thought perhaps they were going to a wedding. Then I read the caption underneath:

Todd Roth and Madeline Elgin announce their engagement.

Their engagement?

Seventy-seven days ago—not that I was counting—*our* engagement had ended. And he'd already proposed to someone else? For fuck's sake, she wasn't even the woman I'd caught him cheating on me with.

It had to be a mistake. My hand shook with anger as I moved the mouse around and clicked to Todd's home page. But, of course, it wasn't a mistake. There were dozens of congratulatory notes—and he'd even responded to a few. He'd also posted a picture of their joined hands, showcasing the engagement ring on her finger. *My. Damn. Engagement. Ring.* My classy ex hadn't bothered to have the setting changed after I threw it in his face while he was still zipping up his pants. There was no way he'd changed the mattress we'd slept on for two years before I moved out. In fact, *Madeline* was probably already a buyer at the Roth chain of department stores—sitting at my old desk, doing the job I'd quit so I wouldn't have to look at his cheating face every day.

I felt . . . I wasn't sure what I felt. Sick. Defeated. Aggravated. *Replaceable.*

Oddly, I didn't feel jealous that the man I'd thought I loved had moved on. It just really hurt to be so easily substituted. It confirmed that what we'd had wasn't special at all. After I'd broken things off, he'd vowed to win me back—told me I was the love of his life and that nothing would stop him from proving we were meant to be together. The flowers and gifts had stopped after two weeks. The calls had stopped after three. Now I knew why—he'd found the love of his life, *again*.

Shocking even myself, I didn't cry. I just felt sad. *Really sad.* Along with my life, my apartment, my job, and my dignity, Todd had robbed me of the ideal I'd always believed in—true love.

I leaned back in my chair and shut my eyes, taking a few deep, cleansing breaths. Then I decided I wasn't going to take this news lying down. *This is crap!* I had no choice but to take action. So I did what any scorned girl from Brooklyn would do after discovering her ex-fiancé didn't wait for the bed to cool before bringing home another woman.

Finish off the bottle of wine.

◆ ◆ ◆

Yep. I was drunk.

Even if my speech hadn't been slurred, the fact that I was sitting in a feathered wedding gown with the zipper wide-open at the back, while slugging directly from a wine bottle, might have been a dead giveaway. I tilted my head back in a very unladylike manner and emptied the last drops before slamming the bottle down on the table. My laptop jolted, causing it to spring to life from sleep mode. The happy couple greeted me.

"He's going to do the same thing to you." I wagged my finger at the screen. "You know why? Because once a cheater, always a cheater."

The damn feathers on the gown tickled my leg again. It had happened a dozen times over the last hour, yet each and every time, I swore it was a bug crawling up my leg. When I reached down to swat again, my hand brushed against something, and I realized what it was. *The blue note.*

Lifting the hem, I pulled the inside of the dress up and read the note again.

> *To Allison—*
> *"She said, 'Forgive me for being a dreamer,' and he took her by the hand and replied, 'Forgive me for not being here sooner to dream with you.'"—J. Iron Word*
> *Thank you for making all of my dreams come true.*
> *Your love,*
> *Reed*

My heart let out a yearning sigh. *So beautiful. So romantic.* What had happened to these two that this special dress had wound up on some drunken girl instead of being cherished and passed down to their daughters? It was a long shot, but I couldn't stand to look at Todd's face anymore anyway. So I typed into Facebook: *Reed Eastwood.*

Imagine my surprise when two popped up in New York. The first guy was probably midsixties. Although the dress was a little sexy for a bride his age, I stalked to be sure anyway. Reed Eastwood had a wife named Madge and a golden retriever named Clint. He also had three daughters and cried while walking one down the aisle last year.

Even though part of me really wanted to stalk Reed's daughter's wedding photos to torture myself a little more, I moved on to the next Reed Eastwood.

My pulse jolted me back to sobriety when his profile picture popped up on the screen. *This* Reed Eastwood was drop-dead gorgeous. In fact, he was so incredibly handsome that I thought it could possibly be a model's photo someone had used as a joke or to catfish. But when I clicked into the photos, there were others of the same man. Each more gorgeous than the last. He didn't have too many, but the last one I clicked on was of him and a woman, taken a few years back. It was an engagement photo—Reed Eastwood and *Allison* Baker.

I'd found the author of the blue note and his love.

◆ ◆ ◆

My cell phone was dancing like a Mexican jumping bean on the night-stand. I reached over and grabbed it just as it went to voice mail. Eleven thirty. Damn, I'd really been out. I tried to swallow, but my mouth was drier than the desert. I needed a tall glass of water, Motrin, a bathroom, and the bedroom blinds drawn to block the god-awful, glaring sun.

Dragging my hungover butt to the kitchen, I forced myself to rehydrate, even though drinking made me queasy. There was a distinct possibility the water and pills were going to travel in the opposite direction in the near future. I needed to lie down. On my way back to the bedroom, I passed my laptop on the kitchen table. It was a painful reminder of the fuzzy night before—of why I'd finished a bottle of wine alone.

Todd is engaged.

I was pissed at him because I felt like crap today. And even more pissed at myself that I'd allowed him to ruin yet another day of my life. *Ugh.*

My memory was hazy, but the picture of the happy couple was, of course, clear as day. A sudden panic came over me—*God, I hope I didn't do anything stupid that I don't remember.* I tried to ignore the thought, even made it back to my bedroom door, but I knew I'd never be able to rest with the unsettled feeling I had. Returning to the table, I woke up my laptop and went directly to my messages. I breathed a sigh of relief finding I hadn't messaged Todd and then crawled back to my bed.

It was early afternoon before I finally started to feel human and took a shower. When I was done, I pulled my cell from the charger and sat on my bed with my hair wrapped in a towel, going through my texts. I'd forgotten my phone had woken me up earlier until I saw I had a new voice mail. Probably another temp agency that wanted to waste a day interviewing me when they didn't have a job to offer. I hit "Play" and grabbed my brush to comb out my hair as I listened.

"Hello, Ms. Darling. This is Rebecca Shelton from Eastwood Properties. I'm calling in response to your request to view the penthouse at Millennium Tower. We have a showing today at four. Mr. Eastwood will be on-site if you would like to tour the space after, perhaps around five this evening? Please give us a call to confirm if this works with your schedule. Our number here is . . ."

I didn't catch the telephone number she'd left since I'd dropped the phone on the bed. *Oh God.* I'd completely forgotten that I'd stalked the blue-note guy. Bits and pieces rolled back in through the fog. That face. *That gorgeous face.* How could I have forgotten that? I remembered clicking through his pictures . . . , then his bio . . . , which led me to a website for Eastwood Properties. But then I couldn't remember a damn thing.

Grabbing my laptop, I searched my history and called up the last website I'd visited.

Eastwood Properties is one of the largest independent brokerage firms in the world. We connect the most prestigious and exclusive properties with qualified buyers, assuring the utmost privacy for both parties. Whether you're in the market for a luxury New York City penthouse with a view of the park, a waterfront Hampton estate, or an enchanting chateau escape in the mountains, or you're ready for your own private island, Eastwood is where your dreams begin.

There was a link to search properties, so I typed in the name of the place the woman had mentioned in the voice mail: *Millennium Tower.* Sure enough, the penthouse popped up for sale. For only $12 million, I could own an apartment on Columbus Avenue with sweeping views of Central Park. *Let me write you a check.*

After drooling through a video and two dozen photos, I clicked on the button to make an appointment to view the property. An application popped up, the top of which read: *For the privacy and safety of our sellers, all prospective buyers are required to complete an application to view properties. Only buyers that meet our stringent prequalification criteria will be contacted.*

I snorted. *Great prequalification criteria you have there, Eastwood.* I wasn't sure I had enough money to take the train uptown to get to that swanky place, much less buy it. God knows what I'd written that had qualified me.

I closed the website and was just about to shut my laptop and go back to bed again when I decided to take one more peek at Mr. Romantic on Facebook.

God, he was gorgeous.

What if . . .

I shouldn't.

No good ever came out of ideas formulated while drunk.

I couldn't.

But . . .

That face . . .

And that note.

So romantic. So beautiful.

Plus . . . I'd never seen the inside of a twelve-million-dollar penthouse.

I really shouldn't.

Then again . . . I'd spent the last two years doing everything I *should* do. And where had that gotten me?

Right here. It'd gotten me right damn here—hungover and unemployed, sitting in this crappy apartment. Maybe it was time I did the things I *shouldn't* be doing for a change. I picked up my phone and let my finger hover over the "Call Back" button for a while.

Screw it.

No one would ever know. It could be fun—getting all dressed up and playing the part of a rich Upper West Sider while satisfying my curiosity about the man. What harm was there?

None that I could think of. *Still, you know what they say about curiosity . . .*

I pressed "Call Back."

"Hi. This is Charlotte Darling calling to confirm an appointment with Reed Eastwood . . ."

CHAPTER 3

CHARLOTTE

"Feel free to start looking around, or you can stay here in the foyer—whichever you prefer. Mr. Eastwood is just finishing up with his previous appointment and should be with you shortly."

Apparently it took more than one person to show a fancy penthouse. Not only was Reed Eastwood somewhere in the vicinity but a hostess was also assigned to greet me and hand me a glossy booklet with information on the property.

"Thank you," I said before she disappeared.

I stood in the foyer, clutching my kelly-green Kate Spade purse that I'd scored in the clearance section of T.J.Maxx and feeling like this might've been a very big mistake.

I had to remind myself *why* I was here. What did I have to lose? Absolutely nothing. My life was a mess, and at the very least, I could satisfy my curiosity about the author of the blue note and put this whole thing to rest. I just needed to know what had become of him—of them—and I would be on my merry way.

Thirty minutes later, I was still waiting. I could hear muffled talking on the other side of the space but hadn't seen anyone emerge yet.

Then came the sound of footsteps echoing along the marble floor.

My heart beat faster, only to slow down again upon the sight of the hostess walking a wealthy-looking couple through the foyer and to the exit. No Reed Eastwood.

The woman, holding a tiny white dog, smiled at me before the three of them disappeared into the elevator.

Where is he?

For a moment, I wondered if he'd forgotten about me completely. It was so quiet. Was there a back exit? Even though I probably should have just stayed in the foyer, I decided to wander a bit and made my way into a grand library.

Dark, masculine wood lined the space. Open bookshelves covered every wall from floor to ceiling. Under my feet lay a Persian rug that likely cost more than I could make in an entire year.

The smell of old books was intoxicating. Meandering over to one of the shelves, I picked up the first one that caught my eye—*The Adventures of Huckleberry Finn* by Mark Twain. I remembered hearing about this book in school years ago but couldn't recall for the life of me what it was about.

"The first great American novel, depending on who you ask."

My body shook at the sound of his deep, penetrating voice. It was the kind of voice that sliced right through you.

My hand over my chest, I turned around. "You scared me."

"Did you think you were alone?"

I froze—absolutely froze—as I took him in. Reed Eastwood was as dark and intimidating as this room. One look, and my knees were shaking. He was even taller than I'd imagined, and he wore what I was certain had to be a dress shirt custom-tailored for him. It fit the curves of his chest like a glove. He also wore a bow tie and suspenders, which on anyone else might have been deemed nerdy. But on this man—on that muscular chest—they were incredibly sexy.

He just stood in the doorway, observing me and holding a folder. I thought that was kind of rude, but honestly, I had no experience in this scenario. Doesn't a Realtor normally extend his hand to a client? Apologize for being late?

"Have you read it?" His voice once again vibrated through me.

"What?"

"The book you're holding. *The Adventures of Huckleberry Finn.*"

"Oh. Um . . . I have. I think . . . yes, in school, years ago."

Shivers ran through me as he approached, giving me a skeptical look as if he could see through my answer. That made me very uneasy. His eyes were like dark chocolate—the deepest shade of brown. As they scrolled once down the length of my body, my nipples hardened.

"What made you pick out that book in particular?"

Answering honestly, I said, "The spine."

"The spine?"

"Yes. It's black and red and coordinates very well with the room. It popped . . . stood out to me."

His mouth curved into a slight, cynical smile, although he didn't laugh. He seemed to be studying me. His intensity made me want to just run. Forget this whole crazy endeavor. He was *nothing* like I'd pictured, based on the sweetness of that blue note.

This was *not* what I'd signed up for.

"At least you're honest, I suppose." He tilted his head. "Right?"

I was sweating. "What?"

"Honest."

He said it like he was challenging me.

I cleared my throat. "Yes."

He inched closer and took the book from my grasp, his fingers brushing against mine. The slight touch felt electrifying. I couldn't help checking his left hand for a wedding band; there was none.

"This was a controversial book in its time," he said.

"Why was that, again?" *Again.* Like I ever knew the answer in the first place.

As I waited for his answer, I breathed in the rustic scent of his musk.

Reed ran his long fingers along the other books on the shelf, not looking at me as he spoke. "It's a satirical account of the social atmosphere in the South just before the turn of the century, but the author's take on racism and slavery is interpreted differently by many. Thus the controversy." He finally faced me. "You were probably taught that in school when you weren't paying attention."

I swallowed.

First discovery about Reed Eastwood: condescending asshole.

Condescending asshole—who's right. I hadn't been paying attention.

He placed the book back on the shelf and looked at me. "Do you read?"

Every question came out of his mouth in a challenging way.

"No. I . . . used to read romance novels. But I got out of the habit."

He cocked a mocking brow. "Romance novels?"

"Yes."

"So tell me, Ms. Darling, how is it that someone who doesn't read—aside from the occasional romance novel—comes to be interested in a penthouse property featuring a library that takes up twenty-five percent of the entire space?"

I said the first thing that came to mind—anything to avoid awkward silence with this man.

"I think the library adds character. Being surrounded by books is very sexy . . . cozy . . . I don't know. There's just something intriguing about it."

God, that was a stupid answer.

He continued looking at me inquisitively, like he was expecting more. His gaze made me very uncomfortable, not only because he was so serious but also because he was so *attractive*. His dark hair was parted to the side, and unlike the rest of him, it wasn't perfectly coiffed. He was also sporting three-day scruff on his chin. Reed had a dangerous energy about him that contradicted his proper attire. Something in his eyes told me he'd have no trouble bending me over and smacking my ass so hard that I'd feel it for days. At least, that's where my mind went.

Being in the quiet of the library, coupled with the power of his stare, was making me tense.

He finally said, "Shall we tour the rest of the space?"

"Yes . . . please. That's why I'm here."

"Right," he muttered.

I breathed a sigh of relief, grateful for the change of environment. The library had started to feel like a dungeon.

Reed was equally impressive from the back. Watching the curve of his ass move against his tailored pants, I tried to fight the sexual thoughts in my head.

He led me into the impressive kitchen. "We have mahogany floors. As you can see, it's gourmet—designed with the chef in mind and recently renovated. Countertops are granite, center island is marble. Bosch stainless steel appliances. Everything is top-of-the-line. Cabinets are custom white lacquer. Do you cook, Ms. Darling?"

Straightening my black sheath dress, I said, "I do, on occasion, yes."

"Great. Well, feel free to look around. You can let me know if you have any questions."

Was he starting to act normal with me? My pulse began to calm down a bit.

I strolled around the massive kitchen, my heels clicking throughout the room. He leaned his muscular forearms against the center island, his body still as his eyes followed me. The break in his intensity had apparently been short-lived. It was back.

Forcing my eyes away from him, I nodded. "Very nice."

"Questions?"

"No."

"Ready to move on?"

"Yes."

The next stop was the master suite. The room was dim, but the large window in the space that displayed a spectacular view of the city more than made up for that.

"This is the master suite. Take a moment to look inside the generous walk-in closet. The en suite bath features a steam shower, Jacuzzi tub, and marble floors. And as you can see, this room has the best view in the entire place."

I took my time, looking at everything in a last-ditch effort to appear serious. He followed close behind me, which put my body on alert. I was highly sensitized to his sexuality, and I didn't like it. This man was not nice. He was not Reed—or at least not the Reed I'd fantasized about. My Reed was supposed to give me renewed hope. This one was slowly sucking the life out of me.

Once we circled back into the main space of the bedroom, he looked at me. "Questions? Comments?"

I needed to just end this. *Say something.*

"I'm thinking . . . um . . . that this might be too much space for me."

He sat down on the bed and crossed his arms, the ever-present folder still in his hand. "Too much space . . ."

"Yes. I'm thinking it might be a lot for just me. I . . . work a lot. And . . . won't have time to enjoy it."

He glared at me—like, full-on glared. "Oh, that's right. The dog-surfing instruction."

Dog what?

"Excuse me?"

He tapped the folder with his index finger. "Your occupation. You filled out the application and submitted all of your information. That job sounds very involved—*dog surfing*. How does one come to teach that?"

Oh shit.

What have I gotten myself into?

At this point, lying was simply easier than explaining the truth.

I started speaking out of my ass. "As you said . . . it's very . . . involved. It takes . . . a lot of schooling. A lot of practice."

"How does it work exactly?"

19

How does dog surfing work? Beats the hell out of me.

"You stand at the back of the board and . . . the dog stands on the front . . . and, um . . . he . . ." I lost my train of thought.

"Surfs." The word came out in a laugh.

"Yes."

Reed stood up from the bed and approached me. "So it pays well?"

Swallowing, I shook my head. "It doesn't, no."

His questions came faster.

"You have old money, then?"

"No."

"If your occupation doesn't allow you to afford a place like this, how do you plan on paying for it?"

"I have other ways . . ."

His stare became icy. "Really? Because your credit report says you *don't* have ways. In fact, it pretty much says you don't have a pot to piss in, *Charlotte.*" My name rolled off his tongue like an obscenity.

He took a piece of paper out of the folder and held it in front of my eyes.

"Where did you get that?" I hissed, snatching it from him. "You looked me up?"

His tone turned angrier. "Do you really think I'm going to show someone a twelve-million-dollar apartment without a background check? You can't be that naive."

Humiliation overwhelmed me. "But you can't do a background check on me without my permission."

His eyes narrowed. "You gave me permission when you clicked the box to submit your viewing application. What a surprise, that fact seems to escape you."

I loosened my defenses in concession. "So you knew from the very beginning?"

"Of course I knew," he spat. "Let's look at some of the other things you can't seem to remember entering on your application."

Oh no.

Reed opened the folder. "Occupation: dog-surfing instructor. Hobbies and interests: dogs and surfing. Previous employment: night manager at Deez Nuts." He tossed the folder aside—more like whipped it across the room. The contents went flying.

"Why are you here, Ms. Darling?"

I literally peed in my pants a little. "I just wanted to see . . ."

"*See . . .*" He gritted his bright-white teeth as he spoke.

"Yes. I came to see . . ." *You.* "And I wasn't expecting you to be so mean."

His laugh was angry. "Mean? You have no regard for the value of a person's time, walk in here with a completely fake profile, and you're calling *me* mean? I think you need to look in the mirror, Ms. Darling. Surprisingly enough, it seems that *is* your real name. Why you lied about everything else and gave your *real* name is beyond me, not to mention idiotic. So, no. If I were *mean*, I'd be calling security right now."

Security?

I snapped.

How dare he go there? I'd only come to see *him*. To make sure he was okay, that *they* were okay. And while I couldn't admit that, his turning this nasty really flipped a switch in me.

"Okay. You want to know the truth? I was curious. Curious about this place . . . curious about what seemed to be the complete opposite of the life I've been dealt lately. I wanted a change. I've been down in the dumps for weeks, so I got a little drunk one night. Looked online and found this listing—found you. I wanted to come *see*, not for malicious reasons, not to waste your time. I just wanted a little bit of hope that things might turn around someday. Maybe I wanted to pretend things aren't as miserable as they really are. I don't even remember entering that ridiculous information, okay? All I know is that I got a call confirming this appointment, and I took it, thinking maybe it was fate—that I should come and experience something out of the ordinary."

Reed was silent. So I continued.

"And I *do* read, *Reed*. I was embarrassed to tell you the truth. I still read romance, but only the books with hard-core sex since I'm not getting any at the moment because I don't trust anyone enough to let them near me after my fiancé cheated on me. So, yeah . . . I read, Reed. I read a lot. And I would use the shit out of that library, except the books on my shelves wouldn't be anything you'd be able to display to stuffy prospective buyers."

His mouth curved up a bit.

"And if you can throw it in a Crock-Pot, I can cook it. But I would never actually use that kitchen. It's way too much. This bedroom, though? Absolutely. It would be a dream. Just like this whole experience. It's all a dream, nothing I'll ever really get to live. So sue me for being a *dreamer*, Eastwood."

I stormed away, but not before tripping on the rug on my way out.

CHAPTER 4

CHARLOTTE

"Goddamn it!" I'd managed to keep my tears in until I found a bathroom in the lobby of Millennium Tower. I'd even somehow succeeded in keeping them at bay while I went into one of the large stalls to pee. But then there was no toilet paper, so I opened my purse and started to dig for a tissue while I was still hovering. My hands hadn't stopped shaking from the ass-chewing I'd just experienced, and I wound up bumbling the damn thing, causing the entire contents to spill all over the floor. And . . . my phone cracked as it smashed against the fancy tile. That was when I broke down and cried.

No longer giving a rat's ass about germs, I sat down on the toilet seat and let it all out. It wasn't just a cry because of what had transpired upstairs. It was a cry that was a long time coming—a big, fat, ugly cry. If my emotions were a roller coaster lately, this was the part of the ride where you put your hands up and careened down at a hundred miles an hour. I was glad the bathroom was empty, since I had the terrible habit of talking to myself when I was really upset.

"What the hell was I thinking?"

"Dog surfing? God, I'm such an idiot."

"Could I have at least embarrassed myself in front of a less intimidating man? Perhaps one that wasn't a tall, dark, confident Adonis with an attitude?"

"Speaking of men, why are the good-looking ones always such jerks?"

I wasn't really expecting an answer, although I got one anyway.

A woman's voice spoke from somewhere in the bathroom on the other side of the stall. "When God was making the mold for good-looking men, he asked one of his angels what else he should add to make a man more attractive in her eyes. The angel didn't want to be disrespectful by using foul language, so she simply said, 'Give him a big stick.' Unfortunately, the added piece was put on backward, and now all good-looking men are born with a large stick up their tuchus."

I laughed through an unattractive sniffle. "There's no toilet paper in here. Would you mind passing me some?"

A hand appeared under the stall door with a wad of tissue. "Here you go."

"Thank you."

After using half the paper to blow my nose and dry my face and the other half to wipe myself, I took a deep breath and began to collect the contents of my purse from the floor. "Are you still out there?" I asked.

"Yes. I figured I'd wait to make sure you were okay. I heard you crying."

"Thank you. But I'll be okay."

The woman was seated on a bench in front of a mirror when I finally emerged from hiding in the stall. She was probably in at least her seventies, but she was dressed in a suit and groomed to the nines. "Are you alright, sweetheart?" she asked.

"Yes. I'm fine."

"You don't seem fine. Why don't you tell me what upset you?"

"I don't want to trouble you with my problems."

"Sometimes it's easier to talk to a stranger."

I suppose it's better than talking to myself. "Honestly, I wouldn't even know where to start."

The woman patted the seat next to her. "Start at the beginning, dear."

I snorted. "You'll be here until next week."

She smiled warmly. "I've got as much time as we need."

"Are you sure? You look like you're about to go to a board meeting or get honored at some charity event."

"It's one of the only perks of being the boss. You set your own hours. Now, why don't you start with dog surfing. Is that actually a thing? Because I have a Portuguese water dog that might be interested."

◆ ◆ ◆

". . . and then I just ran out. I mean, I don't blame the guy for being upset that I wasted his time. It's just that he made me feel like such an idiot for even having dreams." I'd been talking to my new friend, Iris, for more than an hour. Just like she'd said, I'd started at the beginning. We'd been through my engagement, the breakup, my job, Todd's new fiancée, my drunken apartment application, and the resulting ass-chewing that landed me in the bathroom in tears. For some unknown reason, I'd even told her I was adopted and how much I longed to find my birth mother someday. I didn't think that fact had anything to do with everything that was upsetting me today, but nevertheless, I found myself unloading that piece of information along with my tale of woe.

When I finally finished my story, she sat back. "You remind me of someone I knew a long time ago, Charlotte."

"Really? So I'm not the first unemployed, single, broke hot mess to have a near nervous breakdown while you were trying to wash your hands?"

She smiled. "It's my turn for a story, if you have a little time."

"I literally have nothing *but* time."

Iris began. "In 1950, a young seventeen-year-old girl graduated high school and had dreams of going to college to study business. Back then, not many women went to college, and very few studied business, which was widely considered a man's field. One night shortly after graduation, the young woman met a handsome carpenter. The two had a whirlwind courtship, and before long, the girl had immersed herself in his world. She accepted a job as a secretary answering the phones for the family business that the carpenter worked for, spent her evenings helping his mother take care of their home, and put her own passions and dreams on the back burner.

"On Christmas Day in 1951, the man proposed, and the woman accepted. She thought by the following year she would be living the American dream of being a housewife. But three days after Christmas, the young man was drafted into the army. Some of their friends were also drafted, and many of them were getting married to their sweethearts before they were shipped off to the military. However, this woman's carpenter didn't want to do that. So she vowed to wait for his return and spent the next few years working for his father's carpentry business. When her soldier finally returned home four years later, she was ready for her happily ever after. Only on his first day back, he informed her that he'd fallen in love with a secretary on base and was breaking off their engagement. He even had the audacity to ask for the ring he'd given her back so that he could offer it to his new girlfriend."

"Ouch," I said. "Did I mention that Todd's new fiancée is wearing my engagement ring? I wish I'd never thrown it at him."

Iris went on. "I wish you hadn't, too. That's what this girl did. She refused to return the ring, telling him she was keeping it as payment for four lost years of her life. After a couple of days of licking her wounds, she dusted off her dignity, held her head high, and promptly sold the ring. She used the money to pay for her first business classes at college."

"Wow. Good for her."

"Well, the story doesn't quite end there. She finished up college but was having the worst time trying to secure a job. No one wanted to hire her to run a business when her only experience was secretarial work for her ex-fiancé's family carpentry company. So she embellished her résumé a bit. Instead of saying she was the secretary of the carpentry company, she wrote she was the manager; and instead of listing her duties as typing up quotes and answering phones, she listed preparing bids and negotiating contracts. Her improved résumé got her a job interview at one of the biggest property-management companies in New York City."

"Did she get the job?"

"No. Turned out that the personnel director knew her ex-fiancé, knew she had lied about her responsibilities with the carpentry company, and berated her during the interview."

"Oh my God. Like what happened to me today with Mr. Stick-Up-His-Ass."

"Precisely."

"So what happened?"

"The world has a funny way sometimes. A year later, she had worked her way up in a rival, smaller property-management company, and she received a résumé from Mr. Locklear, the man who had berated her during that first interview. He had been downsized from his position and was looking for a job. So she called him in with the intention of giving him back as good as he'd given it to her. But in the end, she took the high road and hired him because he was qualified and, after all, she had lied on her résumé."

"Wow. Did Mr. Locklear at least work out?"

She smiled. "He did. After the woman removed the stick up his ass, they worked together quite nicely. In fact, eventually they started their own property-management company, and it grew into one of the largest firms in the state. Before he died, the two of them celebrated forty years in business, thirty-eight of which they were married."

By her smile, I knew. "I guess your name is Iris *Locklear*?"

"It is. And the best thing that ever happened to me was having that soldier break our engagement. I was never meant to be a housewife. I'd forgotten all about my own dreams. Was being a buyer at a department store your dream career, Charlotte?"

I shook my head. "I went to college for art. I sculpt."

"When was the last time you sculpted?"

My shoulders slumped. "A few years ago."

"You need to get back to it."

"It doesn't exactly pay the bills."

"Maybe. But you need to figure out how to love the life that you have, while you work on the life that you want. So you'll find a job that pays the bills and sculpt at night. And on weekends." She smiled. "That'll keep you from trolling the internet and submitting fake real estate applications."

"That's true."

"Everything happens for a reason, Charlotte. Take this time to reevaluate your life and what you want out of it. That's what I did. You can only find true happiness within yourself, not inside of other people, no matter how much you care about them. Make yourself happy, and the rest will come. I promise."

She was absolutely right. I'd been so busy being miserable and sulking that I'd forgotten there were things I loved that made me happy. My *own* things. Sculpting, travel . . . I had the oddest urge to run home and make a list of things I wanted to do. "Thank you so much, Iris." I engulfed her in a big hug, not caring that she had been a stranger an hour ago.

"You're welcome, my dear."

I washed my hands and, using the mirror, did my best to wipe away my smeared makeup. When I was done, Iris stood. "I like you, Charlotte."

I snorted. "Of course, I remind you of *you*."

She extended a business card to me. "I have a position open for an assistant. It's yours if you want it."

"Really?"

"Really. Monday morning, nine a.m. The address is on my card."

My mouth hung open. "I don't know what to say."

"Don't say anything. But bring me a piece of pottery you make this weekend."

CHAPTER 5

CHARLOTTE

This place made my old office look like a dump.

I knew from the clothes that she wore, not to mention the fancy cream business card with gold-leaf lettering, that Iris Locklear ran a successful business. I just had no idea she was *this* big of a deal.

I looked around the reception area in awe. A giant, sparkling chandelier, floor-to-ceiling windows overlooking Park Avenue, and space—so much wide-open space. The lobby was bigger than my entire damn apartment. An attractive brunette called my name as I gawked out the window. I tried to hide the shake of my hands as I walked toward her.

"Hi, Charlotte. I'm Liz Talbot. I'm in charge of Human Resources. Mrs. Locklear said I should expect you this morning. She's at a meeting but should be here in about an hour. Why don't I take you back and show you around, and you can fill out all your employment paperwork in the meantime."

"That sounds great. Thank you."

Locklear Properties occupied the entire floor and employed more than a hundred people, including forty property managers, thirty real estate agents, a marketing department of ten, and dozens of other support staff. Iris hadn't been kidding when she said she'd worked her way up. After the grand tour, we went by Liz's office, and she gave me a stack of paperwork in a folder that had my name typed on it.

"I'll take you to your office, and then you can get started on this stuff. Your employment agreement is in there, along with information on your choice of health-insurance plans, information on our 401(k) options, direct-deposit forms, and your W-4 and I-9, which we'll need filled out and returned by Wednesday. Paydays are the first and fifteenth of the month." She tapped her finger to her lips. "I feel like I'm forgetting something. But it's Monday, and I've only had one cup of coffee so far, so I probably am."

Liz opened a drawer to her desk and took out a large ring of keys before leading me to where I'd be working. She unlocked an office door and flipped on the lights. "Here we go. I'll order a nameplate for the door and get an extra set of keys made up this afternoon."

"Umm. I think maybe you're confusing me with someone else."

She furrowed her brow. "You are Charlotte Darling, right?"

"Yes. But shouldn't I be in a cubicle somewhere? This looks like an executive office. It has a couch?"

A look of understanding crossed her face. "Oh." She chuckled. "I've been working here so long that I forget how unusual some things at this place can seem. The assistant takes care of all of the personal needs of the Locklear family. You're going to have access to a lot of confidential and personal information, and the family is very private. They wouldn't want that information left out in a cubicle where everyone could see."

"Oh. Okay. That makes sense." Although it still seemed a rather large space for an assistant. But who was I to complain about a private, posh office on Park Avenue? Everything almost seemed too good to be true—a job where I could learn from a woman like Iris, a steady paycheck with benefits, and no Roth family to deal with. Even though I'd enjoyed my job working for Todd's family, I'd always felt that some people looked at me like I'd gotten my job because of the man who slept in my bed. Iris had given me so much more than a job when we met, and I was determined to show her she hadn't made a mistake.

"I'll let you get started. You know where my office is if you need anything at all. I'm extension 109 if you want to call with questions."

"One-oh-nine. Got it. Thanks."

Liz smiled and walked toward the door. She stopped when she reached the couch and tapped her hand along the back of it. "By the way, just a heads-up—woman to woman—Max can be a bit of a flirt. He'll be lying in here on this couch trying to chat you up before the day ends. But he's harmless. Don't let it freak you out."

"Max?"

"Mrs. Locklear's grandson. He's not around often. Only comes in on Mondays, most weeks. I think his weekend runs Tuesday through Sunday. He and his brother run the property-sales side of the business. Well, mostly his brother runs it. Mrs. Locklear runs the property-management side of the business. They're separate corporations with separate names, but a lot of the staff, like you and me, work for both companies."

"Oh. Okay. And thanks for the tip on Max."

My head was spinning after Liz left me alone. I gave myself a minute to take a few deep breaths and then started on my pile of paperwork. Iris and I had never even discussed a salary. So admittedly, I was curious about what my new position paid. It was a good thing I was sitting when I found out. *Seventy-five thousand dollars!* That was more than I'd made at Roth's. This entire thing seemed like a dream.

Almost exactly an hour later, the woman who'd started me down a new path in life knocked on my new office door.

I stood. "Iris. Uh . . . Mrs. Locklear." I'd noticed that Liz had called her the latter.

"Call me Iris, dear. How are you this morning?"

I thought maybe she was nervous I was emotionally unstable. "I'm good. I won't have a breakdown in here. I promise. I'm normally pretty levelheaded."

Her smile hinted at amusement. "I'm glad to hear that. Did Liz give you a tour?"

"She did. The office is beautiful."

"Thank you."

"She also gave me this paperwork. I'm not finished yet, but I can finish it tonight."

"Why don't you take your time and come down to my office when you're done. I need to make a few phone calls anyway. We can go through some of your responsibilities. Did you get to meet my grandsons?"

"Not yet. Their office doors were closed when we passed by. Liz said they weren't in but should be shortly."

"Okay, then. We'll introduce you when we get started. I'll see you in a little bit."

She was at the door when I remembered something. "Iris!"

"Yes?" She turned around.

I opened the desk drawer where I'd stashed my large Michael Kors tote bag and reached inside to the bundle of newspaper. "I made this for you this weekend. Remember, you told me to make you a piece of pottery?"

Iris walked back to my desk as I unwrapped the vase I'd made. Since I was rusty at the wheel, it had taken me a dozen tries to get the shape right. But in the end, it had come out even better than I'd expected. I'd spent all weekend at the Painted Pot, where I'd bisque-fired and painted the vase, but it still needed to be glazed and go back into the kiln. "It's not done. It needs more finishing and more baking, but I wanted you to see it and know that I made it for you."

Iris took the vase from my hand. I'd painted it with vibrant purple irises. I was happy with the way it looked but suddenly nervous about giving it to her. Even more so since I'd gotten a look at the fancy art pieces around the office.

"This is magnificent. You really made this yourself?" She turned the vase to get a look at the full piece.

"Yes. It's not my best work. I'm sort of rusty."

She looked up at me. "Then I'm dying to see your best work, Charlotte. This is stunning. Look at the detail and shading on the flowers, and the delicate shape of the piece. You don't make pottery—you make art."

"Thank you. Like I said, it's not done yet. But I wanted you to know I'd kept my word and made it."

She handed it back to me. "This means a lot to me. I go with my instincts, and I wasn't wrong about you. I have a feeling today is the first day of great things for you."

After she left my office, I felt like I was on cloud nine. I finished filling out all the forms Liz had given me and then decided to go get some tissues to wrap the vase in before covering it with the newspaper. Since the vase wasn't glazed yet, the bottom of it had a little ink smear that must've rubbed off from the paper. I didn't want it to get any other ink stains. So I took the vase with me to see if I could clean it before packing it again.

Stepping out of my office, I turned left to head to the kitchen before realizing that I'd gone the wrong way. I stopped and started to walk in the other direction. Only, I hadn't looked where I was going first. On the second step, I crashed right into someone.

I fumbled the vase in my hands as I rebounded off a hard chest. I'd almost made it, almost steadied myself back upright and avoided dropping the product of my entire weekend. But then I made the mistake of looking up at the person I'd collided with. The vase slipped from my hands, right before I went down on my ass.

What the . . .

The man sank down in front of me. "Are you alright?"

I could only blink in response, stunned into silence amid shattered ceramic pieces.

He looked so different without the scowl on his face that it made me wonder if perhaps I was mistaken—perhaps it was just a man who looked eerily similar. *Until he got a good look at me.* A slow and wicked smile crossed his handsome face.

There was no mistake. The man that sucked the breath from my body a second time . . . was definitely Reed Eastwood.

CHAPTER 6

REED

Blinking my eyes wasn't working. She was still here. I wasn't seeing things.

It was really her.

In my place of business.

That platinum-blonde hair.

Those icy-blue eyes.

Nordic Barbie from the other day—Charlotte Darling—was flat on her ass before me, looking scared, like she'd seen a ghost. I stood, extended my hand, and helped her up.

If I scare her so much, why does she continue to stalk me?

There wasn't much time to think before the words exited my mouth. "Are you taking your show on the road, Miss Darling? I don't recall buying tickets to Crazytown. What are you doing here?"

"I . . . ugh . . ." She shook her head as if coming out of a daze and placed her hand on her chest. "Reed . . . Eastwood. What are *you* doing here?"

What kind of a game is she playing?

"You're asking *me* what *I* am doing at my own company? Who let you into my offices?"

Seeming flustered, she looked down and adjusted her skirt. "I work here."

She what?

My blood was pumping.

Even though I'd let her come to that penthouse appointment to berate her for playing games and wasting my time, afterward I'd regretted acting so harshly. But she was totally justifying how I'd acted.

"You know, I actually felt a little sorry for you when you stormed out of the Millennium upset the other day. But your coming here is out of line. How did you get through security?"

My mention of the *S* word triggered something in her. The same woman who had been cowering a few seconds ago straightened her body and glared at me. I should've remembered from last time that the one sure way to get her to snap was to mention security.

Leaning in, she raised her voice. "Stop threatening to call security on me. Did you not hear me say that I *work* here?"

The smell of something sweet on her breath made me lose my train of thought for a brief moment. *Glazed doughnut, maybe.* I was quickly snapped out of that momentary loss of focus when she closed her eyes and began moving her fingers frantically as if she were . . . typing. Actually, that's exactly what she was doing—typing something in the air.

I had to ask. "What in God's name are you doing?"

She continued the motion as she spoke. "I'm typing all the things I really want to say to you, to get it all out without actually having to say the words. Trust me, this is what's best for both of us." Her fingers kept moving.

I couldn't help but laugh under my breath. "You'd rather look like a complete spaz than say what's on your mind?"

She finally stopped moving her fingers. "Yes."

"Did you remember to hit 'Send'?" I mocked.

Charlotte didn't find my sarcasm funny.

"Telling you what I was thinking would have been unprofessional. I don't want to risk losing my job on the very first day."

"I see you learned a lot about professionalism during your time at Deez Nuts."

"Screw you."

"Whoa. Someone needs a 'Backspace' key."

Jesus. Now I was actually enjoying messing with her—engaging the crazy. I needed to remind myself that she was trespassing.

"Tell me again how you got in here, Miss Darling? Because you sure as hell don't work here. This is *my* company. I can assure you I would've noticed if I'd hired you."

My grandmother appeared and interrupted, "Technically, it's *my* company." She turned to Charlotte. "I apologize for my grandson's behavior."

"Grandson?" Charlotte pointed her index finger while looking back and forth between my grandmother and me. "He . . . is your grandson? That's . . . that's the guy I told you about in the bathroom that day—the pretentious asshole Realtor!"

"I'm sorry, Charlotte. Apparently I hadn't put two and two together." Despite her words, my grandmother didn't seem very surprised at all. "I would have never imagined that the condescending prick you described was Reed."

"Bathroom? What are you talking about?" I asked.

Charlotte began to explain, "When I left you at Millennium Tower, I went to use the restroom in the lobby. That was where I ran into Iris. I obviously had no idea she was your grandmother. She saw that I was upset. I told her everything that had happened with you during the showing. We stayed there a bit and talked—bonded—and that's when she offered me the personal-assistant position here."

Oh, hell no.

Hell. No. This woman was certifiable. There was no way she was going to have access to my personal dealings.

"Grandmother, can we speak in my office for a moment, please?"

"Of course." She smiled before looking over at Charlotte, who had bent down to pick up the pieces of the broken vase. "Why don't you head back to your office, Charlotte, and get acclimated to the company database. I've asked Stan from IT to meet you in your office if you have any questions. I'm sorry that the beautiful vase you made for me broke. You don't have to clean it up. I can get someone to do that."

"It's okay. I've got most of it. We may need someone to vacuum the shards, though." She stood up and dumped the broken pieces into a nearby trash can before turning to me with glaring eyes. "Maybe Stan can work on getting a sensitivity chip installed into your grandson. He seems to be missing one."

I snapped my fingers. "They must have forgotten to put it back in when they installed my bullshit detector."

I really need to stop enjoying this.

Charlotte's eyes lingered on my stern gaze before she turned away from me. A strange feeling bubbled in my chest as I watched her blonde locks moving back and forth while she walked away. I knew it was guilt creeping in. My reaction to her was the only sensible one, given her craziness, but somehow, I felt like a total asshole now.

My grandmother quietly followed me into my office.

I shut the door behind us. "You know your day is going well when your own grandmother calls you a prick."

"Well, you certainly act like one sometimes." She seemed amused by my anger. "She's pretty, isn't she?"

Sure, if you consider expressive eyes, luscious lips, and a body like a 1950s pin-up "pretty." More like kryptonite.

Charlotte's physical beauty was undeniable. But there was absolutely no way I was going to acknowledge it. "Crazy" eclipses beauty.

I grimaced. "Grandmother . . . what are you trying to pull here?"

"She'll be a great addition to our staff."

Pointing back toward the door, I yelled, "That woman? That woman has no experience. Not to mention, she's crazy and a known liar. You should've seen the ridiculous things she put on her application to see that penthouse."

She grinned mockingly. "Dog surfing, I know."

"You *know* about that, and you hired her anyway?" I started to pace, my blood pressure rising. "I'm sorry, but you need your head examined. How can you be okay with having her handle some of our most sensitive and personal business?"

My grandmother took a seat on the sofa across from my desk, then said, "She didn't know what she was doing when she filled out that application—didn't even remember doing it. It was a drunken lapse in sanity. We've all had nights like that. At least, I have. I'm not going to tell you everything we discussed because it's private, but there was a very good reason for her actions. I saw something in her that reminded me of myself. I think she has a determined spirit, and that's the type of vibrant energy we need here."

Is she kidding?

Vibrant.

To me, Charlotte was like blinding sunlight shining into your face after a hangover. Vibrant, maybe—but most unwelcome.

My grandmother was a kind and empathetic person who saw the good in people. I respected that but had to wonder if she was being manipulated here.

"She's a liar," I stressed again.

"She lied . . . but she's not a habitual liar. There's a difference. She made a mistake. Charlotte opened up to me—a complete stranger. She didn't have to do that. She's one of the most honest people I've ever met."

Crossing my arms, I shook my head in disbelief. "I can't work with her."

"Her employment status isn't up for debate, Reed. You have plenty of money to hire your own personal assistant if you don't want to use the shared one, but I'm not firing her."

"She's going to have access to all of my personal information. Shouldn't I have had a say in this?"

"Why? Do you have something to hide?"

"No, but—"

"You know what I think?"

"What?" I huffed.

"I haven't seen you this passionate about anything in a long time. Actually, not since the Christmas concert at Carnegie Hall."

I cringed. "Can you please not remind me of that?"

She loved bringing up my short stint in a boys' choir as a kid. I used to get *really into* the gleeful songs until I started to mature and began to see choir as a dorky hobby. I dropped out, and my grandmother continued to harp on the fact that I'd missed my calling.

"Good or bad, that girl has lit a fire inside of you," she said.

Glancing out the window at the traffic below, I refused to acknowledge any truth to that statement as heat permeated my skin. "Don't be ridiculous . . ."

My grandmother had touched a nerve. I knew deep down she was right. Charlotte *had* triggered something in me. It manifested itself as anger on the outside. But on the inside, it felt like this indescribable excitement. Yes, she had pissed me off for wasting my time during the showing that day. But by the time she'd lashed out at me and stormed out of the bedroom, she'd made an impression on me that I couldn't quite explain. I hadn't been able to stop thinking about her that entire night. I'd worried that I'd been too rough on her, that I'd inadvertently caused some kind of mental breakdown. I imagined her stumbling all over Manhattan with runny mascara, tripping over her own feet in those freaking heels. Eventually, I'd stopped thinking about it and hadn't thought about her again until she'd literally bumped into me moments ago. And just like that, all that bizarre energy rose to the surface again, once again expressing itself as anger toward her. But why? Why did I even care enough to let her get to me?

My grandmother interrupted my train of thought. "I know that what happened with Allison really killed your spirit. But it's time to move on."

The mention of Allison made my stomach ache. I wished my grandmother hadn't brought her into this.

She continued, "You need a change of scenery. Since you're not going anywhere, I brought it to *you* by hiring Charlotte. I would rather see you out there bickering with her than alone in your office."

"You can't bicker with someone whose mode of communication is to silently air-type her side of the argument."

"What?"

"Christ, you didn't see her doing that?" I couldn't help but chuckle. "She said she didn't want to *tell* me what she was really thinking for fear of losing her job, so she pretended to be typing in the air like a loon to get it out of her system. This is the whack job you hired."

My grandmother bent her head back in laughter. "That's a great idea, actually. Some politicians should take lessons from her. We could all stand to learn from thinking before we speak, even if it means typing it instead of saying it. That's what I mean about her. She's unique."

I rolled my eyes. "She's unique, alright."

Her expression softened as she placed her hand on my shoulder. "Can you do me a favor and at least *try* to make her feel welcome?"

"Doesn't sound like I have a choice." I sighed in exasperation.

"I'll take that as a yes. You can practice in the Hamptons tomorrow. She's going to be helping you at the Bridgehampton estate. Lorena is out all week. As we've done in the past, the company PA fills in when Lorena can't be there to assist during showings."

Great. An entire day with her.

She got up and headed toward the door before turning around one final time. "Charlotte knows a thing or two about a broken heart. You have more in common with her than you think."

It irked me whenever my grandmother alluded to my breakup with Allison. Not only did it have no place in this discussion, but it also forced me to have to think about things I was trying to forget. I'd really been making an effort to move on from the pain that went along with the end of that relationship.

I stood staring out the window for the better part of the next half hour, twiddling my thumbs and trying to make sense of the fact that Charlotte now worked here. Her ending up here was definitely a bizarre coincidence. There was just no way we were going to be able to work together every day without constantly butting heads.

I decided to head down to her office and set some ground rules—outline what my expectations were for the time she'd be working under me tomorrow.

Under me.

I quickly shook away the visual of her petite body beneath me. That was the funny thing about having disdain toward someone who was physically attractive. It was like a battle between mind and body that under normal circumstances the body would be destined to win.

But these weren't normal circumstances. Charlotte Darling was far from normal, and I needed to keep my guard up.

Readying to give her a piece of my mind, I stomped down the hall and took a deep breath before opening the door to her office without knocking.

The sight of my brother, Max, with his feet up on the couch threw me for a loop. Although it shouldn't have been a surprise that he rushed to make an impression on the attractive new assistant. This was typical Max.

"Can I help you, Mr. Eastwood?" she asked coldly.

Max smirked. "Charlotte, I know you two have already met, but let me formally introduce you to my older brother, otherwise known as our evil overlord."

Great.

Manwhore Ken had wasted no time moving in on Nordic Barbie.

CHAPTER 7

CHARLOTTE

The mood had completely changed the second Reed entered the room. The vibe sort of reminded me of when I was in elementary school and the teacher would suddenly turn off the lights to calm the rowdy class down. The fun was officially over.

Suddenly, my palms were sweaty again.

Taking a sip of the iced caramel macchiato Max had brought me from the Starbucks across the street, I tried to compose myself, but it wasn't working. Everything about Reed intimidated me—his stature, his bow tie and suspenders, his deep voice. But what I found most intimidating was the fact that I suspected he hated me. So, there was that.

His brother, Max, on the other hand, was the total opposite—charming and down-to-earth. If this were high school and not Corporate America, Max would be the class clown. Reed would be the cranky teacher.

Max had managed to help me momentarily forget about Reed's chastisement earlier. But the reprieve was short-lived.

Reed flashed Max a dirty look. "What are you doing in here?"

"What does it look like I'm doing? Welcoming our newest employee, which is more than I can say for you."

Reed's eyes were like daggers. He looked even more perturbed that I'd told Max about what had happened out there. But I couldn't help it. Max had asked me what was wrong, and I'd decided to be up front about it. What was *wrong* was Reed Eastwood.

The younger Eastwood, on the other hand, had told me not to take anything his older brother said or did personally, that Reed could sometimes be tough even on him. He'd assured me that Reed was not as mean as he might appear. He'd just apparently had a rough year. It was really hard to imagine that he was the same person who'd penned that heartfelt blue note. Which made me wonder about Allison. Had she left him because of his attitude? It certainly wasn't out of the realm of possibility. I felt a twinge of guilt knowing about his failed wedding and that he had no clue how I'd really come to find him.

Reed gestured toward his brother. "Don't you have—I don't know—to go get your shoes shined or something, Max?"

Max crossed his arms. "Nope. Actually, I'm good. My schedule is clear for today."

"Big shocker."

"Come on . . . you know I'm president of the welcoming committee." Max took a sip of his coffee and settled himself deeper into the black leather couch.

"Funny how the welcoming committee seems to be very selective. I don't see you down in accounting welcoming the new bookkeeper who just started today."

"That was gonna be my next stop."

"Right." Reed glared at his brother.

The two of them were similar but different. Although they resembled each other and both had dark good looks, Max had longer hair and seemed wilder and more carefree with a shit-eating grin. Reed was put together and perpetually angry. The latter shouldn't have appealed to me, but there was something about the unattainable that I'd always found attractive. Through his heavy flirtation, Max made it clear that I could probably have him if I wanted him. And that sort of turned me off. On the other hand, I wasn't even sure if Reed hated me, yet I was captivated by his mysterious personality.

"Well, I need to talk to Charlotte," Reed said. "About actual business, unlike whatever it is you call what you were doing just now. Give us some privacy, please."

◆ ◆ ◆

I sat up straighter in my chair as Reed closed the door behind his brother. Unlike Max, he didn't take a seat on the couch. No, *this* brother preferred to stand with his arms crossed while looking down his nose at me. And I wasn't putting up with it anymore. I stood, kicked off my heels into the air, and climbed up on top of my chair.

"What do you think you're doing?" He squinted at me.

Mimicking his posture, I folded my arms across my chest and glared at him over my nose. "I'm looking down at *you*."

"Get down."

"No."

"Ms. Darling, get the hell down before you fall and get hurt. I'm sure your years of practicing balancing with a dog on the front of your surfboard has made you think you're capable of riding a chair with wheels, but I can assure you that falling and cracking your skull on the edge of the desk is going to hurt."

God, this man was *such* a pompous ass.

"If you want me to get down, then you'll need to take a seat to speak to me."

He sighed. "Fine. Get down."

Just for shits and giggles, I pretended to wobble before I got down. Reed ran to my side to catch me. *Well, whaddya know, Mr. Meanie has a chivalrous side.* I couldn't hide my smirk.

He scowled. "You did that on purpose."

I jumped down and extended my hand toward the chairs on the other side of my desk. "Why don't we both have a seat, Mr. Eastwood?"

He grumbled something I couldn't make out, but sat.

I folded my hands on my desk and flashed him my pearly whites. "So what is it you wanted to discuss?"

"Our trip tomorrow."

Iris had mentioned that I'd need to assist with a property showing out east tomorrow, but since I'd had no idea he was her grandson at the time, I still hadn't put the pieces together. *Great, a whole day with the man who hates me.* And here I thought I was getting a fresh start at this perfect new job. Instead, I'd have a man who couldn't wait for me to screw up watching me like a hawk every second.

"What would you like to tell me about the trip?" I took out a note-pad and readied a pen.

"Well, for starters, we leave at five thirty, sharp."

"In the morning?"

"Yes, Charlotte. People tend to want to visit large estates with acreage during daylight hours."

"You don't have to be so condescending. I'm new, you know."

"I'm painfully aware of that fact, yes."

I rolled my eyes and wrote down five thirty on my notepad, adding the word SHARP in all caps with a double underline while he watched. "Five thirty it is," I said. "Will I be meeting you at the train station?"

"We'll be driving."

"Okay."

"I have a seven a.m. phone call with a client in London. When Lorena and I go out for the day, I usually drive for the first hour or so. When we hit the end of the LIE, we grab some breakfast, and she drives the rest of the way so that I can take my calls and work on emails before arriving at the property."

"Uh. I don't drive."

"What do you mean, you don't drive?"

46

"It means I don't have a license, so I won't be able to take a shift."

"I wasn't asking the question literally. I was asking why a twenty-something-year-old woman doesn't have her license yet?"

I shrugged. "I just don't. A lot of people who live in the city don't drive."

"Have you never attempted to learn?"

"It's on my to-do list."

Reed let out another loud sigh and shook his head. "Fine. I'll drive the entire trip. Email me your address, and I'll pick you up. *Be ready.*"

"No."

His brows rose. "No?"

I was guessing that this man was not acquainted with being told no too often. "I'll meet you at the office."

"It's easier for you if I pick you up at home at that hour."

"It's okay. I don't feel comfortable with you seeing where I live."

Reed scrubbed his hands up and down his face. "You do know that I can go into the employee database and look up your address anytime I want, right?"

"That's fine. But *knowing* where I live and *seeing* where I live are two different things."

"How so?"

"Well . . ." I sat back in my chair and gestured to the outfit I wore. "You *know* I'm naked under here. But that doesn't mean I have to *show you* my breasts."

His full lips curved into a wicked smile as his eyes dropped down to the hint of cleavage that my shirt displayed. "I don't quite think those are the same thing. But whatever you say."

This man had the ability to unnerve me with one look. I straightened my spine and held my pen to the notebook again. "What else?"

"We're showing the Bridgehampton estate to two families. This is a seven-million-dollar property, and our clients expect privacy. You'll need to position yourself at the front door so that no one enters the house during the showing. If the second family arrives too early, you're responsible for limiting them to the sitting room in the front that is off the main hallway."

"Okay. I can handle that."

"Have the caterer set up in that room so you can offer the clients something while they wait. Of course, you should offer both families something when they arrive. But it's also a discreet way of getting buyers who show up too early to move into a room while I finish a showing."

"Caterer?"

"Citarella. They're in the vendor directory. You should download the contact information to your phone in case there are any issues."

I tilted my head to the side. "How come the Bridgehampton prospective buyers get food and I didn't? My penthouse had a higher price tag."

Reed smirked. "That would be because I told Lorena not to offer you any food since I'd already figured out that you were a fake."

"Oh."

"Yes. *Oh.*"

"Please also dress accordingly. Nothing so tight that it's distracting."

I took offense to that comment. I was always dressed appropriately for work. "Distracting? What's that supposed to mean? And . . . distracting for who?"

Reed cleared his throat. "Never mind. Just wear something like you're wearing now. It's a workday and not a day trip to the Hamptons for fun. And . . . it would be *whom.*"

"Who? What?"

"You said, 'distracting for who.' It would be 'whom.'"

I rolled my eyes. "You went to one of those all-boys prep schools, didn't you?"

Reed ignored my question. "There's a glossy prospectus on the property in the file. You should become acquainted with the amenities so that you can answer any questions that might arise if I'm not available."

I jotted down a note. "Okay. Anything else?"

He reached into his pants pocket and took out his cell. "Program your number in, in case there's a change of plans."

I started to type.

First name: *Charlotte*

Last name: *Darling*

Company: I inwardly smirked as I ruminated over typing in *Deez Nuts* but then thought better of it. At least *I thought* I'd inwardly smirked.

"What are you doing wrong?" Reed craned his neck, peering over to look at his phone.

"Nothing."

"Then why did I see a flash of the devil on your face for a moment?"

I extended my hand with the phone in it to him. "My grandmother always said a lady gave an angel's smile and kept her devilish thoughts to herself."

He grumbled and stood. "No wonder you and Iris hit it off so easily."

Without saying he was finished with our conversation, Reed walked to the door. "By the way, I was looking down at my phone while walking earlier when I crashed into you. My grandmother said it was a vase in your hands that broke all over the floor. Bring me the receipt, and I'll reimburse you for it."

I shook my head. "No need. The supplies were only a few dollars. I made it."

His brows drew down. "You made it?"

"Yes. I sculpt. And make pottery. Well, I used to anyway. When Iris and I met in the bathroom, I'd mentioned that and said I missed doing it. She encouraged me to start back up, get back on track with things that make me happy. So I spent the weekend at the wheel making it. It had been a few years and, well, she was right. I need to focus on things that make me happy instead of dwelling on the past, which I can't change. Making that vase was the first step in the right direction for me."

Reed stared at me funny for a long time, then turned around and walked out the door without a word. *Such an asshole.* A gorgeous, arrogant asshole who looked just as good going as he did coming.

Later that afternoon, I noticed a blue note sitting on my desk. It really caught me off guard and made me pause for a moment before picking it up. That's because it was the same exact blue stationery as from inside of the wedding dress.

Shivers ran down my spine. I'd almost forgotten about that beautiful note and the emotions I'd felt back when I first discovered it. I couldn't imagine the unpleasant man I'd come to know could ever be such a romantic. The Reed I encountered was pragmatic and cold. It made me even more curious about what had soured a man who was once so sweet.

I sighed.

A blue note from Reed.

Meant for me.

This feels surreal.

At the top were the embossed letters that read *From the desk of Reed Eastwood.* I took a deep breath and read the rest:

> *Charlotte,*
> *If you have any further questions about Bridgehampton,*
> *feel free to air-type them up for me.*
> > *Reed*

CHAPTER 8

REED

I pulled up to the light at the corner fifteen minutes early. Charlotte was already there, standing out in front of the building. Since the light was red, it gave me some time to observe her from a distance. She looked at her watch and then glanced around at the sidewalk before walking to a nearby empty water bottle lying at the curb. She picked it up, then looked around some more.

What the hell was she doing? Looking for bottles on the streets of Manhattan to return for a five-cent deposit? This woman was definitely out there. Who had time for this crap? I watched as she walked over to something else, bent to collect it, then walked a few feet away and did it again. *What the . . .*

The light turned green, so I proceeded to turn right and pull down the one-way street in front of our building. Charlotte took a cautious step back, then bent down to see who it was. The woman was collecting germ-infested treasure from a New York City street and was worried that the Mercedes S560 pulling up might be trouble. I rolled down my tinted window. "You ready?"

"Oh. Yes." She looked right, then left, and held up her pointer finger before wandering halfway down the block. "One second." My eyes followed as she walked to a garbage can and tossed in the crap she'd collected. *Great. Not only does she clean city streets at the ass-crack of dawn but her ass in that skirt looks fantastic as she's doing it.*

She opened the passenger door and hopped in. "Good morning."

Chipper, too. Perfect.

I pointed to the glove compartment. "There are wipes in there."

Her little nose wrinkled in confusion.

I sighed. "To clean off your hands."

That devilish smirk was back. Charlotte held up her hands, palms toward me, and waved them in front of my face, taunting. "Are you a germaphobe?"

"Just wipe them off." This was going to be one long-ass day.

I pulled away from the curb and started toward the tunnel as she cleaned her hands. Neither of us said another word until we were out of the city and in line to pay the toll on the other side of Manhattan. "Don't you have one of those passes?" she asked, looking at the large sign overhead that read CASH ONLY.

"An E-ZPass. Yes. But last time I used it was in my other car, and I forgot it there."

"Is your other car a work van or something?"

"No. It's a Range Rover."

"Why do you need two cars?"

"Why do you ask so many questions?"

"Geez. You don't have to be so rude. I was just trying to make conversation." She stared out the window.

The truth was, the Rover had been Allison's. But I wasn't opening that can of worms with this woman. There were two cars ahead of us in line, so I reached into my pocket to grab a twenty and realized I'd tossed my wallet into the glove compartment. "Could you take my wallet out of the glove compartment for me?"

She continued to stare out the window. "How about using 'please' in that sentence?"

Frustrated, and faced with only one car between me and the toll collector, I leaned over and grabbed my wallet myself. That position, unfortunately, also gave me a spectacular view of Charlotte's tanned, toned, shapely legs. I slammed the glove compartment door shut.

Once we were through the toll and onto the Long Island Expressway, I decided to test how well our new assistant followed directions.

"How many bedrooms and baths does the property we're showing today have?"

"Five bedrooms and seven baths. Although I have no idea why anyone would need seven bathrooms."

"Pool construction?"

"Gunite. Heated. In the shape of a mountain lake with imported Italian tumbled-marble decking and a waterfall."

She'd done her homework . . . although . . . I'd lofted some softballs her way.

"Square footage?"

"It's 4,752 for the main house. An additional 650 for the pool house, which is also heated."

"Number of fireplaces?"

"Four inside, one outside. The interior are all gas, outside is wood burning."

"Appliances?"

"Viking, Gaggenau, and Sub-Zero. There's actually a separate Pro Series Sub-Zero refrigerator and freezer in the main kitchen and another combined unit in the pool house. And, in case you were wondering, the three refrigerators, combined, cost more than a new Prius. I checked."

Hmmm. I wanted her to get one wrong, so I slipped in a question that wasn't in the prospectus. "And the interior decorating was done by who?"

"Carolyn Applegate of Applegate and Mason Interiors."

I had the strangest battle being waged inside of me. Even though I'd wanted to trip her up so she'd get one wrong, a part of me also inwardly fist-pumped that she'd gotten it right.

"And 'whom' . . . ," she mumbled, her voice trailing off.

"Pardon?"

"You said, 'And the interior decorating was done by who?' It would be 'whom.'"

I had to pretend to cough to hide my smile. "Fine. I'm glad you've done your homework."

We arrived at the Bridgehampton estate an hour before the first showing. The caterers were busy setting up. I needed to make a few phone calls and answer some emails, so I told Charlotte to tour the property to get herself acquainted with it. Half an hour later, I found her in the great room studying a painting.

I walked up behind her. "The owner is an artist. None of the paintings are part of the sale."

"Yes. I read that. She's pretty amazing. Did you know she goes around to nursing homes and listens to stories of how people met their spouses and then paints the image that she sees from hearing their love story? I wonder if this is one of them. It's so romantic."

The piece depicted a couple on a date in a restaurant, but the woman seemed to be looking at a different man, one sitting at a table across from her, and sneaking a smile. "What part is romantic? The part where the woman is eyeing a different guy than the one picking up the bill, or the part where the poor schlep she's checking out doesn't yet realize she'll be doing the same thing to him in a few months?"

I looked at the painting and silently sympathized with the unsuspecting fool. *Trust me, buddy, you're better off finding out now that she isn't loyal.*

Charlotte turned around and faced me. "Wow. You're really a breath of fresh air, aren't you?"

"I'm a realist."

Her hands went to her hips. "Oh really? Tell me something positive about me, then? A realist can see *both* positive and negative in people. The only thing you've seen in me since we met is negative."

Charlotte was short, even with the heels she had on. And from the close proximity in which we were standing, I had a view straight down her silky blouse. I didn't think she'd appreciate the positive thoughts I had at the moment. So I turned and walked away. "I'll be in the kitchen when the first clients arrive."

◆　◆　◆

Even assholes give a compliment now and again when due. And maybe I'd just been too tough on Charlotte. But something about her riled me up. She had an innocence that I had the urge to shatter, and I wasn't quite sure why. "You did a great job today." I locked up the front door and put my hand out for Charlotte to walk down the steps before me.

Being her usual pain-in-the-ass self, she couldn't just take the compliment. Holding a hand to her ear, she smirked. "What was that? I didn't quite catch it. You'll have to repeat yourself."

"Wiseass." We walked toward the car together. I opened the passenger door and waited until she got in before closing it.

Backing out of the long driveway, I asked, "How did you know all that stuff about Carolyn Applegate anyway?" The first client hadn't been initially sold on the interior design of the house, but after Charlotte name-dropped a dozen celebrities who'd recently had their homes redone by the same designer, the woman seemed to view the place through rosier glasses. That little soft sell she'd done might've changed the entire outcome of today's visit.

Charlotte was unusual, that was for damn sure, but I had to admit my grandmother's instincts were usually right. She hadn't gotten to where she is today by accident. Iris reads people well, and it was starting to look like her read on Charlotte wasn't totally off base. Perhaps I'd let my feelings for another beautiful blonde taint my initial judgment somewhat.

"Google," she said. "I put in the name of the current owners and found them listed as clients on the designer's website. Then I stalked through some of their other clients. When I'd mentioned the designer had also done Christie Brinkley's place a few miles away, Mrs. Wooten's eyes lit up. So I called up the website and showed her that the photos from Christie's house had a similar fabric on the couch throw pillows."

"Well, it worked. You changed her initial view of the house. And with the second couple, pretending to like their little monster worked like a charm."

She frowned. "I wasn't pretending. The little boy was adorable."

"He was yelling the entire time."

"He was *three*."

"Whatever. I'm glad you could shut him up."

She shook her head. "You're going to make one unlucky woman a miserable husband and impatient father someday."

"No, I won't."

"Oh? Are you nicer to women you date?"

"No, I just don't plan on getting married or having children." My knuckles turned white from the death grip I held the steering wheel in.

Charlotte was quiet, but a quick side-glance at the expression on her face told me that I'd hit upon a topic she planned to analyze for the entire car ride home. I needed to nip that shit in the bud, so I turned the focus back to business. "I'll need you to send a follow-up email from me to both couples. Thank them for coming out to view the property and secure a time that we can speak on the phone in the next week."

"Okay."

"Also, call down to Bridgestone Properties in Florida. Ask for Neil Capshaw. Tell him you're my new assistant and ask the status of the Wootens' Boca property they're selling. We refer a lot of business to their agency, so they'll be happy to share information. If the Wootens have a buyer for that, they might be more inclined to purchase the Bridgehampton summer home sooner, rather than later."

She'd taken out her phone and started to type notes into it. "Okay. Follow-up emails to buyers. Call Capshaw. Got it."

"There's also an appointment on my calendar for tomorrow that I need moved from four o'clock. See if you can push it back to four thirty."

"Okay. Who is the four o'clock with tomorrow?"

"Iris."

Charlotte looked up from her typing in her phone. "You want me to call Iris—*your own grandmother*—to change an appointment?"

"Yes. You're my assistant. That's what assistants do. They make appointments, change appointments, and even cancel appointments on occasion. Did you not get the memo on that being part of your job function?"

"But she's your *grandmother*. Not every relationship should be treated like business, even when it's business you're discussing. Shouldn't you call yourself?"

"Why?"

Charlotte shook her head and exhaled. "Never mind."

Luckily for me, we drove in silence for a little while after that. Traffic was light, and we managed to make it to the expressway without Little Miss Sunshine telling me how to do my job. I was about to merge onto 495 when Charlotte crossed and uncrossed her legs in the passenger's seat, and my eyes drifted from the road for a fraction of a second. It couldn't have been longer than that. Yet the next thing I knew, Charlotte was screaming and grabbing for something to hold on to.

"Watch out!"

Instinctively, I jammed on the brakes before I'd even had an opportunity to figure out what the hell I was watching out for. Everything that happened after that came in slow motion.

I looked up.

A furry little creature scurried across the road in front of us.

My car came to a screeching halt, and I got a look at what I'd nearly hit.

A squirrel.

A damn squirrel.

She'd scared the crap out of me because a rodent had crossed the road.

Unbelievable. I was just about to give her a piece of my mind when a huge bang stopped me. Startled, it took me a minute to realize what had happened.

Someone had hit us from behind.

CHAPTER 9

CHARLOTTE

"Shit!" Reed spewed before exiting the car and slamming the door. He hadn't been able to move the car to the side of the road. Whatever happened had rendered it undrivable.

My heart was pounding.

It's okay.

We're okay.

The squirrel, too.

Everyone is fine.

Still in shock as I got out, I was vaguely able to register the muffled sounds of Reed arguing with the driver of the red SUV that had rear-ended us.

"What can I do to help?" I asked.

"Call the police. We're going to need a report. Then look up the nearest tow company while I get this guy's insurance information." He took something out of his wallet. "Here's my AAA card. Tell them we're just off Exit 70 in Manorville."

An hour and a half later, the police finally left and a tow-truck driver arrived and drove us to the nearest mechanic.

After a long wait, the mechanic came out to see us. Unfortunately, the verdict on Reed's Benz was not good.

Wiping some grease off his forehead, he said, "You have a dented rear bumper that's rubbing against your tire. I should be able to get this fixed for you by tomorrow morning."

A look of concern flashed across Reed's face. "Tomorrow morning? We need to get back to the city tonight."

"This is the fastest service ya gonna get around here. Most people would probably tell you a couple of days or more."

Reed let out a deep sigh of frustration before raking his fingers through his hair.

"How are we gonna get back?" I asked.

"I don't think we *are* going back tonight. You can call a car service for yourself and bill the company if you don't like the idea of staying here in town. Otherwise, book us a couple of rooms nearby. It doesn't make sense for me to rent a car and drive two hours back to the city if I have to pick up my car here in the morning."

The shop owner called Reed away to discuss payment while I mulled over what I wanted to do. Even though he had a tendency to get under my skin, I didn't think that leaving my boss out here in the middle of Long Island was a way to make a good impression. I wanted to demonstrate that I was a team player, show him I was dedicated to my job. There was a lot of potential for growth at the company, and I needed to use every opportunity to prove myself—especially given my rough start. What I had to do was clear. I got to work looking up some phone numbers for local hotels.

Reed looked even more frustrated when he returned from the front desk. "Did you decide what you're doing?"

"I booked us two rooms at the nearby Holiday Inn."

"Holiday Inn? Are there no other options?"

"I'm sure you're probably used to Gansevoort or The Plaza. But I love the Holiday Inn. What's wrong with the Holiday Inn?"

He muttered something, then said, "Nothing. There's nothing . . ." He hesitated, then took a deep breath. "It's fine. Thank you."

"I've also ordered us an Uber. It will be here in a few minutes."

He smiled through gritted teeth. "Great."

I could tell he was pissed at this whole situation. The thought of spending more time with me than necessary probably annoyed him. It pissed me off, too, because we'd been getting along pretty well today. I was actually surprised by how well we worked together. This situation put a damper on what was otherwise a really productive day.

Unfortunately, the Uber driver that showed up to get us drove a Mini Cooper. Reed and I were barely able to fit in the back seat. He grumbled under his breath as we squished together. His long legs were cramped. The driving was erratic, too. Sharp turn after sharp turn, I was thrust into Reed's hard body. I tried not to think about the fact that my own body reacted with every bit of contact.

I spoke to the driver. "Can you stop at that Walmart up ahead? I promise I'll be quick."

Reed's frustration was through the roof. "What do you need at Walmart?"

"A few personal-care items, a bathing suit, and some snacks for the room."

His eyes widened. "A bathing suit?"

"Yes. The hotel has a heated, indoor pool." I smiled.

"What are you . . . ten? This isn't a vacation. Shall we do Chuck E. Cheese for dinner?"

He was so condescending sometimes.

"Adults can enjoy swimming, too, you know. It's a great way to relax and unwind from a stressful day, and living in the city, I rarely have the opportunity to swim in a pool. So you can damn well bet I'm gonna get my money's worth at this hotel. Well, *your* money's worth." I paused before exiting the car. "Do you want anything?"

"No."

"I'll be back in five," I said before slamming the door.

Fifteen minutes later, Reed looked miffed when I returned to the car with my stuff. "That was not five minutes."

"I'm sorry. The man ahead of me in line was arguing with the cashier about the price of nose-hair clippers."

"Are you serious?"

"I couldn't make that up if I tried."

Reed let out an exaggerated sigh. As mad as he looked, he was still so gosh-darn handsome, sometimes even more so when he was angry. He was dressed a bit more casually today, in a navy-blue polo that fit snug across his broad shoulders and a pair of khakis. He looked damn sexy.

I dug into the Walmart bag and took out the candy I'd bought. Opening it, I stripped off a piece of the strawberry licorice and held it up in front of his face. "Twizzler?"

He shook his head and chuckled, finally seeming to concede to the situation he was forced to endure. To my surprise, rather than mock me again, he took the Twizzler and began to devour it. His teeth sunk into it so good as he pulled that I could practically feel the bite in my flesh. I shivered. When he finished, he stuck out his hand in a silent request for more. For the first time, it was evident that he had a lighter side buried beneath that stuffy exterior. That made me hopeful about the possibility of a better working relationship with him.

The Mini screeched to a halt, letting us out at the Holiday Inn.

Reed got us our keys, and just as he was paying, his wallet slipped out of his hands, falling onto the marble floor. A photo that must have been tucked into it lay on the ground. I recognized it immediately as the engagement photo from his Facebook profile.

Oh my God. He still carries her photo.

Why?

This was the first time I truly realized that the same man who'd written the blue note was still somewhere inside of him. Maybe he really hadn't changed all that much. Maybe he was just *pretending* to have changed.

I needed to know more but had to act nonchalant so that he didn't suspect I knew anything I wasn't supposed to.

Bending down to pick up the wallet and photo, I played dumb as I handed everything to him. "Who is that woman?"

"It's no one."

My heart was pounding as we made our way to the elevator. We took it up to our floor in silence.

He walked me to my room, which was three doors down from his.

That was it? He was going to just pretend that he was carrying a photo in his wallet of someone who meant nothing to him? He expected me to believe that?

My excitement at the prospect of figuring out a missing piece of the Reed Eastwood puzzle caused me to push further. "I don't believe you when you say that was a picture of no one."

"Excuse me?"

The words vomited out of me. "I stalked you once on Facebook. This was your engagement photo. Her name is Allison. I know it's none of my business, but that's how I know that you're lying."

Oh. Shit.

What is wrong with me?

"You what?" he spewed.

"I'm sorry. But you can't tell me you've never done that . . . looked someone up."

"No, I haven't. I'm not a career stalker like certain people."

I was almost afraid to ask. "What happened to her?"

He ignored my question. "This is out of line."

"I often wonder if she's the reason you are the way you are."

"Excuse me? The way I am?"

"Closed off and bitter. You seemed so happy in that photo."

And then . . . there was the blue note. That was what I wanted to say.

I had just dug myself into a deeper hole.

His eyes darkened, and this wasn't boding well for me.

"You're crossing a very dangerous line, Charlotte."

Despite his harsh words, I somehow thought if maybe I shared the fact that I could relate to getting my heart broken, that maybe he'd open up a little.

"I . . . I don't know what happened with you and her . . . but I understand what it's like to be hurt by someone you cared about—or thought you cared about. Maybe if you talk about it, you can let out some of the anger."

His voice echoed through the long hallway. "The only person making me angry is you. You've been nothing but trouble from the moment you weaseled your way into my life."

He shut his eyes as if he immediately regretted the harshness of his words. But it was too late. The damage was done. Even though I felt ashamed for putting him on the spot like that, his continuing to insult me was not acceptable. I wasn't going to sit around and take it tonight. Shit, I wasn't even on the clock anymore.

Screw this.

"I'm done being spoken to that way. I'm out of your hair for the rest of the evening. We can meet for the continental breakfast in the morning. Starts at seven a.m. It's free . . . not that you care."

I could feel tears forming in my eyes, but I fought them. I refused to let him see how upset his words made me.

Reed walked a little way down the hall to his room. He stood in front of his door, watching me as I kept unsuccessfully scanning my room card. A red error light repeatedly flashed.

Are you kidding me right now? Way to make a swift exit from this scene.

Footsteps approached me. Humiliated, I refused to look at him. He took the keycard from me, and the brief touch of his hand didn't go unnoticed. The door beeped, flashing a green light as he opened it.

Of course he was able to get it on the first try.

I still wouldn't look at him as I whispered, "Thank you."

He started to walk away when I stopped him. "Wait."

I'd bought three packages of Twizzlers. Taking an unopened one out of the Walmart bag, I handed it to him before disappearing inside and shutting the door.

CHAPTER 10

REED

My thoughts were racing in the shower as the water poured down on me. No amount of hotel soap could wash away how shitty I felt.

Then she had to go and hand me those damn Twizzlers, making me feel like an even bigger asshole.

Who does that?

Who gives candy to someone who just treated them like a piece of shit?

Charlotte Darling does. Bright-eyed, bushy-tailed, spirited, blindingly optimistic Charlotte Darling. And I'd done nothing but try to dampen her spirits from the moment we'd met to ensure that none of her fucking sparkle rubbed off on me.

Her bringing up Allison forced me to put up my guard worse than ever. Because the only truthful answer to her question about what happened would have required me opening up to her. Only immediate family knew the truth about what had gone down between my former fiancée and me. I needed to keep it that way.

I'd honestly forgotten I even had that photo stashed away in my wallet. But I understood how it must have made me look—like a sentimental sap. Maybe I *was* one before Allison made me lose my faith in love. Charlotte must have figured my carrying the photo gave her a ticket to try to get me to spill my guts.

With a towel wrapped around my waist and my hair soaking wet, I lay back on the bed and pondered just falling asleep that way. But I hadn't eaten anything besides that entire package of Twizzlers. I had to leave the room to get food. At least, that's what I told myself. The real reason was that I couldn't shake Charlotte from my mind. Maybe I'd sleep better tonight if I apologized for lashing out at her.

I put my clothes back on before venturing a few doors down to Charlotte's room.

Taking a deep breath in, I knocked on her door a few times. Several seconds passed with no answer. I knocked again. Still no answer.

Well, without a car she couldn't have gone very far. I took the elevator down to the lobby and peeked into the sports lounge, but there was no sign of Charlotte.

The only other restaurant within walking distance was a Ruby Tuesday. As I exited the front sliding doors of the Holiday Inn, drizzle hit my face. Raindrops glistened on the cars as I walked across the windy parking lot to the restaurant.

Once inside, I saw that the hostess station was empty. It was late, probably close to closing time, so there were merely a few patrons. It only took a few seconds before my eyes landed on Charlotte. She was sitting in a corner booth, looking pensive as she chewed on the end of her pen. She then began writing something on a napkin. I chuckled, thinking that maybe the words were expletives and that she was cursing me.

I knew I needed to apologize, but in that moment I much preferred just watching her without her knowing it. I could put my guard up as much as I wanted in front of her, but lying to myself was a lot harder; it was impossible. There was no part of me that truly disliked this woman. I only disliked the fact that she reminded me of all the things I was trying to forget. It was more than just her prying that got to me. Plain and simple, the joyful attitude that always resonated from Charlotte reminded me of a time in my life when I was happy. That was painful to think about, particularly the fact that a part of me still yearned for that happiness.

I made my way toward her and decided to bust her balls. "Did they run out of coloring books?"

She jumped. Whatever she was writing down, she was so into it that she hadn't noticed me standing just to her right.

She flipped the napkin over. "What are you doing here?"

"I heard there was an all-you-can-eat salad bar. And I could use a drink."

"And a chill pill."

"I can't mix the two, so I'll settle for a beer." I sat down across from her. "Am I allowed to join you?"

"I'm not sure if I like the idea of you trying to *weasel* your way into my dining experience, Eastwood."

Weasel. She was using my own terminology against me. Fuck. I deserved it.

Sucking up my pride, I forced out an apology. "I'm sorry that I used that term in reference to you, earlier. And I'm sorry that I lost my temper."

"You could've just said you didn't want to talk about it. You don't have to be so mean about everything." Her face was red. She was really angry.

"You're right."

Charlotte's brow furrowed. "You're agreeing with me? That's a first."

"There were a lot of firsts for me today."

"Like what?"

The waitress came by to take my order, interrupting my ability to address Charlotte's question. When we were alone again, she pushed for an answer.

"So, what firsts?"

"Well . . ." I scratched the scruff on my chin. "This is the first time I've ever set foot inside a Ruby Tuesday." I laughed. "Today also featured the first time I've ever ridden in a Mini. First time I've ever stayed in a Holiday Inn. First time I've ever been in a car accident . . ."

She looked shocked. "Really?"

"Yes. Thanks to you."

"Thanks to *me*? You were the one driving."

"You distracted me."

"You weren't paying attention. That's why you didn't see the squirrel."

That's right. I wasn't paying attention because my eyes were glued to your legs. Just like they're currently glued to your lips.

"Maybe I was a little distracted." Our eyes locked for a moment of silence before I changed the subject. "So what were you writing down?"

She placed her hand over the napkin, preventing me from taking it. "I'm not sure I really want to tell you."

"Why is that?"

"For some reason, I think you'll make fun of me," she said, her expression serious.

Boy, she really had me pegged as an insensitive asshole.

"Nothing with you really surprises me anymore, Charlotte. I'm well prepared for anything at this point. Try me."

She flipped the napkin over and hesitantly slid it in front of me.

It was a numbered list she had started. At the top it said *Fuck-It List*.

"'Fuck-It List'? What is this?"

"It's like a bucket list. But I'm calling mine a Fuck-It List because that's how I truly feel. Life is short, and we should never just assume we have all the time in the world to do the things we want to do. So fuck it! I mean, we almost *died* today."

Her comment caused me to belt out in laughter. "We almost *died*? Isn't that a little bit of an exaggeration? It was a chain-reaction fender bender at best. What would we call our demise . . . like . . . Death by Squirrel?"

"You know what I mean! It could have been a lot worse. None of us know when our time is going to come. So this whole experience today has motivated me to think about doing some of the things I've been putting off."

"Are these in order of importance?"

"No. Just in the order that they came to my mind. I've only just started. I have to really think about the rest."

"I was going to say . . . I hope these aren't the most important things to you . . . because number one—*Sculpt a Nude Man*—is certainly bizarre."

"That might seem bizarre to you, but for me, it would be one of the most challenging and exhilarating projects I've ever undertaken as an artist. The opportunity would be a dream."

That reminded me of the vase she'd made—the one I'd caused her to break. From what I remembered, it looked like she definitely had some talent.

Number two was even more . . . interesting.

"*Dance with a Stranger in the Rain?*"

"That came from a romance novel I read once. It started out with two strangers, and the man pulled the woman in for a dance. Then it started pouring on them. I think it would be cool to randomly dance with a stranger, doesn't even have to be romantic. Music and Mother Nature bringing two people together. They bond over the mere fact that they're both alive. Doesn't matter what their political or religious beliefs are. They know nothing about each other. All that matters is that they're unified in that amazing moment, one they'll each never forget for as long as they live."

"So some unsuspecting person is going to be doing the tango with you this year . . ."

"Maybe . . . if I have the guts to follow through."

"I have no doubt you have the guts. But how do you know when it's the right moment to pull the trigger?"

"I believe that you just *know*. That's how a lot of things are in life."

"So that's it? Just these two?"

"Well, the rest haven't come to me yet. You interrupted my brainstorming. I have to come up with nine."

"Why nine?"

"Well, it's really ten. But I feel like I should leave one permanently open because there's probably something I don't yet realize I want. So, nine for now."

This woman was truly like no one I'd ever met before. In many ways, it was like she was wise beyond her years, and in other ways, like she was born yesterday.

On some level, I agreed with her *live for today* attitude, because you never know when life will throw you a curveball. I'd imagined myself married, living in the suburbs, and picking out dog names by now. In actuality, my situation was far different. I suppose the time to grab life by the horns is when things are going well instead of waiting for them to implode.

"Where did you come from, Charlotte?"

She paused for the longest time before her expression turned serious. "I don't know."

"My question was sort of rhetorical," I clarified. "But what do you mean, you don't know?"

Letting out a deep breath, she said, "Well, your question was ironic, then. Because I really *don't know* where I came from."

"Adopted?"

"Yes."

"It was a closed adoption?"

"Pretty much as closed as they get." She glanced out the window at the rain droplets, then said, "I was abandoned. Someone left me at the local church. They rang the doorbell to the rectory and fled, leaving me on the doorstep."

I could hardly believe it. My body stiffened. That was heavy and not something I was prepared to respond to. There were no words. I couldn't fathom how anyone could abandon their child. My own feelings of abandonment seemed trivial compared with that.

"I'm sorry. Wow."

"Don't be." She paused, looking reflective. "It wasn't a tragedy. I ended up with two great parents. But obviously, knowing how I came to be with them is something I can't exactly forget. And I do feel like a huge part of me is missing. Whoever she is, I forgive her. She must have been pretty desperate, but she made sure I was safe. I'd just like to find her so that I can tell her I forgive her, in case she feels guilty."

Her response blew me away. What an interesting outlook. I couldn't say I'd feel the same if my parents had done that.

"Have you ever considered hiring a private investigator to help figure it out?"

"Sure . . . if I could pay him in . . . what . . . peanuts? I'd never be able to afford that."

That was definitely a dumb question, and I immediately regretted it. When you came from money, it was easy to forget that not everyone had the world at their disposal.

"Fair enough."

She placed a twenty-dollar bill on the table. "I've got to go."

"Why?"

"The pool is closing in a half hour."

"Keep your money. I've got the bill."

"Well, I didn't want to be presumptuous, but thank you." She took the twenty back.

Charlotte began to make her way toward the door when I called after her.

"Charlotte."

She turned around. "Yes?"

"Why did you give me those Twizzlers?"

"What do you mean?"

"I mean . . . I had just barked at you. You were angry. But then you handed me the candy as if nothing had happened."

She seemed to ponder that, then said, "I could see that you were upset. I knew it had nothing to do with me but rather what my question prompted you to have to think about. I didn't take your anger personally—aside from your using the term 'weaseling.' Your anger was directed toward me, I suppose, but it really wasn't *meant* for me. And the truth is . . . as curious as I may be about you . . . what happened isn't any of my business."

I cocked a brow. "Why are you so curious about me?"

Her eyes seared through mine. "Because from the moment I met you, I knew you weren't the person you were portraying."

"How would you come to that conclusion so fast?"

Apparently I'd asked one question too many, because she simply walked away without an answer.

◆ ◆ ◆

I told myself I wasn't going to venture over to the pool on my way back to the room. But I had to pass it anyway in order to get to the elevators.

Maybe just one little peek.

If she was swimming, I'd just pop my head in and say hello.

Feeling the steam emanating from under the crack of the door, I stood outside of the entrance to the indoor pool and peeked through the glass window. Charlotte had it all to herself. Her blonde hair swayed in the water. She reminded me of a mermaid, moving with smooth precision. She stopped at one point to push her wet hair back off her face, offering me a glimpse of her drenched cleavage. It was like watching water streaming down the most beautiful mountain. My eyes darted away from her rack, not because I didn't want to see it, but because this somehow felt creepy and voyeuristic given that she had no clue I was watching her.

She resumed swimming back and forth across the length of the pool.

I envied her ability to lose herself in the water. The more I watched her, the more tempted I was to jump in.

I actually laughed out loud at that thought.

Could you imagine? If I just jumped in and joined her?

Charlotte would probably have a heart attack. She thought she had me pegged as a guarded, miserable person. She'd been trying to figure me out from the moment she first met me, evidently. The one thing I was certain of—if I jumped in that pool, it would be the last thing she would ever expect me to do.

That was exactly why I wished I had the balls to do it.

Maybe it was her little list that influenced me—not sure. But I suddenly felt motivated to step out of my comfort zone—and my pants.

CHAPTER 11

REED

Charlotte Darling, I typed into the search bar.

It had been at least six months since I'd even signed on to Facebook. Social media wasn't my thing. But it was after midnight, and I still couldn't fall asleep. Surprisingly, the bed was comfortable enough in the standard economy hotel room my whack-job assistant had booked me into. I just felt restless and couldn't fall asleep for some reason.

Since Charlotte had invaded my privacy and stalked me, I figured I'd return the favor. I started with her pictures. The last picture she'd posted was a few hours ago—an arty-looking shot of the hotel pool with some kind of a filter on it. The caption underneath it read *Just keep swimming*. Those three little words pretty much summed up Charlotte Darling's outlook on life. Her ability to see the positive in a negative situation drove me nuts, yet I couldn't help but admire it in some way.

Fender bender and stuck in the sticks at a three-star hotel? While I groaned and thought "inconvenience" and "bed bugs," Charlotte picked up her pom-poms and cheered "*hotel pool*" and "*Ruby Tuesday!*"

I clicked to the next picture. *What the fuck? Is that . . . me?*

She must've snuck and snapped the picture on the drive out here. The picture was only of my hand, so no one except me would even know who it was. But, of course, I recognized my own damn hand. My fingers were wrapped around the steering wheel, gripping it so tight that it looked like I was attempting to choke the shit out of it. My knuckles were white, and the veins in my hand and forearm were bulging. Why was I strangling the damn steering wheel? My eyes dropped to the caption she'd given the shot: *Let it go.*

What the hell? She had some nerve taking a picture of me and posting it on social media, even if no one would recognize it was me. *Let it go.* I had the urge to march three doors down and let *it* go, alright.

What else might Ms. Darling have posted about me? I clicked to the next photo. It was a shot of a vase painted with bright purple flowers. The caption read *Create your own happiness. Create irises.* This was probably the vase I'd knocked from her hands that she'd made for my grandmother. I zoomed in on the photo. *Wow.* Charlotte had talent if she'd made this—it was actually beautiful.

The next photo was a close-up of Charlotte and an older woman that I thought might be her mother. Their cheeks were pressed together, and their smiles were wide. The caption read *Because of you, I am.*

The next photo was of her and a woman about the same age standing on the beach, wearing bikinis and big straw hats while holding up drinks with umbrellas. *Damn.* Charlotte had some body—a lot of curves for a tiny girl. She wasn't stick thin like Allison. And unlike Allison, who had perfectly plumped, round, fake tits, Charlotte had full, natural, feminine breasts. I might've zoomed in on that shot for a while, wondering how much softer they'd feel in my hands.

Fuck.

This was a bad idea.

I clicked back to my own Facebook page to escape getting sucked into the little blonde vortex any further. Only there wasn't much to see there. The last pictures posted were of Allison and me out on a boat last summer. I remembered when she'd taken that last shot on my phone and admired it. We looked happy. At least I thought we did at the time. What a goddamn fool I was. I gazed at her like she was the sun causing the warmth on my face. Little did I know, I should've doused myself in sunscreen because I was about to get burned.

I blew out a deep breath. Why hadn't I posted anything since then?

Then again, what the hell would I post? Me at the office at eleven o'clock at night? A picture of takeout Chinese for one? Maybe a shot of my dog and me? *Oh, that's right.* Allison took him, too, when she packed the rest of her shit.

I couldn't stand to look anymore. I began to close my laptop but stopped myself and instead clicked back to Charlotte's page. She had a shitload of recent pictures. Not knowing what I was looking for yet unable to stop searching, I clicked for the next picture, then the next, then the next.

A shot of Charlotte in the arms of some guy caught my attention. They were all dressed up, and his arms were locked around her little waist as they kissed. She had one hand wrapped around his neck and the other was holding out her hand to the camera with her fingers splayed wide. My eyes dropped to read the caption, *I said yes,* before returning to the photo to examine the rock on her finger. She wasn't wearing that ring anymore. Maybe Little Miss Crazy and I really did have something in common after all . . . other than we both liked her in a red bikini.

◆　◆　◆

The next morning, I went in search of coffee downstairs in the hotel. I stopped short, spotting Charlotte inside the small gym, and watched through the top of the glass door. *What the hell is she doing?* She was alone in the tiny mirrored room. Only she wasn't exercising. She was sitting on one of those big exercise balls, bouncing up and down, while watching the television hanging on the wall and chewing on a Twizzler.

I shook my head and chuckled. *God, she's so nuts.*

When I opened the door, her head whipped around to look at who had walked in, and it must've thrown off her balance. She bounced up and then hit the corner of the ball with her hip, causing her next bounce to land her flat on her ass on the floor.

Shit.

I walked over and extended my hand. "Are you okay?"

She smacked at her chest with her hand and spoke with a strained voice. "I just swallowed a piece of Twizzler down the wrong pipe because of you."

"Because of *me*? How is it *my* fault?"

"You scared me."

I arched a brow. "It's a public gym in a hotel, Charlotte. People are going to come and go. That's how facilities open to the public work. No appointment necessary."

She clasped my extended hand and gave it a yank that was harder than necessary to get up. "God, you're so condescending. Do you hear yourself?"

Standing, she brushed imaginary dirt from her clothes and hands. That's when I got my first look at her outfit. I'd been so preoccupied watching her bounce up and down on that stupid ball that I hadn't noticed it before.

"What the hell are you wearing?"

She looked down. "Betsy gave me this. They keep a stash of new clothes donated from local businesses for emergencies. You know, like when guests lose their luggage on flights and stuff."

"Betsy?"

"The woman at the front desk who checked us in? She introduced herself to you and wears a name tag."

Whatever. Charlotte's outfit was interesting, to say the least. She wore a black T-shirt with the Applebee's logo emblazoned across the front, coupled with a pair of men's Gold's Gym shorts that were rolled at the waist yet still fell to her knees. But the most intriguing part of the getup was her exercise footwear—white terry cloth slippers that were four sizes too big, with "Holiday Inn" written across the front.

"You can't use the equipment in that. It's not safe."

She rolled her eyes. "I know. That's why I was exercising on the ball instead."

Both my brows shot up. "Exercising? Is that what you call sitting on the ball and bouncing while eating candy?"

Her hands went to her hips. "I just *finished* exercising, and I was taking a break."

"To eat Twizzlers . . ."

"I bet if you look at the product information on a package of Twizzlers compared to a bottle of Gatorade, it's not all that different."

"Gatorade provides hydration and has electrolytes and potassium. Twizzlers are straight-up sugar."

She scowled at me. "God, you're so annoying."

Apparently we were done talking again because she opened the door and walked out without another word.

◆ ◆ ◆

It looked like shit, but it ran. The mechanic had managed to secure my cracked bumper that had hung down and rubbed against my tire, but the car would need to go into the dealership for bodywork when we got back to the city.

I was just about to merge onto the expressway at the spot where Squirrelgeddon had happened yesterday. Shaking my head at the memory, I asked my passenger, "Is the coast clear? I wouldn't want a field mouse to run across the road so that I wind up with another ten grand's worth of damage."

She glared at me. "Today a field mouse or a squirrel, tomorrow I'll be reading about your plowing into an old lady crossing the road."

I hid my smirk. "You have a vivid imagination. Tell me, Charlotte, did you speak to your old boss this way? No wonder you were unemployed."

I side-glanced and saw her face drop. *Shit.* I'd been joking around, but it looked like my snide comment had hit a sensitive spot. She stared out the window as she answered.

"My boss at Roth Department Stores was a pig. He deserved way worse than a little teasing."

I felt a knot tighten in my chest. My eyes flashed to Charlotte and then back to the road. "He harassed you?"

"No. Not really. Not in the way you think, anyway. Although I did catch his secretary bobbing for apples one night under his desk, and it wasn't even Halloween."

"You walked in on him getting a blowjob?"

She continued to stare out the window. "Yep."

"Crap. What did you do?"

She sighed. "I threw my engagement ring in his face."

It took a few seconds to realize what she'd said. "Your boss was your fiancé?"

"Well, he wasn't my direct boss. But he was my boss's boss."

"Shit. Sorry."

She shrugged. "Better to find out before the wedding than after."

That I knew firsthand to be true. "What kind of work did you do before this?"

"I was an assistant buyer at Roth's in the women's department. My ex-fiancé is Todd Roth. His family owns the chain."

"Did you quit, or did the asshole have the nerve to fire you?"

She smiled at my term of endearment. "I quit. I couldn't work for him and his family after I broke off the engagement. Plus, I honestly never intended to do that type of work to begin with, so it wasn't like I was working at my dream job anyway. Although in hindsight, I probably should have lined up another job before quitting. I wound up taking crappy temp jobs for months, and it killed me financially."

"His loss," I said.

She smiled sadly. "Thanks."

I wasn't the best at expressing empathy, even though I could relate to Charlotte's situation. You don't just lose a partner; you realize you never had one to begin with. I was relieved when Charlotte's phone buzzed and diverted her attention. She spent a few minutes typing before speaking again.

"The Wootens have an offer on their Florida property. Neil Capshaw said it's an all-cash deal with a quick close. I also set you up with a call for Friday morning with Mr. Wooten and moved your appointment with Iris like you requested."

I glanced at the time on the dashboard. It wasn't even eleven yet, and she'd gotten everything done even though I'd given her the list of things to do yesterday afternoon right before the accident. "Great. Thank you."

She put her phone back in her purse. "Are we going straight to the office?"

"I wasn't planning on it. We should be back in the city by one. I don't have anything on my calendar until three, so I thought I'd go home to shower and change. But you can take the rest of the afternoon off. Yesterday was a long-enough day."

"No, I'd rather not take any time off. But thank you for offering. Iris gave me some things to do when I get back, and I want to get started. Although I'd love to run home and shower quickly, too, before heading back in."

"Okay. I'll drop you wherever you want and then see you back at the office later."

She was quiet for a moment. "Would you mind dropping me at my apartment? I'm not too far from the office, but they're doing midday work on the A train that slows everything down, and I want to get back to the office quickly to get started."

"Of course. No problem." Remembering her logic as to why she wouldn't let me pick her up yesterday morning, I said, "I take it you're okay with me seeing you naked now?"

Her face pinked up. "What?"

"Relax." I laughed. "I wasn't propositioning you. I was using your analogy from the other day when you were okay with me knowing where you lived but not seeing your building." Although I suppose she'd figuratively shown me herself naked in the last twenty-four hours, too. I knew the details of her breakup, that she was adopted, even some of the things on her crazy Fuck-It List. It troubled me that learning all that made me feel closer to her.

"Oh." Charlotte laughed and sat back into the passenger's seat. "Yes, I suppose I'm okay with you seeing me naked now."

After that, she relaxed for the rest of the ride to the city. I, on the other hand, definitely did not relax, with thoughts running through my mind that Charlotte was okay with me seeing her naked.

CHAPTER 12

CHARLOTTE

The office was eerily quiet.

It was early, but not so early that I expected to unlock the front door to the office suite. Even though I'd stayed until after seven last night, I hadn't gotten as far as I'd wanted to with Iris's project list. So I'd come in at six thirty this morning to get a jump on the day.

After flipping on all the lights and booting up my computer, I headed to the break room to make a pot of coffee. While I waited for it to brew, I decided to clean some spills inside the refrigerator that I'd noticed on Monday. It looked like a container of orange juice had spilled on the shelf at one point, and no one had bothered to wipe it up. I grabbed some paper towels and Formula 409 spray from underneath the sink and bent to clean the glass on the middle shelf while the smell of coffee percolating filled the air. The back wall of the refrigerator had some hardened orange gunk, too, which I could only reach by pulling the shelf slightly out and stretching my entire arm inside and up the rear wall. That was exactly the position I was in, my body bent as I scrubbed the inside of the refrigerator and my ass prominently on display, when a man's voice from somewhere behind me scared the shit out of me.

"What the hell are you doing?"

I jumped and whacked my head on the shelf above where I was cleaning.

"*Ouch!* Shit."

Attempting to stand, I realized that not only had I banged my head, but I'd also managed to get the top of my hair stuck on something inside the refrigerator.

"What the fuck, Charlotte?"

Of course, it had to be Reed.

Visualizing what he was seeing, I took a deep, cleansing breath before speaking. "I'm stuck."

"You're what?"

I waved my hand, pointing to where my hair was caught. "My hair. It's stuck on something. Can you take a look?"

He mumbled something I couldn't make out and then came to stand behind me. Leaning down, he had to bend over my ass to see what my hair was caught on.

"How the hell? Your hair is wrapped around the lever that you crank to make the shelf higher and lower."

"Can you just unwrap it? Or cut the piece off if you have to. This isn't exactly a comfortable position."

"Stay still. Stop squirming. The way you're moving around is making it tighter."

I stayed as immobile as I could while Reed had one hand on my head and the other working to untangle whatever I'd snagged. It wasn't easy, considering my body was acutely aware of the close proximity of his. But once I stopped moving, it took only a few seconds for him to free me.

Rubbing my head where the root had been yanked, I stood. "Thank you."

Reed folded his arms over his chest. "Do I even want to know?"

"I was cleaning a spill and my hair must've gotten caught."

"You came in before seven in the morning to clean out the refrigerator. We do have a cleaning crew, you know."

"No. I came in here to make coffee. But while I waited, I figured I could clean the spill since I'd noticed it the other day."

The coffee machine beeped, signaling the brewing was done, so I turned and grabbed the mug I'd brought in and poured a cup. Turning back to Reed, I held up the pot. "Do you have a mug?"

"No. I just use the Styrofoam ones we keep up in the cabinet."

I frowned. "Those things are so bad for the environment. You need to get a mug."

Reed squinted at me. "Did Iris tell you to say that?"

"No. Why?"

He reached over my head, opened the cabinet, grabbed a Styrofoam cup, and then took the pot from my hand. "Because she's been harping on me about that for years."

I offered him a sugary smile before sipping my coffee. "Maybe you should listen for a change."

Allowing him to consider that thought, I left him in the break room alone.

◆ ◆ ◆

While Reed and his brother primarily focused on real-estate sales, Iris's side of the business managed properties that the Eastwood family owned and provided management for clients who owned commercial buildings. Although there was some crossover where the brothers kept a building to manage if they had sold it or had a relationship with the owner.

One of the projects on Iris's list was to compile one database of all the cleaning-company vendors that they used so she could solicit bids for managing multiple properties for a cost savings. In order to do that, I had to go into each of their individual folders on the system and pull up information on every property. While Max's files were a disaster, with Word documents and Excel spreadsheets strewn all over the place and no clear file-naming system in place, Reed's were as organized as I would have expected. Each property had a separate folder named with the building's street address, and inside each folder were separate subfolders that were logically organized, such as the one labeled MAINTENANCE, where I found most of the information I needed.

It took me a few hours to compile almost everything. Information from only one property of Reed's was missing: 1377 Buckley Street. After checking the property's folder a second time, I clicked around to check a few other folders that were not labeled with addresses. One such folder was simply labeled PERSONAL. Inside there were a dozen subfolders. I perused the titles for anything that might be misfiled and found folders such as MEDICAL, CONTRACTS, LEGAL . . . there was even one labeled WEDDING. Curious, I left-clicked on the mouse to look at the last time the folder had been opened. It hadn't been accessed for more than six months. I was just about to close out and take a walk over to Reed's office to ask him if he knew where I might find the information for the remaining building when I saw there was one lone, unfiled Word doc. This file was labeled BUCKET.

Thinking nothing of it, I clicked to check out the contents. What I found shocked the crap out of me. Reed had made a fuck-it list of his own.

◆ ◆ ◆

Throughout the entire morning, I couldn't get Reed's list out of my head. Although it wasn't necessarily the contents of his list but more the fact that he'd made one at all that boggled my mind. The man had laughed when I'd told him I was working on my list. Yet he'd made his own bucket list? And I'd checked the time on the file. It had been created at eight o'clock last night and last updated a little after ten. He'd still been in the office when I left around seven. I just couldn't imagine that he'd stuck around for hours, working on his own list. It seemed too out of character for him. There were definitely two sides to Reed Eastwood—a side that he showed me and the rest of the world, and a side that he kept hidden. I could totally see the man who penned the beautiful blue note having a bucket list of things that he wanted to achieve in life, but certainly not the condescending Reed that he was to me most of the time. Then again, there were these brief moments when I felt like I was catching a glimpse of the other Reed. But they never lasted for very long.

I strolled the aisles of the dollar store on my lunch hour with a basket in my hand, lost in thought. I'd come to pick up silver baking trays, paper towels, and rubber gloves—three things I used in excess when I worked with pottery clay—but I never left the dollar store without a bunch of junk I didn't really need. My basket had tissues, a few plastic bowls, hair ties, and a bunch of spices that were too cheap to pass up even though I didn't have a clue what I'd use them for. When I arrived at the shelving with seasonal mugs, I decided to pick one up for Reed so he'd stop using the Styrofoam ones for his coffee.

Fingering through mugs with Halloween pumpkins, Valentine's hearts, and menorahs on the front, I snorted when I picked up one particular red mug. It was Christmas-themed, and the cartoon picture on the front was of a group of boys wearing sweaters and scarves while singing Christmas carols. I couldn't resist buying it, considering what he'd written as number three on his bucket list.

Sing in a Choir.

◆　◆　◆

Sometime in the middle of the afternoon, it dawned on me that maybe Reed had planted that list on the server to screw with me. Could he be poking fun at me? Or did he have an epiphany after hearing about my list and truly decided to make his own? I couldn't very well come right out and ask him since I'd be admitting that I'd snooped in his personal files. Well, *I could*, of course, but last time I did that he'd gotten pretty pissed off. So I decided that I'd gauge his reaction to the mug I'd bought him. If he'd planted that list and made up the crazy part about singing in an all-male choir, I might be able to see it in his face. So around five o'clock, I made a fresh pot of coffee and fixed a cup just for my boss in his new mug.

Reed was looking down at a stack of papers when I knocked on his open office door. It was the first time I'd seen him wearing glasses. They were a tortoiseshell-colored, rectangular pair—very studious— that really worked with his chiseled face. *God, he looks like a sexy Clark Kent.* They must've been only for reading, because he took them off when he looked up.

"Did you need something?"

In that moment, quite a few unprofessional answers popped into my head. I shook the thoughts away and stepped forward with the full mug of steaming coffee. The picture on the front was facing me still. "I thought you could use some coffee."

He looked at me, then the mug, then back to me and tossed his glasses on the desk. "You found me a mug, I see?"

"I did, actually. I went to the dollar store at lunch and picked you up one so you can skip the Styrofoam."

"That was nice of you."

I smiled. "No problem. It's from their off-season seasonal merchandise. Hope you don't mind a little Christmas spirit in July." I turned the mug so he could see the picture on the front and focused on his face so I could observe if he had any reaction.

Reed just stared at the caroling boys on the mug for the longest time. Blinking in confusion, it was clear that I'd caught him off guard. Without a hint of laughter coming from him, I knew there was no way that he had planted that list for my amusement. He would've gotten the joke if that were the case.

He peered up at me. "Why did you pick this one?"

Uh . . .

Oh no.

I could feel a case of the nervous giggles coming on. Occasionally, when I'm put on the spot, I just laugh. And once it starts creeping in, there is no stopping it from happening.

This was not good.

Rather than answer him, I fell into a fit of laughter that gradually went from slight to hysterical. Tears were forming in my eyes. "I'm sorry. I'm so sorry," I said as I tried to stop. This went on for almost a minute—me laughing and Reed just watching me incredulously.

He finally asked, "What the hell is so funny about this mug, Charlotte?"

Oh my God.

Either I admit to him that I was snooping and found his bucket list or he's going to think that I'm making fun of his choir wish.

Never! I would never be so cruel as to laugh at someone's dreams. I mean, I thought this was a joke on *me*—that he'd planted that list. Now that I knew it was real, I could never make light of something he truly wished for. My laughter was more about getting caught in a sticky situation. I was laughing at myself . . . but he wouldn't know that.

There was only one way out. I had to tell the truth.

"I'm sorry. This is a misunderstanding."

"Care to explain?"

"I . . . stumbled upon your bucket list. The one that you saved on the company server."

Reed's expression soured. My heartbeat accelerated in anticipation of his response.

He let out a breath, then said, "It was on the server, yes, but it was in a *personal* folder, Charlotte."

"That's right."

"You were snooping in my personal files, and this mug is your way of poking fun at what you discovered?"

"No! You have it all wrong. You see . . . I just couldn't believe that you would be making a bucket list in the first place. You were sort of making fun of me for my own. I didn't want to have to admit that I'd opened that file, even though I figured that anything on the company server couldn't be that private, even if marked 'Personal.' But I apologize. I was wrong. Anyway, I thought maybe you left the list intentionally for me as a joke. I was trying to gauge your reaction with this mug to see if my suspicions were correct. But it's become apparent that I was very wrong. I wasn't laughing because you want to sing—at all. Please know that. I was laughing at the situation I'd gotten myself into. It was nervous laughter. And now I'm rambling. I'm sorry."

He just sat there staring at me while he took a few sips of coffee from the mug. I caught a hint of a slight smirk. It seemed that he was enjoying watching me sweat.

When he finally spoke, he said, "You're a real pill, you know that?"

Unleashing the smile I'd been holding back, I said, "So . . . it's true? You started to make a list because you *wanted* to? It was real?"

He placed his mug down, then rubbed his temples. His deep brown eyes seared into me when he looked up and said, "Yes."

"Really?"

"Did I not just say yes?"

Taking a seat in front of him, I crossed my arms and leaned into his desk. "What made you do it?"

"You made some good points, okay? I never said your list was stupid. I never made fun of you for it, either, like you seem to think. So yes, you did motivate me to think about a similar list for myself."

I got chills. Once again, he was proving that the more sensitive man I'd originally imagined him to be when I'd found the blue note was in there somewhere.

"Wow. That's so amazing."

Reed rolled his eyes at my enthusiasm. "The concept of a bucket list is not that amazing."

"What I mean is . . . I didn't even think you *liked* me. Meanwhile . . . I inspired you? That's so cool."

He got up out of his seat suddenly, walking to the other side of the room. "Let's not get carried away." It looked like he was pretending to sift through files just to avoid this conversation.

"So, I noticed that you only jotted down a few things. Will you tell me why you chose them? *Climb a Mountain* makes total sense to me. I mean, I would imagine that's simply exhilarating. But the men's-choir thing . . . do you sing?"

He let out a deep breath, then turned to me. "I'm not going to get out of this question, am I?"

"Not a chance."

Reed returned to his seat at the desk and downed the rest of his coffee. "Yes, Charlotte. I sing. Or rather, I *sang* . . . when I was younger. But my teenage ego stepped in, and I abandoned the hobby. I'd prefer not to get into it in great detail, except to say that the image on this little mug here pretty much sums it up . . . scarily so. If you ever want to hear about my singing, Iris will be happy to tell you *all* about it. She has quite a few cassette tapes of it as well that she's been known to threaten me with."

"Really? I'm definitely going to ask her about it."

"Great."

"You know . . ." I smiled. "A bucket list is useless if you don't actually attempt to take action. Let me help you arrange one or two of these things."

"I'm all set."

"Everyone needs motivation. I can help you follow through. We can sort of be like bucket buddies . . . or in my case, fuck-it buddies."

That sort of sounded bad—like "fuck buddies." Sweat started to permeate my forehead.

"Why would you even want to bother, Charlotte? What's the catch here?"

"There is none. Well, I suppose the catch is, you have to help keep me on track with my own goals. We can be each other's cheer captains."

He bent his head back in laughter. "Okay, let's calm down a bit."

"Will you at least *consider* letting me help you? I mean, you employ me. Why not take advantage of me?"

His voice lowered, causing my skin to prickle. "You want me to take advantage of you?"

Iris walked in at that inopportune moment.

She clasped her hands together and smiled gleefully. "Ohhh . . . glad to see you two are finally getting along."

Clearing my throat, I said, "Hello, Iris."

She addressed Reed. "I just heard about this car accident out in the Hamptons. You never told me about it. What happened, exactly?"

"Charlotte tried to save a squirrel and set off a chain-reaction crash."

"Well, that was very noble of you, Charlotte."

"What can I say? Someone needs to look out for them. The squirrels love me for it." I shrugged, then moved on to a more pressing topic. "Iris, is it true that Reed used to sing?"

My question seemed to surprise her. "Why yes, it is, but I can't believe he admitted that to you. Reed's pretty secretive about it." She closed her eyes and sighed. "He had the most beautiful voice, a perfect tenor. I would have funded any musical education he wanted. Such a shame that he didn't continue."

Reed was quick to change the subject. "To what do I owe the pleasure, Grandmother?"

"Actually, I was hoping to catch Charlotte before she left for the day. I've decided to move the annual company summer party to the house in Bedford, so I'll need her help making some of the arrangements."

Even though she lived in Manhattan, Iris kept a family home in the suburbs. It was where the Eastwoods and Locklears had large family gatherings, and where they celebrated the holidays. Reed's parents also lived there part of the year when they weren't traveling the world. Apparently Mr. and Mrs. Eastwood had decided to retire early down in Florida and enjoy their lives a bit, whereas Iris was too much of a workhorse to ever pass off her responsibilities at the company to someone else.

"I thought we were renting a venue in the city for that this year," Reed said.

"I decided against it. The Bedford estate worked really well the past couple of years. We'll need to rent some large white tents and work on moving the caterer. Jared will also be in town that weekend, so it's perfect timing."

I looked at her. "Jared?"

"My grandnephew from London—my sister's grandson. He's only visited the States a couple of times, so I'm going to actually be relying on you quite a bit during his stay, Charlotte, to make sure he's well cared for."

Reed didn't seem to like that idea. He grumbled, "Why does Jared need a babysitter?"

"He doesn't. I just thought he and Charlotte would get along well. She could show him around the city, take him to the hip places—you know, wherever young people go these days."

"I'll be happy to show Jared all of my favorite haunts."

"Thank you, dear. I'm certain Jared will love that. Don't you think, Reed?"

I kept waiting for a response from him, but Reed offered nothing but a death stare aimed at Iris.

CHAPTER 13

REED

My grandmother was really pushing it.

Jared Johansen was one of London's most notorious bachelors; Iris knew that when she decided to pawn him off on Blondie. This was entirely about getting me worked up and had nothing to do with his suitability for Charlotte.

Jared was a commodities broker by day and a playboy by night. With a penchant for fast cars and even faster women, there was no way he was going to let an opportunity to sack a beauty like Charlotte pass. One look at her striking, curious eyes and killer body, and he'd quickly see her as the perfect summer catch. My only hope was that she could see through his façade.

It had been a few years since he'd last visited the United States, but Jared was more than capable of finding his way around New York City. Iris was playing games, trying to once again light a fire under my ass when it came to Charlotte. But I refused to play along.

During the afternoon that Jared arrived, I kept a low profile the entire time he and Charlotte were gallivanting around. And by low profile, I mean following Charlotte's social media for a virtual map of their whereabouts, which included stops at the Museum of Modern Art's Pottery Exhibit and Magnolia Bakery for cupcakes.

I hated that I cared, that I was attracted to her. I hated that she made me feel more alive than I had in a long time. But most of all, I hated the fact that Charlotte was probably still better off with that philandering cousin of mine than she would be with me. That hurt to admit. But it was the truth. He'd be able to give her towheaded little children and the life she deserved someday.

As much as I wished I could skip the party, the Eastwood/Locklear summer event wasn't something I could just blow off. Believe me, I searched for a way out of it, but bailing was kind of hard when you owned the company. I was not only expected to be there and smiling but also to give a speech and pass out employee appreciation awards later in the evening. My grandmother had delegated the latter task to me a few years ago because, in her words, I was the best speaker in the family. It was the one night of the year that I schmoozed with my employees, and that made for one mentally exhausting evening. Add Charlotte and Jared to the mix, and I was definitely eager for the night to be over before it even started.

◆ ◆ ◆

I lingered in the upstairs master bedroom of my family's estate for as long as possible, looking down on the festivities. Five gigantic tents were spread about the massive front lawn while a jazz band played live music. Guests mingled at sunset while waiters passed out hors d'oeuvres. Fiddling with my watch, I gave myself a mental kick in the ass and ventured downstairs to face the music.

Charlotte and Jared were at the bar. She was playing with the thin red straw in her cosmo. Jared was using the loud music as an excuse to lean in to her ear while talking. I knew that trick. It was just an excuse to get close to her. He was practically sucking her ear off with every word.

Turning a blind eye, I walked past them and over to a group of employees to make small talk.

After finishing my obligatory speech, I kept moving around the lawn, making the rounds so that I could get to that point where I could just drink without having to worry about talking to anyone else. Every time my eyes would wander over to Charlotte, I'd notice that she was looking right at me. In fact, she didn't seem very into whatever Jared was saying at all.

Max interrupted my thoughts when he snuck up behind me. "Goldilocks looks bored as fuck." He handed me a vodka on the rocks.

"Well, she's not exactly eating up the bullshit porridge Jared is trying to feed her, thankfully."

"What was Grandmother thinking anyway—sending her out with him today?"

I squinted at my brother. "I'm surprised you even know what's going on around here. I haven't seen you in days."

"I follow her on Insta," he said.

"I should've known."

"Anyway, it pisses me off."

I suddenly wanted to punch him. "I didn't realize you had such a vested interest in Charlotte."

"I wouldn't mind getting to know her better." He must have seen the anger in my eyes. "Why do you look like you're ready to kill me right now?"

"What are you talking about?"

"As soon as I said I was interested in her, your face did a one-eighty. Is there something you want to tell me?"

"I shouldn't have to remind you about our nonfraternization policy," I said, downing the vodka.

"We don't have a nonfraternization policy."

"We do now."

With a smug grin, I handed him my glass and promptly walked away before he could push me any further into an awkward conversation in which I forbade him from going near Charlotte without a rational explanation. My feelings were complex, and Max was beginning to figure out my interest in her. That was a subject I didn't want to have to get into with him, especially when Charlotte wasn't someone I could seriously pursue.

It was apparent I was going in the wrong direction because Charlotte was making her way toward me.

"Eastwood, is it just my imagination, or have you said hello to everyone here tonight but me?"

I hadn't realized my actions were so obvious. "You tell me, since you've been watching me all night."

"Hello, by the way," she said.

"Hi." Clearing my throat, I said, "How was your day?"

"Busy."

"Yeah? Stuffing your face with cupcakes can be pretty tiring."

"How do you know about that?" She snapped her fingers. "Ah . . . you were on my Instagram page."

"Well, it's public, unlike—oh, I don't know—sifting through someone's personal files."

Charlotte laughed. "You're a stalker."

"Takes one to know one, I suppose."

Jared interrupted us. "Cousin! Good to see you."

With his blond hair, blue eyes, and tall stature, Jared was decent-looking. I wished that weren't the case.

"Jared." I spoke through gritted teeth. "Long time no see. How's your trip so far?"

"Brilliant. Charlotte here took real good care of me today."

You wish.

Jared turned to her, practically undressing her with his eyes. "Let's dance, shall we?"

Pissed off, I started to walk away. "I'll let you two be."

She placed her hand on my arm to stop me. "Wait. You said we were going to discuss that business thing."

Is she winking at me?

Charlotte Darling was apparently trying to use me to get out of dancing with Jared. That pleased me despite understanding that feeling that way would be to my own detriment.

I decided to fuck with her. "Oh yes. Project Squirrel. That's right. We were going to meet about that."

Jared looked perplexed. "A business meeting now?"

Charlotte wasted no time elaborating. "Just something we need to discuss before tomorrow. Do you mind?"

"Not at all. Iris has been fancying another dance with me anyway. I'll catch you in a bit, Charl."

When Jared was out of earshot, she looked at me. "I hate when he calls me 'Charl.' Thank you for going along with that. I just needed to get away from him for a bit. I suspect he thinks something's going to happen between us just because I've been nice to him, but he's sorely mistaken. I don't want to insult your grandmother, but I don't date guys whose nails are better manicured than mine. Not to mention, all he does is talk about his cars and his gigantic garage back in England. I couldn't care less."

And just like that, Charlotte went up another notch on the respectometer.

Pausing to really take her in, I inhaled deeply to squelch the ache in my chest. Charlotte looked simply breathtaking under the outdoor lighting and starry night sky. She was wearing a pale-pink dress that was not too much darker than her skin. With her hair up, she reminded me of a ballet dancer—with a belly-dancer body. That dress did nothing to hide Charlotte's killer curves.

I should've just walked away. Instead, my eyes fell to her cleavage before the words exited my mouth. "Can I get you another drink?"

"I would love one."

"I'll be right back."

I flashed a mischievous grin that stayed glued to my face the entire walk to the bar.

However, my smile quickly faded upon the sight of a familiar brunette walking toward me, the same one who'd happened to rip my heart out two years earlier. All the energy was suddenly sucked out of me.

Allison.

CHAPTER 14

Charlotte

I couldn't believe my eyes.

It was her. Reed's ex-fiancée, Allison. At the bar.

What is she doing here?

My curiosity got the best of me as I inched my way closer to where they were standing.

Allison had blonde hair that was darker than mine. She was tall, almost Reed's height. But she was gorgeous, and I couldn't help the twinge of jealousy I felt as I saw them together for the first time.

For two people who had been so in love, though, they definitely seemed uncomfortable around each other at the moment.

My need to know what had actually happened between them was stronger than ever. I kept my eyes on them as if I would be able to figure something out from just observing them.

Reed looked distressed, fidgeting with his watch as they made small talk.

She took a deep breath, then exhaled. "You look good."

"Thank you," he said without making eye contact.

"I happened to see all of the tents set up as I was driving to my parents' and thought I would stop by to say hello, see how you're doing."

I noticed he went to straighten his tie, but he wasn't wearing one. It was like he didn't know what to do with his hands.

It wasn't my place to interrupt, but my instinct told me that he wanted a way out of the conversation. No, he *needed* it.

"I'm very sorry to interrupt, Mr. Eastwood, but we really need to discuss Project Squirrel. I have to leave soon and really don't want to miss the opportunity to pick your brain."

Allison looked between us. "Project what?"

Reed seemed like he didn't know whether to laugh or cry. "Ah yes, very important. I need to attend to this. Allison. It was great seeing you. We'll have to catch up again some other time."

"Great seeing you, too."

Reed followed me, and we just kept walking in silence until we were far away from the festivities. It felt like we'd walked at least a half mile.

They had so much land. And there were outdoor lights all throughout the multi-acre estate.

We finally stopped at a small lake that ran along the property. I sat down on the grass and Reed joined me.

He looked up at the sky as he spoke. "How did you know I needed a way out of that conversation?"

"Your face. You seemed very uncomfortable talking to her. I figured I would at least try getting you out of it. I told myself that if I was mistaken, you didn't have to go along with it."

"Thank you."

"Was she supposed to be here?"

He simply shook his head no.

"Why did she come?"

"Her family's estate is just down the road. She stopped by to say hello. Security knows her and probably let her in, thinking she was invited."

I wanted so badly to ask again what had transpired between them, but then I remembered what had happened back at the hotel on Long Island when he snapped at me.

Reed was gazing up at the stars. To my surprise, he partly answered the question in my head without my having to even ask.

"She hurt me very badly when she realized the future she thought we were going to have was going to look a bit different than she'd always imagined it to be. Without going into details, she showed me that her love was definitely conditional."

"There is no such thing as conditional love."

"You're right," he said. "But it was difficult for me to realize that. I believed that I loved her unconditionally. When love is not returned, you have to learn to unlove the other person. The mind tells you that you're not supposed to love them anymore, but the heart isn't listening so easily."

"Do you still love her?"

"Not in the same way, but my feelings are complicated."

My heart broke for him, but at the same time, I envied Allison for having been the recipient of true love. Todd had never loved me. I knew that now. Knowing that Allison's love for Reed was conditional definitely shattered the idea I'd had about them when I first discovered the blue note. I was realizing I didn't really know anything at all, but I was afraid to pry too much. At the same time, seeing that he was still struggling with his feelings warmed my heart and gave me hope that there were men out there who were truly capable of love.

I stared at Reed's profile. God, was there really anything sexier than a gorgeous man who just wanted to be loved by a woman?

He picked at the grass. "I really wish she hadn't shown up."

My eyes stayed glued to his long, masculine fingers on the ground. "I'm glad she did, because you have to be able to face her to move on. It was good practice. Plus, did you see the look on her face? She was really confused when you left. And that made it all worth it."

"Project Squirrel." He laughed under his breath.

I chuckled. "Project Squirrel. Definition: the nonexistent, top-secret business venture that hereby serves as the perfect way out of any uncomfortable situation."

He sighed. "I could really use that drink, but I don't feel like walking back just yet."

I started to stand up. "Want me to go get us drinks? You can stay here."

"No." He placed his hand on my leg, prompting me to sit back down.

We sat in silence for a while. "Does this lake belong to you?"

"Yes. It's part of our property."

"Wow."

Something amazing occurred to me in that moment. Well, I wasn't sure if Reed would consider it amazing. But the wheels in my mind were turning. Apparently my joy was transparent.

"What do you have going on in that head of yours, Charlotte?"

"I feel like I'm ready to burst. I'm getting this urge to do something crazy."

"Now?"

"I added a couple of things to my Fuck-It List recently. And one of them involves a lake. It just feels like the opportunity is being presented to me right now."

"What you mean, 'involves a lake'?"

"*Go Skinny-Dipping in a Lake at Night.* I'm never at a lake at night. God knows when it would happen again. This just feels like fate. But I don't want to freak you out if you'd prefer I didn't do it."

"You seriously didn't just make that shit up? That was really on your list?"

"I swear."

He shocked me when he said, "Then I think you should do it."

"Really?"

"Yes. It would be the most fitting ending to this bizarre night."

"Do you think anyone will venture down this far? I wouldn't want to get caught."

"I doubt it. But make it fast. I'll stand guard. And I won't look."

"You're really encouraging me to do this?"

"Call me insane, but I need all the distraction I can get tonight, even if it comes in the form of your crazy. I don't feel like going back to the party yet, so we might as well pass the time. I'm turning around now."

His back faced me. I squealed in delight as I swiftly got out of my clothes before jumping into the water, which was surprisingly warm.

Once my body was immersed, I called out, "Safe to turn around!"

Reed stood with his hands in his pockets as he watched me bounce around the water. He didn't move from his spot and kept his eyes on me, occasionally looking back to make sure no one was coming.

I yelled over to him, "See . . . that's one of the differences between a fuck-it list and a bucket list—the spontaneity factor. The fuck-it list is more spur of the moment. Part of the mantra of the fuck-it list is that if the opportunity comes to you, you need to take it. And that's what I'm doing."

It felt exhilarating to be naked at night on this property. It was also thrilling because it seemed so naughty, given that Reed was standing just feet away from me. My nipples hardened at the thought.

I was proud of myself for seizing the moment. I likely wouldn't have considered doing something so spontaneous during the time I was engaged to Todd. In that sense, surviving the breakup had not only made me stronger but also more adventurous.

After I'd had my fill, I said, "I'm coming out!"

Reed turned his back to me. I slipped my dress back on over my wet body while the reality of what I'd done started to sink in.

"How do we explain why you're all wet?" he asked.

"I don't know. How are *you* going to explain it, Reed?" I grinned impishly.

"You're going to put this on me, Darling? Is that a challenge?"

"If you want to take it."

When we arrived back at the party, thankfully, it seemed Allison had left the premises.

People were looking at us, confused, particularly Max and Jared. Everyone was perplexed except for Iris, who was beaming.

"What on earth happened to you, Charlotte?" she asked.

I looked at Reed and waited for his response, trying my best not to lose my shit.

He finally answered his grandmother's question.

"Charlotte and I took a walk to discuss business. She sees this squirrel run right into the lake. It was dark, and the rodent was flailing its little arms and legs for dear life, trying to stay afloat. She then decides to go and pull a Charlotte, didn't even think twice, jumped right into the lake and saved it . . . set it free, saved its life."

Reed deserved an Academy Award, because he delivered that ridiculous story with unwavering seriousness.

"Charlotte, you never cease to amaze me," Iris said.

"Yeah, she's pretty amazing." Reed smiled.

I kept waiting for him to add something to ruin that sweet sentence, something like "pretty amazing for a crazy person." But he never did.

◆　◆　◆

I felt like I owed Reed big-time. He'd assisted me with my lake jaunt and played along so well after. Now that I knew how great it felt to knock that first item off my list, I was even more motivated to start helping him with his own bucket list.

The following Wednesday, I stayed at the office late to research choirs in the state of New York.

It felt like I'd hit the jackpot when I stumbled upon the Brooklyn Tabernacle Choir. I immediately sent an email to inquire as to whether they were accepting new members.

The choir director returned my email right away and provided me with some dates for their upcoming open-enrollment tryouts.

Printing out all the materials, I wondered how Reed was going to react. When I got to his office, he wasn't there, so I left all the information in a folder on his desk with a note that read: *Paying you back. Let's do this!*

The next morning, I got to the office early to find another blue note from Reed sitting on the center of my desk.

Anytime I'd see this stationery, it would give me goosebumps and remind me about discovering that blue piece of paper inside of the dress.

I eagerly picked up the note and read it.

> *Dear Charlotte:*
> *Do you know why squirrels love you so much?*
> *Because you're NUTS.*
> *Reed*

I shook my head and whispered to myself, "These are the kind of love notes you're doling out now, Eastwood?" I laughed. "More like a hate note."

CHAPTER 15

REED

I hadn't planned on showing up.

At least that was what I'd told myself. The fact that I'd set up an appointment with a prospective seller in the Cobble Hill section of Brooklyn had nothing to do with open tryouts going on twelve blocks away the very same day.

My meeting happened to end at six thirty, and driving up Smith Street took me right past a certain massive church. Next thing I knew, I had parked and was following a herd of people like a mindless sheep.

"Welcome to the Tabernacle." An older man at the entrance handed me a brochure with a warm smile. "Talent is a gift from God. Sharing it here is your gift back. Good luck tonight."

While the inviting gesture should have made me feel at ease, it made me feel the exact opposite. I wanted to run the hell out of here. But since I'd come this far, I tamped down the urge to flee, took a seat in the very back row, and watched all the excited faces pile into the front pews of the church.

"Mind if I sit next to you?" The guy who'd greeted me stood in the aisle at the end of the pew I sat in. I glanced around the church. There had to be thirty completely empty rows in front of me.

He read my face. "I like to sit next to the door in case there are any interruptions or latecomers that make a ruckus."

I nodded and slid over in the pew to make room. It was after seven. People had stopped piling in, but auditions hadn't started up yet.

"You new? Don't think I've seen you around here before."

"I just stopped in to . . ." What the hell *was* I doing here? ". . . to check things out."

"So you don't sing?"

"No. Yes. No. Yes. I mean . . . I used to. A long time ago."

He nodded. "What made you stop coming to church?"

I hadn't said I'd stopped coming to church. I'd only implied I once sang and didn't anymore. "How do you know I don't go to a different church?"

He smiled. "Do you?"

I couldn't help but laugh a little. "No. I don't."

He motioned to the back pews. "When people first come back after a long absence, they tend to sit in the back rows."

I nodded. "Makes the escape easier."

"How long's it been?"

"Since I sang?"

He shook his head. "No. Since you've been to God's house."

I knew the answer without having to think about it. The last time I'd stepped foot inside of a church had been with Allison. We'd gone to mass before our scheduled meeting with the deacon. It had been two weeks before our wedding day, and we'd given him the readings and song choices we'd picked out for the ceremony. Ironically, the day we'd gone to God's house had been the night that she'd chosen for her come-to-Jesus moment. "It's been a while."

"I'm Terrence." The man extended his hand. "Welcome back."

"Reed." I shook. "And I'm not sure I'm actually back."

"Every journey begins with a first step. You planning on trying out for the choir?"

"I haven't made up my mind yet. Figured I'd watch tonight and see how things go. There's a second tryout night next week, isn't there?"

"That's right."

The church doors opened, and a guy in a maintenance uniform walked in. Spotting Terrence, he said, "Got an issue with the boiler in the basement. Could use a few hands to help me move the file cabinets that Miss Margaret made us store down there. They're blocking access to the system."

Terrence nodded and turned to me. "A volunteer's work is never done around here." He stood and patted me on the shoulder. "I hope you find what you're looking for."

A few days later, I still hadn't decided if I was going back for the only other audition night at the Brooklyn Tabernacle. But when I went into my online calendar, I noticed that an appointment had been booked for that night. The scheduler showed that Charlotte had entered the appointment, although the only information on the blocked-out time was a bunch of letters that spelled nothing: *SFBGITS*.

I picked up the phone and called her extension.

She answered on the second ring, "Bonjour, Monsieur Eastwood. *Je peux vous aider?*"

What the . . . "Charlotte?"

"Oui."

Then it dawned on me. When I'd stalked her Fuck-It List online the other day, *Learn French* had been added. I'd seen her in the break room earlier, eating her lunch with earbuds in while mumbling to herself. Now it made sense. Well, sense for Charlotte Darling. She'd been listening to phrases and practicing speaking them.

Luckily, I'd taken some French myself. *"Ne tenez-vous pas la langue anglaise assez?"* Translation: Don't you butcher the English language enough? I covered the phone and chuckled, because I had no fucking clue if my own translation was even correct.

She responded, "Umm. Huh?"

I chuckled. "That's what I thought."

"I'm still learning."

"I never would've guessed . . ."

"Shut up. Did you call for a reason, or did you just get the urge to poke fun at someone so you automatically dialed my extension?"

"Actually, I called for a reason. You just make it so easy to poke fun."

"What did you want?"

"There's an appointment on my calendar for Wednesday at seven. It's labeled *SFBGITS*. Do you know what that is?"

"Of course. SFBGITS—'Sing for big guy in the sky.' I wrote it in code so no one would figure it out except us."

I shook my head. "Except *you*, you mean."

"Whatever. Are you excited? Have you been practicing?"

"I'm not auditioning, Charlotte." Even if I'd decided to do it, there was no way I'd have let her know about it. I hadn't sung in years, and the people at those tryouts were really good. I doubted I could even make the cut. Besides, if by some long shot I did make it through tryouts, I envisioned her sitting in the first row of every performance. She'd probably invite the entire office staff and a few janitors I've never met from the building, too.

I could imagine the pout on her face when she spoke. "Why not?"

"Just because I made the list doesn't mean I'm planning on attacking it like it's a race."

"Oh." She was quiet for a moment. Then again said, "Why not?"

"Just take the appointment off my calendar, Charlotte."

"Fine."

After I hung up, I felt slightly bad about being a dick toward her. So I opened up her calendar, called up all her appointments and reminders for the next week, and began to translate them all from English to French for her to work through.

One appointment read "Iris flight landing at 5pm. Call to confirm at 4." So I translated it to: *Le vol d'Iris atterrit à 17h. Appelez pour confirmer à 16h.* Then I decided to add a few tasks of my own for her to do: *Prendre rendez-vous avec rétrécis.* Translation: Make appointment with shrink. At least that's what I attempted to write.

Another reminder she had read "Victoria's Secret sale ends. Order new unmentionables after getting paycheck!" I laughed out loud at that one. Charlotte was definitely the only twentysomething-year-old I knew who would use the word "unmentionables." I gave her a good translation for that.

Commandez des pantalons et des soutiens-gorge. Order granny panties and support bras.

I was enjoying myself, getting into screwing with her, until I came to the next appointment. "Blind Date at 9."

An unexpected anger bubbled up inside of me. Even though I had no right to feel that way, it didn't cool the burn in my throat. Some asshole was going to take full advantage of Goldilocks. I wasn't jealous—I was . . . protective. Deep down, buried underneath all that crazy, was a woman who believed in fairy tales. Her asshole fiancé had been dipping his pen in the company ink at the place *she worked*, and Charlotte still posted shit on Facebook like *Just keep swimming* and *Create your own happiness.* Some people never learn. She wouldn't see that her knight in shining armor was an asshole wrapped in tinfoil until after he screwed her over. And it pissed me off that she was so blind. That feeling became immeasurably worse when I realized that her little Victoria's Secret shopping spree likely directly correlated to her big blind date.

"Leave it on my desk," I bit out without looking up. I'd smelled her walk into my office. And that only served to irritate me even more—that I knew her scent. That I liked the way she fucking smelled.

Charlotte placed the report she'd been working on for me down and turned around to walk out. Only she stopped in the doorway. "Did I do something wrong, Reed?"

I'd been giving her an attitude for a few days—since the afternoon I'd made the mistake of opening her calendar. "Nope. Just busy."

"Can I get you some coffee or something?"

"Nope." I motioned to the door without looking up from editing the brochure I was working on. "But you can shut my door on your way out."

After my door clicked closed, I tossed my pen on the desk and sat back in my seat. The goddamn entire office smelled like her now. A few minutes later, I was still unable to concentrate, so I opened my laptop and fired off an email to my annoying assistant.

To: Charlotte Darling

Subject: You.

I would be most appreciative if you could reduce the quantity of perfume that you bathe yourself in. My olfactory receptors set off my allergy sensors twenty feet before you arrive in a room. Besides, a woman wears subtlety best.

Getting that off my chest, I was able to return my focus to actual work. Until a few minutes later, when a soft chime notified me a new email had arrived. I knew who it was from before waking my computer from the screen saver.

To: Reed Eastwood

Subject: Your olfactory receptors

It's a shame your olfactory receptors are so sensitive. Have you tried exposing yourself to the allergen in order to desensitize the effect? Perhaps it might help if on occasion you would stop and smell the roses instead of trampling on the garden? The world is filled with bouquets of women. Besides, a man wears manners best.

The next evening, before I left for the night, I stopped by Charlotte's office to drop off some receipts so she could prepare my monthly expense report. It was nearly eight, and I'd assumed she'd left already. Her voice stopped me right before I reached her door.

"And what's the price of a sleeper cabin?"

Quiet, and then, "Hmm. Okay. And how big are the beds in the cabin?"

More silence.

"Wow. You don't have something to fit two? Maybe a queen or something?"

She laughed. "Okay. Well, I guess that's always an option. I'm not ready to book at this time. But thank you very much for the information."

I didn't want to get caught eavesdropping in the hall, but I also couldn't resist being an asshole. Strolling into her office, I dropped my expense envelope on her desk and said, "Using a company phone at work to make vacation plans. Not very professional, Charlotte."

She glared at me. I found her wrinkled nose, squinty eyes, and the pink heat rising in her cheeks to be cute. Wisely, I kept that thought to myself.

Charlotte picked her cell phone up from her desk and waved it in my direction. "I was using *my* cell phone, not the company phone. And my workday ended *three hours ago*. So technically, the only *company thing* I'm using is *this chair*."

I hid my smirk. "Taking a trip somewhere? I didn't realize you had earned vacation time already."

"Not that it's any of your business, but I was only getting information for a train ride in Europe. I like to daydream about things I want to do, and sometimes the visual of what that looks like helps."

It clicked. *Under the Tuscan Sun*. Yesterday she'd added *Make Love to a Man for the First Time in a Sleeper Cabin on a Train Ride Through Italy* to her Fuck-It List. If she knew I'd been stalking her list on the server, she'd take that to mean I was interested in being her bucket-list buddy, so I didn't mention I knew what she was talking about. Instead, I chose a different path to walk. One that surely led straight to hell. "Perhaps if you spent more time working and less time daydreaming, you'd be more productive and wouldn't have to stay until eight o'clock at night."

Her eyes flared wide. She stared at me for a moment, then opened her desk drawer and ripped her purse out of it, slamming it down onto her desktop before banging the drawer back closed. Shutting her laptop, she stood and tugged her purse to her shoulder. She then proceeded to march toward the door where I was still standing. Not expecting her to stop when she reached me, I took a cautious step back, anticipating getting reamed out.

Instead, her eyes closed, hands raised, and her fingers frantically began typing in the air.

Seriously. Fucking. Nuts.

And so beautiful when her nostrils were flaring.

She hit what I presumed was the imaginary "Enter" button, took a deep breath, opened her eyes, and walked out of the office without another word.

I might've watched the sway of her ass the entire way out.

We both needed goddamn counseling.

CHAPTER 16

REED

After a few more days of avoiding her at all costs, it was no longer possible when Iris showed up at a business lunch with Charlotte in tow. Matthew Garamound, our CPA, my brother, and I were already seated. Even though I was annoyed at her presence, I stood when she walked toward the table. Nodding my greeting, I pulled out the empty chair next to me, while Garamound did the same for Iris. "Charlotte."

"Actually, I'm going to sit next to Max on the other side of the table if he doesn't mind. I wouldn't want my perfume to bother your allergies."

Iris's eyes narrowed. "You don't have a perfume allergy."

"It's something I recently developed."

Max flashed his annoying-as-shit megawatt smile and stood to pull out a chair. "My brother's loss is my gain." He leaned toward Charlotte, closed his eyes, and inhaled dramatically. "You smell amazing."

I grumbled something about his unprofessionalism under my breath as the five of us sat down. It quickly became apparent that Charlotte was going to avoid eye contact with me, which I initially thought was perfect until I realized that when she wasn't looking in my direction, it permitted me unlimited opportunity to stare at her face. She was so goddamn distracting. I had to force my eyes to pay attention to something else, so I studied our CPA.

Matthew Garamound had to be ten years older than my grandmother. His hair was silver, his skin tanned, and he always wore a tie with an American flag pin. He'd been the company's CPA since Iris had opened her doors, and the four of us got together four times a year like clockwork—two weeks after the end of each quarter. Only we'd just had our quarterly meeting a month ago, and we never brought an assistant to these types of things.

After the waitress took our drink order, Matthew folded his hands on the table and cleared his throat. "So . . . you're probably wondering why we're getting together today."

Max leaned to Charlotte and whispered, even though we could all hear him, "I'm actually wondering what perfume you're wearing."

I answered through gritted teeth. "How about you try to keep the harassment of employees limited to when you're lying on the couch in their offices."

Matthew looked between the two of us. While I sported a scowl, my comment seemed to please my little brother.

"Yes, well anyway," Garamound continued, "I asked Iris and Charlotte to pull this meeting together today because I, unfortunately, have some bad news to deliver."

I immediately assumed he was sick. "Everything okay with you, Matt?"

"Oh." He realized what I thought. "Yes, yes. I'm fine. This is about the business and one of your employees. Namely, Dorothy."

"Dorothy?" I furrowed my brow. "Dorothy's sick?"

Iris took over the conversation. "No, Reed. Everyone's health is just fine. Why don't I start at the beginning? As you know, I've been having Charlotte compile a list of our cleaning vendors so that I could consolidate the number of partners we use and receive a bigger volume discount on services. As part of that project, I had her list all invoices paid for each vendor during the last sixty days."

"Okay, yes, I knew she was working on that."

"Well. She came across a few invoices that were paid wrong—a transposition in numbers. For example, one invoice was for $16,292, yet it was paid for $16,992. Another one was for $2,300, and it was paid for $3,200. None of them were off by a lot—all less than a thousand dollars each. But Charlotte noticed it on four different invoices, so she mentioned it to me. Now, Dorothy is almost as old as I am, and she's been with me as long as you boys have been alive, so I assumed maybe she needed stronger glasses, and I went to speak to her." My grandmother's face fell, and I knew what was coming next. "She acted really strange. So I asked Matthew to look into some of the transactions."

Garamound picked up where Grandmother left off. "I did an audit of her transactions over the last twelve months and found that she'd transposed numbers on fifty-three different invoices. Like the ones that Charlotte found, they weren't very big mistakes and at first glance seemed to be a simple transposition of numbers. But the errors were never in our favor. In total, those fifty-three payments were overpaid by more than thirty-two thousand dollars. When I dug a little deeper, I found that each payment was being made to two different accounts— the right amount was going to the vendor, but there was a separate ACH payment being made for the difference, and all of that was funneled into one account."

I exhaled a deep breath. "Dorothy has been skimming."

Garamound nodded. "Unfortunately so. I haven't gone back to the beginning of time—but it's been going on for at least the last few years."

"Jesus. Dorothy is like family."

Iris had tears in her eyes. "She has a sick grandson."

Swallowing that news, I tasted salt in my throat.

Charlotte chimed in, her own eyes about to overflow. "Choroidal metastasis. It's extremely rare in children. She's been taking him to Philadelphia for experimental treatment that isn't covered by insurance."

"I had no idea."

The mood of lunch took a drastic turn after that. It was one thing to catch an employee stealing, but entirely another to catch a long-term one who had a damn good reason. We all agreed we needed to give the situation some thought and that we'd reconvene at the end of the week to discuss how to handle things.

At the end of lunch, Iris turned to me. "I have an appointment uptown. Could you give Charlotte a lift back to the office?"

Max responded, even though Grandmother hadn't spoken to him. "I can give her a lift."

"It's a Tuesday, you don't usually come to the office." I buttoned my suit jacket. "Don't you have a massage or some other pressing business to attend to?"

My brother slipped his hands into his pockets and rocked back and forth on the balls of his feet. "Nope. I'm free all afternoon."

We already had embezzlement going on at the office; the last thing we needed was a sexual harassment suit. I put my hand on Charlotte's lower back. "We have actual business to discuss. So we'll see you back at the office."

◆ ◆ ◆

Neither of us said a word for the first five minutes of the drive back downtown.

Eventually, I broke the ice. "Good job picking up on that check inconsistency."

She stared out the window and sighed. "It doesn't feel so good. It feels pretty lousy, actually."

"It's never fun to discover that a person you've trusted has betrayed you."

"I know. Believe me, I know. But it's Christian that I feel badly about."

"Christian?"

"Dorothy's grandson. He's only six. And the cancer isn't just in his eye. He spent months sick from the treatment of a tumor in his lungs only to have it metastasize to his eye. He should be playing peewee baseball instead of being home-tutored and living in hotels with his mom while she desperately runs him around like a guinea pig."

I caught myself rubbing at a spot on my chest, but it was inside that hurt. I side-glanced over at Charlotte. "How do you know so much about his illness?"

She shrugged. "We talk."

"You talk? You've only been at the company for what—three or four weeks?"

"So? That doesn't mean I can't make friends. You know that cute picture of him in the Boy Scout uniform on her desk?"

I didn't but skirted the issue. "What about it?"

"Well, I commented about how cute he is on my second day, and she just broke down crying and told me the story. We went to lunch together a few times after that." She paused. "Now I'm the person who got her into trouble."

"That's not on you, Charlotte. She got herself into trouble. I understand you feel badly. But you did the right thing."

Charlotte gazed out the window as a moment of silence passed. She was so damn sensitive to everyone's feelings, which was admirable but also a detriment sometimes when it came to business. Although when you're talking about a kid with cancer, all bets are off. The entire situation was horrible.

"What are you going to do to Dorothy?" she finally asked.

I glanced over at Charlotte and then back to the road. "What would you do if you were in my shoes?"

She took some time to think about her answer. "I wouldn't fire her. She really needs the job. What she did was absolutely wrong, but I don't know that I wouldn't have done the same thing given no other alternative. People aren't perfect, and sometimes we need to balance the one wrong they did with all of the rights they've done. Dorothy has worked for you for a long time and was helping her daughter and grandson."

I nodded. We were both quiet for a long time after that.

It was Charlotte who finally brought us both out of deep thought. She turned to me. "I appreciated the French translations, by the way. I never thanked you. Thank God for Google, though, or else I might've accidentally bought granny panties for my upcoming nonexistent trip to Paris." She rolled her eyes.

"I see you checked my work." I chuckled. "And, *de rien*. You're welcome."

"So why did you stop the French lesson at the point where I scheduled 'Blind Date'?"

Trying to skirt around the question, I said, "What do you mean?"

"You stopped translating my schedule right at that spot. It was like the second-to-last item, and you decided to stop right there. That was random. Is there no French translation for 'blind date'?"

Shit. How was I going to explain that one?

Well, Charlotte, I stopped translating because the idea of you going out with some random man makes me feel violent.

"I was no longer having fun with it, so I stopped." Clenching my jaw, I glanced over at her and asked, "Anyway, why are you going out on a blind date? In this day and age, you have access to so many ways of meeting people. Someone like you doesn't need to resort to that."

"Okay . . . what do you mean, someone like me?"

Of course she wanted me to spell it out.

"Someone . . . attractive and with an outgoing personality doesn't need to go on a blind date. It's too risky, especially in this city. You should really do your homework before you agree to meet someone."

"Like you? Is that what you do? You get background checks done on the people you date? Kind of like how you checked up on me before the Millennium penthouse showing?"

"No. Although I would have no problem doing that. But I wouldn't be going on a blind date in the first place."

"By the way," she said, "I never asked. If you knew I was lying on my application that day, why did you agree to show the penthouse to me?"

"Because I wanted to teach you a lesson, humiliate you for wasting my time."

"You get a rise out of humiliating people?"

"If they deserve it? Yes."

I could feel the weight of her staring at me. My tie suddenly felt like it was choking me. I loosened it a bit.

"What?" I snapped.

"Have you dated anyone since Allison?"

Great. I was trapped in this car and wouldn't be able to escape this question. I had no desire to discuss my dating life with Charlotte.

"That's none of your business."

The truth was, there'd been a few meaningless trysts, but nothing more significant.

"Well, you seem to think that my business is your business, so maybe you should think first before offering me dating advice." She let out a long breath. "'Blind Date' was just code anyway."

"Code for what?"

"I didn't want people to know that I was going out on a date with Max. And before you say anything . . . I know for a fact that the company does not have a nonfraternization policy."

What?

A rush of adrenaline coursed through my veins. The car came to a screeching halt as my foot hit the brakes in the middle of Manhattan traffic, a couple of pedestrians nearly getting hit in the process.

"What?" I spewed, even though I'd heard her loud and clear.

Horns were blaring behind me, but I barely noticed.

She repeated, "Max and I are going out tomorrow night. And you'd better move this car before you get us into *another* fender bender."

She was right. I needed to pull over.

Parking illegally in front of a Dean & Deluca, I put my hazards on.

It was quiet for a few moments before I turned to her and looked her dead straight in the eyes. "You're not going out with Max, Charlotte."

"Why not? He's—"

"Charlotte . . ." Her name exited my mouth in a warning tone. My ears felt like they were burning.

"Yes?" She smiled.

My anger seemed to be amusing her.

It was like a jealous beast that could no longer be tamed had ripped its way through my body. "You're. Not. Going. Out. With. Max."

Without any real justification for my actions, I waited for her reaction. I couldn't articulate the reason why she was forbidden from dating my brother because I didn't even truly understand my rage. I just knew that I couldn't handle even the idea of Charlotte and Max.

I was expecting a big argument, one that included her insisting that I had no right to tell her whom to date. But she surprised me when she said, "I'll tell you what. I'll cancel my date with Max on one condition."

My pulse rate began to slow down. "What is it?"

Whatever it is, I'll fucking do it.

"Tomorrow night is also the last tryout at the Brooklyn Tabernacle. I'll cancel with Max if you go."

Christ. You've got to be kidding me. Now Blondie was an extortionist?

"You're bribing me?"

"Bribery makes more sense than the unwarranted alpha-male behavior you're exhibiting against me with no explanation right now, don't you think?"

There was no way I was going to sit back and do nothing while she went out with my brother, so I gave the only answer I could.

"Fine."

"Fine, you agree with my statement on bribery, or fine, you agree to go to the tryout?"

"Fine. I agree to go to Brooklyn. But I'm going alone. Got it?"

Charlotte looked all too pleased. "Yes."

"Good."

I put the car in "Drive" and pulled out into traffic as we continued our ride back to the office. A slow and satisfied smile spread over her face as she leaned her neck back on the headrest before closing her eyes.

How the hell this car ride had gone from talking about Dorothy's grandson to my suddenly agreeing to try out for the choir was beyond me. But this was typical Charlotte. Typical annoying, insistent, sometimes clever but always . . . beautiful Charlotte. Fucking *beautiful* Charlotte. Fucking beautiful Charlotte who was not going anywhere near my brother.

I could keep her from dating Max—perhaps for now—but I had no right to dictate her life. My need to do so had to end. I needed a distraction from this woman, and I had to figure one out, and fast.

When we returned downtown, Charlotte seemed to be in a rush as she headed back to her office. Meanwhile, I headed straight down the hall to talk to Iris about something that had been on my mind since we'd left the business lunch.

She had just gotten off a phone call when she looked up at me.

"Grandmother, good. You're here. I thought you might still be at your appointment."

She stood and walked around to the front of her desk. "I didn't have an appointment."

Did she forget she'd given that excuse as to why she couldn't drive Charlotte back from lunch? It was then I realized she'd likely made up having the appointment to get me to drive Charlotte. I didn't feel like getting into it with her. So I left it alone.

"Did you just arrive?" she asked. "I figured you'd beat me back here. What took so long?"

"We just walked in. Charlotte and I ran into a little snafu."

She smirked. "I see. That seems to happen a lot with you two."

Yeah.

Taking a seat, I was happy to change the subject. "Listen, we need to talk about Dorothy."

"Yes. I haven't been able to think about anything else all day."

"We need to call her out on the stealing. She can't get away with it."

"I know, Reed, but—"

"Hear me out."

"Alright." She looked worried about what I was going to say next.

"While I think she needs to know that we figured it out . . . I don't think we should fire her. She's going through too much. And she's been a loyal employee up until this happened. I can see how someone in her situation could act in a desperate way. People do strange things when their loved ones are in danger. She stole from us, but I don't think she meant any harm. To her, it was a life-or-death situation."

A look of relief washed over her face. "I agree, and I'm happy and proud of you for seeing it that way."

From the moment I understood what was happening, I knew what I wanted to do. Iris was a charitable person and had always set a good example for me in that regard. It felt good to not only be able to help this family but also make my grandmother proud.

"I'd like to pay for the balance of her grandson's treatment myself."

She seemed taken aback. "Are you certain? That could be a lot of money."

"Yes, I'm sure. I couldn't imagine having a child or a grandchild who was dying and not having the finances to help save him. I mean, is there anything you wouldn't do for a sick grandson?"

My grandmother paused as she looked me in the eye.

"No. No, there isn't."

CHAPTER 17

CHARLOTTE

Out of breath and frazzled when I returned to my office, I pulled up Max's cell-phone number as fast as I could.

He picked up on the first ring. "Well, hello. To what do I owe this—"

"Max!" I interrupted. "Listen. I need a favor. You haven't spoken to Reed since the lunch meeting this afternoon, have you?"

"No. I never ended up going back to the office. I went home. What's up?"

Covering my chest, I let out a sigh of relief.

"I lied to your brother. I told him that I had a date with you tomorrow night."

Max's laughter filled my eardrum. "Um . . . okay. Let me get this straight. I've been trying to get you to go out with me since day one. You turn me down every time, but you're telling people that we're dating?"

"Well . . . yes. But just Reed."

"You're a trip, Charlotte. What . . . were you trying to get a rise out of him? You two have a strange-as-fuck dynamic."

"I was trying to teach him a lesson—sort of. It's complicated. Anyway, he forbade me from going out with you."

"What a dick." He chuckled.

"If he mentions anything to you, will you go along with it for a little while? I'll probably tell him the truth at some point."

"Anytime I can get my brother riled up and out of his funk, I'm happy to do it. Can I tell him you were the one who pursued me if he confronts me?"

"I'd rather you didn't."

He was laughing in my ear. "Okay."

"I made a bargain with Reed. It's not something I'm at liberty to talk about, but my end of the deal was cancelling the date. So I'm cancelling it."

"You're cancelling the date that never existed. Gotcha."

"Yes. And thank you, by the way. I owe you one."

"How about dinner next week?"

"You're relentless."

"Can't blame a guy for trying."

After we hung up, I sat at my desk, thinking about the Eastwood brothers. Max was a carefree playboy, but he was a good guy, and I knew he cared about Reed a lot. Max was definitely the crazier brother. And some might even label him the better-looking one, depending on their taste. He was wilder, too, for sure. But in my opinion, brooding, intense Reed was far sexier. In fact, I'd never found him sexier than in his car today when he turned to me and demanded that I stay away from Max. Todd never gave me that kind of single-minded attention; it felt good to be recipient of it. While some women would have advised me to smack him upside his head in that very moment, I couldn't help but be turned on by Reed's protectiveness. It didn't hurt that the sun was blazing into his beautiful, espresso-colored eyes when he made the demand, or that the car was filled with his intoxicating Ralph Lauren cologne.

My body begged for him to take that intensity out on me in other ways. But there was clearly an invisible barricade that Reed had put up between us.

The next morning, I entered my office to find a blue note staring me in the face atop my desk.

> *From the desk of Reed Eastwood*
> *Charlotte:*
>> *Congratulations on setting a precedent. See the employee manual on the server for the addition of Eastwood/Locklear's new nonfraternization policy. Additionally, I would think long and hard before bribing your boss again. That's grounds for termination, too. P.S. You're late. I got my own coffee, which means it wasn't laden with too much cream for once. Try better to be on time from now on.*
>> *Reed*

Fuming, I decided not to give him the benefit of a reaction, so I kept to myself most of the morning and knocked off the items on my to-do list.

After I cooled off in the early afternoon, I ventured down to his office to feel out his mood and to offer moral support since tonight was his tryout at the Tabernacle.

To my surprise, a gorgeous woman with auburn hair was in there with him, not across from his desk like most visitors, but right *next* to him. She didn't work here, so she must have been a client. She was leaning into him and laughing at everything he was saying.

Wearing those expensive red-bottomed heels and with a string of pearls wrapped around her neck, it was evident she was well off. Her body was against his as he showed her properties on his computer.

The memory of walking into Todd's office and finding him in that compromising position flashed through my mind. It was a horrible feeling to be blindsided and to discover that your entire relationship was just an illusion. That experience would always serve as a reminder that things could change in an instant. The fact that I was experiencing a familiar sense of dread was very telling in terms of my feelings for Reed. We weren't even together, yet I was feeling a hint of betrayal.

My stomach suddenly felt sick as I knocked, making my presence known for the first time.

"Hi," I said. "I was just checking in to see if everything is still on schedule with your appointment tonight and if you needed anything."

Reed looked up. "Yes, it is. And no, I don't need anything." He then turned his attention back to the woman and ignored me.

"Very well, then," I said, basically talking to the wall.

Taking a few steps forward, I introduced myself to Reed's guest. "I'm Charlotte, Reed's assistant. You are?"

"Eve Lennon—a private client of Mr. Eastwood's. He's going to be showing me a few properties today."

Reed finally addressed me. "Charlotte, while I have you, can you call ahead to Le Coucou and let them know I'll be coming there in about fifteen minutes? Have them set up a table for two." He turned to her. "We'll go to lunch first."

I forced a smile. "Of course."

After I lingered at the doorway for a bit, Reed abruptly took off his glasses, looked over at me, and in the rudest tone said, "You can go."

Was he kidding?

He was giving me permission to go? How nice of him!

After begrudgingly heading back to my office to make the reservation, I ventured into the kitchen for some much-needed coffee to cure my splitting headache. Still reeling from the way Reed had spoken to me, I was dropping things left and right—first the open sugar packet, then the stirrer.

Iris was there and must have noticed my slippery fingers.

"Charlotte, is everything okay? You seem frazzled."

Stirring my coffee, I asked, "Who's Eve Lennon?"

"The Lennon family has been a client of ours for years. Why do you ask?"

"Eve is with Reed in his office, and I got the impression that maybe there was something going on with them. She was all over him. Anyway, it's none of my business."

Understanding filled Iris's eyes. "But it is . . . your business . . . because you have to work with him every day, and you work with all facets of our lives. Reed is very much your business, Charlotte." She paused. "You have feelings for him, don't you?"

"Not in that way . . ." I hesitated and let out a breath, realizing I didn't really need to put up a front with Iris. "I don't know. Things are just weird between us . . . all of the time. He's so hot and cold with me. I don't really understand him. You know what he said to me when I went into his office while she was there?"

"What?"

Deepening my voice, I gave my best Reed impression. "'You can go.' Just like that. 'You can go.' He can be so condescending."

Iris seemed upset to see me so bothered by him. She nudged her head for me to join her at one of the tables.

She leaned in. "With my grandson . . . it's a battle between who he really is and who he thinks he should be . . . between what he really wants and what he thinks he deserves. He has his reasons for how he acts sometimes. But one thing I can tell you is that Eve Lennon doesn't hold a candle to you. And if Reed is shooing you away and letting that woman near him, he's using her as a human shield from something he otherwise can't resist."

CHAPTER 18

Reed

I was goddamn rude to Charlotte, and it was eating me up inside.

She'd left my office like a dog with its tail between its legs. She normally bit back at least once. Not this time.

It was bad enough that Eve had been all over me when Charlotte walked in. Even though there was nothing going on between Charlotte and me, I could tell catching me with Eve made her uncomfortable. But I'd volunteered to usher Eve around to three properties for that very reason, hadn't I? To show Charlotte that I had no interest in her and to try to steer my dick into a different direction. After my freak-out over her date with my brother, I'd felt a major diversion was necessary. That diversion was currently trying to rub her foot against my leg under the table at Le Coucou.

I *wished* I wanted Eve. Because she was exactly the type of woman I needed in my life—one I knew would want nothing more from me than sex and expensive things. One who didn't want inside of my head and heart, one who didn't want anything long-term.

Eve had two divorces under her belt and had no desire for marriage and kids. *Perfect.* But as I sat across from her at lunch, I was more than preoccupied.

"So which property are we going to see first?" she asked.

My eyes met hers, but her words hadn't registered. "Hmm?"

She repeated, "Where are we going first?"

"Right. I was thinking the Tribeca loft since it's the closest to here."

She flashed her bright white teeth. "Great."

When Eve got up to go to the ladies' room, I decided to check my phone. Out of habit, I clicked on Instagram and pulled up Charlotte's profile. There was nothing new from today, so I scrolled mindlessly through photos from the past week, coming across one from a week ago that showed a shot of her television while her feet were up on a coffee table. She was wearing fuzzy slippers. The photo was captioned, *It's 9:00 p.m. on a Wednesday night. You know what that means! Blind Date. Best show on TV.*

Everything started to piece together in my brain. The nine p.m. entry of "Blind Date" in her schedule. The fact that Max hadn't waltzed into my office the first chance he got to tell me that he'd snagged a date with Charlotte. I'd thought that was so unlike him, and I'd been too angry to even confront him long enough to feel him out.

Charlotte had lied.

She'd completely fabricated the date with Max to get me to agree to go to the tryout tonight. I didn't know what was worse, the fact that she'd conned me into agreeing to go or that she'd known what kind of reaction threatening a date with Max would garner from me.

The rest of the afternoon was a blur as I ushered Eve to the three showings when all I could concentrate on was confronting Charlotte.

After dropping Eve back at her condo, I slogged through rush-hour traffic, hoping to catch Charlotte if she hadn't left the office yet.

Her office was dark, the only light coming from a small desk lamp. Mostly everyone had left for the day, but Charlotte was sitting at her computer, looking like she was surfing the net rather than working.

When she noticed me standing in the doorway, she jumped a little. "Shouldn't you be heading to Brooklyn? The tryouts are at seven. You need to head out there."

"No," I said as the door latched behind me. "I won't be going to Brooklyn."

Charlotte got up from her chair and crossed her arms. "I thought we had a deal."

"What kind of a game are you playing with me, Charlotte?"

"What do you mean?"

"You lied to me . . . why? So you could see me lose my mind? You knew what kind of a reaction you were going to get. Is that how you get your kicks?"

The guilt on her face was apparent. "How did you know I lied? Did Max tell you?"

"He's in on this, too? Great."

"No . . . I just asked him to . . . um . . ." She lost her train of thought.

I took my phone out of my pocket, opened it to her Instagram post, and placed it in front of her face. "Figured it out. 'Blind Date at nine.' Plus, Max would never keep something like that quiet. He'd look for the first opportunity to rub it in my face. It all makes sense now."

"I just didn't want you to miss the opportunity to try out. That's all."

Charlotte's expression was filled with regret. It wasn't my intent to make her sad. I just wanted to call her out on her lie. But God, the look on her face was making me want to just forget everything and . . . kiss her.

I wanted to kiss her.

I wanted to taste her lips and suck away that sour look on her face, yet I knew that if there was one set of lips on this earth forbidden to me, it was Charlotte Darling's. She wasn't just a pretty face and a hot body. She was someone who wanted inside my soul, and that was never going to happen.

I should have just walked out. Instead, I was completely lost in this moment. The most spectacular skyline may have been visible from right behind her, but there was nothing more spectacular than Charlotte's heaving chest, the sweat beading on her forehead, the reaction she was having toward me. Her attraction to me was palpable.

We were standing about a foot apart, and her damn scent was all I could smell anymore.

A long moment of silence passed.

"What are you doing to me?" I muttered, the words exiting me like a hiccup I had no control over.

"What are you doing to *me*?" she whispered.

I looked down for a moment, and that's when I noticed the pink-striped Victoria's Secret bag on the floor by her desk.

My voice was gruff. "What's that?"

"Iris made me take a break in the middle of the day to clear my head. It was the last day of the sale, so I went shopping."

"Why did you need to clear your head?"

"Because you pissed me off."

God, she was sexy when she gritted her teeth in anger. I wondered what else those teeth could pull on.

Fuck. Stop.

Yet I moved in closer. "Show me what you bought yourself on company time."

Charlotte swallowed, then walked over to the bag. She bent down and took out the contents, removing a sticker on the tissue paper. Returning to the spot in front of me, she opened it up to show me several pairs of lace underwear in a rainbow of colors.

A black lace thong with a tiny silk rose sewn on the top of the waistband caught my eye.

Picking it from the pile, I held it in my hand, relishing the feel of the soft lace and imagining the black against Charlotte's creamy skin. Running my finger along the back string, I also imagined what it would look like inside the crack of her perfectly curved ass. Folding my fingers over the thong, I enveloped it, gripping it in my hand in the same way I wanted to swallow her up whole.

Charlotte was watching me, almost as if in a trance.

And I knew I'd taken this too far. I was her boss, and I'd just demanded to see her underwear. I was fondling it. And if she looked down, she'd also see I was hard. I'd officially lost my fucking mind when it came to her.

A voice of reason inside my head warned me. *Leave!*

I chose to listen to it.

"Good night," I said as I handed her the panties and swiftly exited her office.

Taking the elevator down, I seriously considered heading to a bar and getting piss-ass drunk, even though I rarely drank anymore.

Instead, I drove around for a while and somehow ended up on the Brooklyn Bridge.

◆　◆　◆

Auditions were already halfway over when I slipped inside. Same as last time, I took a seat in the back row by myself and looked around. Over the years, I'd done a lot of business in this part of Brooklyn, so I knew the area well. I'd been a teenager when the church moved to this particular building—the former Loew's Metropolitan Theatre. I must've been about thirteen or fourteen when they started a big restoration on the place. Iris and I had passed by once during that time. She'd pulled over to tell me all about the building. My grandparents had come here on their first date, when it was still a theatre. The way she told the story, how impressed she'd been that he'd taken her to a theatre that had thirty-six hundred seats—the biggest in the country at one time—you'd think my grandfather had built the thing. I smiled at the memory.

Looking up, I could see why she'd been so impressed. Ornate, intricate designs were hand-restored on the multilayers of ceilings, and a mezzanine soared stories high above the orchestra. I sat in awe of the architecture and all the grandeur of the building, something I hadn't stopped to do in a long time. Until my attention was diverted to the front of the stage. A woman with the most incredible, powerful voice sang onstage. *Damn.* She could hold her own against Aretha Franklin. It made me question my sanity for even considering trying out. I was nowhere near as good as these people. Yet I sat there, content to at least watch the show.

During a fifteen-minute break, I was sorting through work emails on my phone when a familiar voice interrupted. "You'll need these."

Looking up, I found Terrence, the older volunteer whom I'd met last time I'd come, holding out some papers to me. I took them. "What are these?"

"Application to the church ministry." He lifted his chin in the direction of the pew I sat in. "Scoot over. Been here all day, and my old dogs need a break."

I slid over to make room but held the papers he'd given me back out to him. "Thank you. But I'm not joining the church."

He didn't lift a hand to take the papers back. "You have to be a member in order to try out for the choir. You'll need to do a membership class and the water baptism, but they'll let you try out if the application is in process. Just fill out those papers, I'll stamp you in, and you're good to go."

"I'm not trying out."

Terrence squinted. "You're not trying out, and you're not joining the church, yet here you are for the second time in a week. What did you come for, then?"

I shook my head and laughed at myself. "I have no clue. Wait, actually, that's not true. I'm here because Goldilocks has me turned inside out."

"*Ah.*" A look of understanding crossed Terrence's face. "A woman. And one that makes you question yourself."

I scoffed. "She makes me question myself alright—mostly whether I've lost my mind."

He smiled. "She sees you for who you are, and it makes you want to be a better man. Don't let go of her."

"It's not like that."

Terrence put his hand on my shoulder. "Would you be here, sitting in this church, if it were not for her?"

I thought about it. "No, probably not."

"Has she made you question how you should treat others?"

Dorothy instantly popped into my head. A few months ago, I'm not so sure I wouldn't have fired her. "She has a unique way of looking at things, which seems to have caused a lapse in my judgment on more than one occasion. But she's an employee of mine, maybe a friend in a loose sense of the word. Nothing more."

Terrence scratched his chin. "What if I told you your Goldilocks was out on a date tonight with a strapping young bachelor?"

My jaw clenched, and Terrence's eyes zeroed right in on it. He chuckled. "That's what I thought. You're still fighting it. I bet you'll come around. And my guess is, this isn't the last time I'll be seeing you in this pew, either." He stood and held out his hand. "But until then, keep the application and take some advice from an old man who has learned from more mistakes than you even realize you're capable of making yet. One man's overlooked blessing is soon another man's gain."

CHAPTER 19

Charlotte

"Reed Eastwood's office. How may I help you?" I answered the phone via my headset and took another giant stride into my next lunge as I waited for the caller to speak. It was my lunch hour, but no one was around to answer the phone, so I'd eaten the salad I'd brought at my desk and then proceeded to do lunges and squats in my office. If the president of the United States could find time to exercise, damn it, so could I.

"Is he in?" the caller snapped.

I scrunched up my nose at the attitude from the woman on the other end of the phone and pushed farther down onto my back toe to tighten the lunge. "No. Mr. Eastwood won't be back until later this after-noon. Can I take a message or assist you with making an appointment?"

The breath of sour air on the other end of the line sighed loudly. "Where is he?"

What a bitch. I stood between lunges. "I'm sorry. I'm not at liberty to disclose that information. But I'd be happy to assist you by setting up an appointment or taking a message."

"Tell him to call Allison as soon as he gets in."

I knew the answer but asked anyway. "May I have your last name and ask what this is in reference to, please?"

Another loud sigh—although somehow I doubted it was because she was doing lunges on her lunch hour while answering a phone and trying to hold her patience with a rude person on the other end. "Baker, and it's in reference to our honeymoon."

Well, that last bit of information was confusing. "Umm . . . okay."

Click.

The bitch had hung up on me.

"Well, you have a nice day, too," I mumbled.

After that, I plugged my headset into my iPhone, turned the music up, and lunged with renewed vengeance.

Chin up.

Chest lifted.

Back straight.

Long stride.

Heel pointed to the ceiling.

And . . .

Hold positioning. God, that woman had nerve. What the hell did she have to be so pissy about? She'd had it all—the feather dress, the gorgeous and wealthy fiancé, a man who wrote her romantic notes. *I* should be the pissy one. What did I have? Her bad-luck dress that I couldn't zip, no man in my life, and her romantic fiancé had turned into a man that now wrote hate notes on his same haughty stationery.

Bitch.

What a bitch.

I'd been lunging around my office for at least a half hour, and my legs were starting to give. Deciding to call it quits, I took one last lunge, closed my eyes, and held my position until beads of sweat formed on my brow and my legs began to shake.

After a minute or two of strenuous balancing, I had the strange sense of being watched. My eyes flashed open to find I wasn't wrong. The door to my office was wide open, and Reed was staring at me.

Startled by the unexpected visitor, I lost my footing and fell straight on my ass.

Reed was at my side practically before I hit the floor. "Jesus, Charlotte. What the hell? Are you okay?"

I slapped away his extended hand and ripped off my headset. "No. *I'm not okay.* You barged in here and scared me half to death. And this isn't the first time you've knocked me over."

His brows lifted. "I didn't barge in here. *I knocked.* You didn't answer. So I let myself in to leave something on your desk. Maybe if you were a little more connected with the world going on around you, you would've been aware of my presence sooner. What the hell were you doing anyway?"

"Lunges."

"Why?"

"So my ass won't look like cottage cheese, that's why."

Reed closed his eyes, mumbled something, and shook his head. "I didn't mean *why* would you perform lunges in general. I do understand the theory of exercising. I meant, *why* were you doing them in your office in the middle of the day?"

I stood from the floor and dusted off my hands and skirt. "Because if the president has enough time, so do I."

"I have no fucking clue what that means."

I glared at him. "What did you need, Reed?" Although I was annoyed, I also couldn't help myself. Unintentional rhymes were just funny. I cracked a small smile that I thought I'd hid pretty well.

Reed squinted at me. "You just amused yourself with a rhyme, didn't you?"

"*Yes.* Good *guess.*" I flaunted a full-blown grin at how entertaining I could be.

He rolled his eyes, but I could see the corners of his lips twitch. "I'll just leave you the invoices that I need processed." Reed made his way to my desk and then turned back to the door. I'd almost forgotten all about the phone call that had lit a fire under my exercise routine.

"Umm . . . you had a call while you were gone. I didn't get to email you the details since I was in the middle of my lunch lunges when it came in."

"That's fine. You can just tell me. Who was it?"

I locked eyes with him to watch his reaction. "Allison Baker."

Reed's jaw flexed, and a scowl marred his handsome face. "Thank you."

He turned and headed for the door again. But I never could leave well enough alone. "She said to tell you it was in regard to *your honeymoon*."

◆　◆　◆

Hours later, I felt bad about the way that I'd treated Reed. I hadn't even asked him if he'd gone to his audition last night, and then I'd zinged him with news about a subject that I knew was a sore one, just so I could watch his face. Basically, I was rude because I was jealous from that one stupid call from Allison.

As I started to close down my computer for the night, I noticed the green dot was lit next to his name on the company internal email, which meant he was still signed on, too. Without overthinking it, I typed using the chat feature.

Charlotte: Hi. I was just about to head out for the night. Can I do anything for you before I leave? Some coffee or anything?

A minute later, a response popped up.

Reed: No, thank you. I'm good.

I chewed on my nail for a minute, then typed:

Hate Notes

Charlotte: Are you busy? Can I ask you something?

Reed: Not busy at all. Just doing lunges in my office.

My eyes widened.

Charlotte: Really??

Reed: Of course not, Charlotte. What kind of a nutjob do you think I am?

I actually laughed out loud at that response.

Charlotte: So . . . about that question . . .

Reed: Spit it out, Darling.

Of course, my last name was Darling, and people had called me by it often growing up. But when I read that last sentence, I'd read it as Reed calling me darling—as in, honey, sweetie, baby, *darling*. I smiled to myself, liking the sound of that, and closed my eyes to try to hear Reed's deep voice calling me darling without it being capitalized.

When I reopened my eyes, there was a new message on my screen from Reed.

Reed: I hope you know I was calling you Darling as in your last name . . . not darling as in the term of endearment.

As much as the thought would kill him, there were a lot of times that our minds were simpatico. I decided to feed him his own line.

Charlotte: Of course not, Reed. What kind of a nutjob do you think I am?

Reed: Touché.

Charlotte: Anyway, about those questions . . .

Reed interrupted with another message as I typed.

Reed: So now it's "questions," not "question"?

I ignored him.

Charlotte: How did your audition go last night?

Reed: I was starting to worry about you. It's been almost twenty-four hours, and you hadn't asked yet.

Charlotte: Aww . . . that's sweet. You worry about me. So how did it go? Did you make it to the next round?

Reed: I went. But I didn't try out.

Charlotte: What? Why?

Reed: To be honest, I'm not good enough. I listened to some of the auditions and realized that it would take hard work to get myself to the point where I would have a legitimate chance of making it.

I was disappointed. But it sounded like he'd at least done some soul-searching by going.

Charlotte: There's always next year. Start on some lessons!

Reed: Maybe I'll do that. And thank you, Charlotte. As much as you annoyed the crap out of me over this, I actually did enjoy going to watch the auditions.

Charlotte: You're welcome. Glad I could put my annoying-as-crap skills to good use and be of some service.

Reed: It's late. Why don't you go home?

I didn't think he was asking a question that he wanted an actual answer to, yet I answered out loud talking to my computer. "Because I have nothing to rush home to."

Charlotte: Can I ask you one more question?

Reed: Why of course. I love personal questions at seven at night that interrupt me while I'm working.

Charlotte: I'm going to guess you meant that sarcastically, but I'll ask it anyway. Where were you planning to go on your honeymoon?

Reed didn't respond. After a few minutes, the green light turned red, indicating that he'd signed off the company email. I'd clearly over-stepped our invisible boundaries again. So I finished shutting down my computer and packed up my desk. I was surprised when Reed appeared at my door, although at least I didn't fall over this time.

He had his jacket over his arm and his leather bag slung over his shoulder. "Hawaii," he said. "We were going to honeymoon in Hawaii."

I must've made a face without realizing it.

He arched a brow. "You don't approve?"

"I'm sure it's beautiful. I just . . . I figured you for something a little more unique. Hawaii doesn't seem to suit you."

Reed scratched at the five o'clock shadow on his chin. "What does suit me?"

I gave it some real thought before answering. "Africa. Maybe a safari."

He smiled. "That's actually where I wanted to go on our honeymoon."

"I take it Allison didn't?"

"No. Allison's idea of a great vacation consists of a five-star spa with daily massages and tanning on the beach while drinking fruity drinks with umbrellas out of a coconut."

"So you did what she wanted to do?"

"I compromised. Her initial choice was worse. At least in Hawaii, I could rock climb while she sunned herself on the beach."

"You rock climb?"

"I used to."

"Why did you stop?"

Reed shook his head. "Good night, Charlotte."

I loved working with Iris. Not only did I learn new facets of the business every time she involved me in a project but also I felt a real woman-to-woman connection with her. When she asked how things were going, I believed she really wanted to hear the answer, unlike most people.

We'd just finished compiling quarterly financial numbers to send over to the accountant when she asked, "How are things at work, Charlotte? Are you happy here so far?"

That was probably one of the only questions that I didn't have to ponder the answer to. "I love it here. I'm really happy, Iris. I've been meaning to tell you that. I know you took a big risk by hiring me, and to be honest, I probably didn't take the job for the right reasons initially, except for that I knew you were a woman I wanted to be around. But I'm learning a lot, and this job feels right for me. I want to learn more. I want to learn everything!"

Iris chuckled. "I'm glad to hear that, dear. We all feel your enthusiasm. You've really invigorated the office. How about your art? Are you still working at it?"

"I am. And I think I finally found its place in my life. I always thought my dream job would be to work with clay all day. But I'm finding that I enjoy it much more when I use it to relax and escape."

"That's wonderful. And my grandsons? How are things going with them?"

"Well, things with Max are great. He's really sweet."

She lowered her reading glasses to the tip of her nose and looked at me over them. "And my *other* grandson?"

I shrugged. "Well, yesterday he knocked me over, and I chatted with his ex-fiancée about their honeymoon, so I probably should answer that things aren't going that well."

Iris blinked twice. "Come again?"

I laughed. "Well, technically he didn't physically knock me over. He just scared me while I was lunging. And my chat with his ex consisted of her huffing a lot and being rude before she hung up in my ear."

Iris smiled. "That sounds like Allison."

"But on the other hand, I got him to go to church twice, and tonight I have my first climbing lesson, so I guess you could say that even though he'll never admit it, we sort of have influenced each other in a positive way."

"Church? Climbing? I think you need to back up a bit, dear. You lost me after Allison acting like a bitch."

"Well, it all started with my Fuck-It List. Excuse my French. You actually helped inspire the start of the list. After our long talk in the ladies' room and you giving me this great new job, I decided to make a list of things that I wanted to do."

"Like a bucket list."

"Yes. Except I'm not planning on dying anytime soon, so I called it a *fuck-it* list."

"Creative. Go on."

"Well, long story short, I told Reed about my list, and one night I found that he'd started his own list."

Something in Iris's face changed. "My grandson made a bucket list?"

"Yeah. I know. I couldn't believe it, either. But that's how I found out about his secret dream of singing in the choir. So I did some research and found out that the Brooklyn Tabernacle Choir had tryouts coming up and told Reed about it."

Iris looked pretty shocked. "And he went?"

"He did. Twice. He didn't wind up trying out because he needs to work on his voice, but I think it was nice that he went. And I added rock climbing to my list after he said he was a climber. I've always wanted to try it. It seems like a badass hobby."

"Reed is taking you rock climbing?"

"Oh. No. I said we're tolerating each other and influencing from a distance. I think we're a long way off from playdates. He just mentioned it was a hobby of his, and I thought I'd check it out. I found an open class over on Sixty-Second Street that starts tonight at seven."

"I see. Well, as long as he isn't being difficult for you."

"He's not. It's funny, the harder he tries to be difficult, the more I see that it's a wall he puts up to keep people out. I know it's none of my business, but I have the urge to slap that Allison for whatever she did to him."

A warm smile spread across Iris's face. "You've got my grandson's number. Do me a favor? Don't give up on him. I promise if he lets you in, it's worth all the effort. Even if it's just friendship."

I nodded.

Since we were done for the day, I cleaned up the papers spread out all over the table in her office and said good night. Iris stopped me on the way out.

"Charlotte?"

"Yes?"

"One last thing. If we ever have the opportunity to slap that Allison, you'll have to get in line behind me."

I grinned from ear to ear. "No problem. Have a good night, Iris."

CHAPTER 20

REED

Apparently I'd decided on a new path to exit the office these days.

Even though I'd been leaving the same way every night for the last eight years—turning left out of my office, right down the long hallway, and straight out the main entrance—now I automatically go right, then left, then right, and weave around cubicles like a rat in a maze to work my way to the front door. It takes twice as long, and I'd never admit that I took the extra steps to pass Charlotte's office, yet there was an unwelcome disappointment inside of me when I saw that her door was already closed tonight.

Grandmother's office was located only a few doors down from Charlotte's, and she walked out carrying her coat just as I passed.

"Oh. Reed. I didn't realize you were still here. I stopped by before, but your light was off."

"I had an appointment downtown but stopped back in to grab some files for my morning showing. Did you need something?"

"Umm. Yes, actually. Do you remember my friend Helen?"

"Bradbury?"

"Yes."

"Well, her grandson has recently taken up rock climbing, and apparently he's bought some second-rate gear. His eighteenth birthday is coming up next week, and you know Helen, she's having a party that is bigger than most weddings. I thought it would be nice if I purchased him some new gear as a gift. I'm sure it would put Helen's mind at ease, too. Only . . . I have no idea what to buy."

"I can help pick some things out. Why don't I show you some sites online tomorrow when I get back in the afternoon, and we can order stuff for next week."

"Oh. Did I say next week? I meant tomorrow. The party is tomorrow."

I squinted. "The big party is on a weekday?"

"Umm . . . yes. Helen is a stickler about having a party on an actual birthday. Anyway, I looked up local places, and there's a store that sells top-of-the-line gear over on Sixty-Second Street—it's sort of on your way home."

I nodded. "Extreme Climb. I know the place. They hold climbing classes and arrange group trips, too."

Grandmother smiled and pointed a finger at me. "That's the one." She looked at her watch. "It's already almost seven, and I have an appointment downtown at eight o'clock. The store closes at nine. I'm worried I won't make it. Could I trouble you to pop in and pick out a helmet for me on the way home tonight?"

"Sure. No problem. I'll grab something and bring it to the office tomorrow."

She hugged me. "You're a doll. And if you happen to see anything of interest while you're there, you should pick it up, too."

"Umm. Okay."

"Have a wonderful evening, Reed."

"You, too."

Extreme Climb hadn't changed much in the two years that I'd been absent. The megagym concentrated more on indoor rock-climbing classes than on gear sales, and even though they had more than ten thousand craggy square feet and three training walls, one reaching forty feet, the place was always packed.

The guy at the front desk remembered me. I'd done a few of their climbing trips when I'd first started out.

"Eastwood, right?"

We shook. "Good memory. Unfortunately, mine's not as sharp."

He smiled. "No problem. It's Joe. Haven't seen you around in a long time. Injury?"

"Nah. Just took a break."

"Back for a refresher lesson? It's beginner night. You probably don't want to hit the twenty-five-foot wall with them. But the back climber is open if you want. I can get one of the guys to spot you."

"Maybe another night. I just stopped in to pick up a helmet for a gift."

"We just got the new Petzl Trios helmet in today in flat black." He whistled. "The thing is sweet. It's not out for display yet, but I can grab you one to check out if you want."

"Yeah. That'd be great."

"Give me a few minutes. If you want to amuse yourself in the meantime, go watch the beginner class. We have a few that strapped the helmet on backward. Should be fun to watch."

I chuckled. "Maybe I'll do that."

When Joe disappeared, I wandered around. Seeing everyone climbing up walls, or excited for their first attempt, made me remember how much I used to love the sport. *Maybe I should give it a shot again.*

A bunch of guys were gathered at the beginner's wall, looking up while a woman climbed. She was almost to the top of the short wall, about twenty feet up the twenty-five-foot climb, and wore hot-pink shorts that displayed a heart-shaped rear from the bottom. I'd thought that was the cause for the giant smiles they wore. Until I heard *the moan*.

Each time the woman climber reached for the next peg, she let out a sound that was an odd hybrid of whimper, moan, and sigh. Sort of like Venus Williams in a tennis match, except way fucking sexier. Clearly it wasn't intentional, because the woman was stretching and trying her hardest to get to the top. But that didn't make the sound any less sensual. She reached again, and the sultry moan shot straight down to my dick. *Damn.* It'd been a long time since I'd heard that sound. *Too long.* For some reason, it made my brain think of Charlotte. I bet she'd make some great sounds in the sack and was pretty damn uninhibited, too. All that pent-up crazy probably translated into one hell of a firecracker in bed.

The woman managed to scale a few more feet and grab on to the top climbing holds with one last, loud moan. She stretched high and rang the bell at the top. The group of guys ogling a few feet away clapped and hooted. The tallest of the group said, "Damn. I'm gonna ask her out. I bet she sounds as good under me as she does overhead." Even though I was no better than him—standing there staring at the woman's ass while thinking about what another woman might sound like in bed—the guy's comment pissed me off.

My attention was diverted back to the climber when she shrieked a resounding *woo-hoo* and flailed her arms in the air like she'd just scaled Mount Everest.

That voice.

Oh no.

Shit.

It couldn't be . . .

The woman cheered once again.

But it was . . .

I'd know that scream anywhere.

She started to make her way down. I watched in amazement, still unable to believe it was her.

"Charlotte?" My voice was louder than I'd intended, practically echoing.

She turned to look at me, pausing for a moment to catch her breath before she completely lost her focus and landed in a twisted position.

"Ow . . . ow!"

Shit!

I rushed over to her, then knelt down. "Are you okay?"

She looked up at me in a daze, her blue eyes glistening.

God, she's beautiful. Even when she is a mess.

"What . . . what are you doing here?"

"Can you move your leg?"

"It's my ankle and foot mostly. But everything hurts."

A couple of employees surrounded us. "Do you need assistance?"

She held out her hand. "No, I'll be fine."

"We can call an ambulance. Are you sure?" one of them asked.

"Yes." She turned to me. "You didn't answer me. What are you doing here?"

Why was she so concerned with that when she could barely move?

"Is that really relevant? Iris sent me here to run an errand for her."

"That's strange. I mentioned to her that I was coming here. Why didn't she just ask me?"

I have my theories.

When she tried to move her ankle again, she cringed. "Ow."

"We'd better get you checked out. I'll drive you to the hospital. Can you stand?"

Blowing out a breath, she said, "Let's find out."

Offering her my hand, I helped her up slowly.

Charlotte immediately winced when she tried walking. "This is not good." She leaned on me as she limped.

I had her wait for me at the entrance while I went to retrieve my car.

Helping her into the vehicle, I said, "I'm surprised you lost control so easily. I was watching you before it happened—before I realized it was you. Your balance was pretty impressive."

"Well, if I'd known you were watching me, I'm sure my concentration would have suffered. And I lost control because you freaked me out when you called my name. You weren't supposed to be there."

I walked around to the driver's seat, then said, "You might want to consider wearing something less revealing. You had quite the cheering squad of men admiring your little hot pants."

"Were you one of them?" She cocked her brow, then moved her seat back before kicking her leg up on my dash.

Hell yes, I was . . .

I refused to acknowledge her question.

She laughed. "The answer is in your silence, Eastwood."

Weaving in and out of traffic, I said, "I'm your boss, Charlotte. All I would need to do is tell you I was admiring you in that way, and you could go after me for sexual harassment."

"I would never do that to you—ever."

I believed her. Charlotte wasn't trying to trap me. She wasn't an opportunist, either. Sometimes I wish she were, so I could find some kind of real fault in her.

Keeping my eyes on the road was always a challenge with Charlotte in the car.

I glanced over at her. "Rock climbing, huh? Right after I told you I rock climbed? Original. I see your stalkerish tendencies are still in full effect. You mean to tell me this was a coincidence?"

"Not at all. You gave me the idea. I have no problem admitting that. I figured if you liked it, it must be worthwhile, since there's *so little* you seem to enjoy."

I chuckled. "What are you basing that opinion on?"

"You work long days and then you go home. There's little room for anything else."

"How do you know what I do after I go home at night?"

"Well, I'm privy to your entire schedule for the most part. I'm assuming there's not a lot of time for extracurricular activities based on your hours. You work a lot of weekend showings, too."

"If I wanted to get something past you, I would, Darling."

"Darling as in my last name, with a big *D* not a little *d*, right? That's okay, I like big *D*s."

She did not just say that.

I bet you do, Charlotte. And in another life, maybe I'd give it to you.

CHAPTER 21

CHARLOTTE

Reed took me to the emergency room at New York–Presbyterian. He'd stepped out to take a phone call when the physician entered the room.

"The results of your X-ray indicate that it's just a sprain. You're very lucky, Miss Darling." He handed the paperwork over to the attending nurse.

"So what do I need to do?"

"Keep off your feet for a couple of days. I'll leave you with this boot and crutches." He helped me slip my foot into the boot before making his way out of the room.

Reed passed the doctor on his way back in from the hallway.

"Would you mind helping me up off the bed?" I asked.

He looked down at my boot, then up at me. "Of course."

"Thank you."

He extended his hand. I took it, selfishly loving that I'd touched Reed more in the last two hours than I had in the entire time I'd known him. He looked particularly hot right now, too. His hair was a bit tousled, and he'd loosened his collar at the top. He'd come to Extreme Climb straight from work in his suit and bow tie, but over the course of the evening, he'd slowly come undone a little. I loved "undone" Reed.

"What did the doctor say?"

"He said it was a . . ." I hesitated, deciding to bend the truth. "He said that I needed to keep off my foot for at least a few . . . weeks. Maybe." The nurse who'd been preparing my discharge paperwork gave me a look from behind Reed's shoulders. She knew I was bullshitting but didn't ruin it for me.

It was an impulsive decision to stretch the truth. I felt bad for lying about the time frame of my expected recovery, but I was able to justify it in my head because it was helping me get closer to Reed. I loved the attention I was getting from him and just wasn't ready for it to end.

"Shit. Okay," he said, rubbing his chin. "What can I do to help you?"

"You can drive me to my apartment."

"Yeah. Alright. Let's get you home."

◆ ◆ ◆

Reed looked around as we entered my place down in Soho. "This is nice. Very . . . homey."

"The décor is shabby chic. Glad you like it."

I didn't believe him. My taste was subtle and feminine and so *not* Reed Eastwood. Although I'd never seen the inside of his place, I had my ideas about what it looked like: dark, sleek, and modern.

Even though my apartment was in the city, the décor was more country with light and airy colors. I had floral linen slipcovers on the sofas and matching custom draperies.

Reed seemed to be hesitant to make his way fully into my living room. He stopped a few feet short of the door.

"You can take as much time off work as you need," he said.

"Thank you. But I still plan to make it in to work. I can just stay off my foot. I may need a ride into the office, though."

"I can arrange that." He slipped his hands into his pockets as he continued standing close to the entrance. "Are you hungry?"

"Yes. Very."

"I can pick up some dinner and bring it back for you."

"Will you stay and eat with me?"

"You need me to stay?"

"I feel like I do, yes. I don't really feel like being alone."

He looked pensive, then sighed. "Then I'll stay for a little while."

Letting out a breath, I said, "Thank you."

"What are you in the mood for?"

"Anything is fine."

"That's not very helpful, Charlotte."

"Just get what you like."

Reed seemed frustrated with me and suddenly made his way toward my kitchen, which overlooked the living room.

"What are you doing?" I asked.

"Going to see what you have in your kitchen."

Reed was rummaging through my cabinets. This felt surreal.

Reed is in my kitchen!

He took out angel hair pasta, a large can of peeled tomatoes, spices, and a jar of kalamata olives.

He looked behind his shoulder at me. "Do you have fresh garlic?"

"Yes. I keep it under the sink."

"Red wine?"

"On the wine rack in the corner."

"Okay, I can work with this."

My eyes widened. "You're really gonna cook?"

"Why not?"

"I didn't see you as the cooking kind."

"I didn't see you as a rock climber."

"Apparently I'm not a very good one."

"You were doing fine . . . until you weren't." He looked back at me, flashed a rare yet genuine smile, then said, "I cook for myself quite a bit."

"I'm impressed."

"When I get home at night, I often don't feel like going out again, so I've taught myself to cook. I enjoy it sometimes."

I lay on the couch in my absolute glory, watching him move as he chopped with his sleeves rolled up. Every movement of his body was a delight for my eyes as he drizzled olive oil, stirred, and tossed the pasta in a pan. The robust aroma smelled so good, better than anything I'd ever smelled before in my kitchen. He'd cracked the window open, letting in a delicate, nighttime breeze. A twinge of sadness hit me. I'd truly missed having a man around, even though I'd certainly never had one who cooked for me. Todd would have just ordered takeout. Unlike my ex, Reed wasn't afraid to roll up his sleeves, get his hands dirty. I was loving that about him.

I could see that he was plating two servings. "Should I come to the table?"

"No. Stay where you are. I'll bring it to you."

This night just kept getting better. Reed placed a glass of wine down on the coffee table and handed me my plate.

"This looks amazing. What is it?"

"My take on spicy pasta puttanesca. Hope you can handle a little heat."

"I can handle more than a little."

Reed cracked another smile. He was definitely loosening up.

"I should injure myself more often if it means getting this kind of treatment." I winked.

He sat on the chair across from me. "I do feel partially responsible for your mishap, so I'm happy to do it."

"You merely said my name. I was the one who freaked out seeing you there."

He took a bite of pasta, then said, "We certainly incite very odd reactions in each other, don't we?"

"Yes, but I enjoy it . . . even when you send me your little blue hate notes. I enjoy every minute of bickering with you."

Reed stopped chewing for a moment. It almost looked like it pained him to hear me say that. He cleared his throat. "Let me get you a napkin."

I stopped him from getting up. "No. I'm good." He sat back down.

"You look like you want to say something, Charlotte." Reed seemed to be able to tell that there was something on my mind.

There was. A question that had been eating away at me. It was none of my business, of course, but I would ask him anyway.

"Why was Allison calling you about a honeymoon you never took?"

Reed paused and placed his fork down, and it clinked on the plate. "We paid for all of the arrangements, and the resort wouldn't give us our money back. They would only give us a credit for a stay at one of their locations. Allison has continuously insisted that I be the one to use it."

"Because she ended it. So she feels like you deserve it?"

"Yes. Evidently the credit expires in three months. I couldn't care less, and I don't have the time. I told her to use it or let it expire."

"Use it, Reed. Make the time."

"I wouldn't use that credit even if I *had* the time," he snapped.

Come to think of it, I probably would've felt the same way if Todd and I had had a trip planned before everything crumbled. Given how strong Reed's feelings for Allison were, it made sense that he wouldn't want to go on what would have been their honeymoon. I suddenly felt bad for suggesting that he go.

"I get it. You're right. I'm sorry for prying."

He lifted his brow. "Are you?"

"Not really." I smiled. "Even though I still don't know what happened with her, because you won't tell me, for the record, I think she made a huge mistake."

"No, she didn't. She dodged a bullet." He suddenly got up and took my empty plate back to the kitchen.

Okay. What was that about?

It was a while before he returned to the living room. Reed walked over to the window and stared out of it for a bit before picking up one of my framed photos.

I reached for my crutches and made my way over to him.

"Are these your parents?" he asked. His back was toward me.

"What tipped you off? The jet-black hair?" I joked. "They are. Frank and Nancy Darling. Best parents I could have asked for."

"They seem . . . like good people from this photo, but yes, clearly they look different from you." He turned around to face me and surprised me when he said, "I noticed you added something interesting to your Fuck-It List the other day."

"Spying on my list, are you?"

"What's on my server is mine, Darling—with a big *D*. It's not spying."

"Yes, I did add something I'd been putting off."

"You want to find out where you came from."

I knew that addition to my list was a lot different from all the others. Lately, figuring out exactly who I am had become somewhat of a focus for me. I'd lost a little of myself when I was with Todd—trying to fit into his career, his lifestyle, his hobbies, instead of what made me happy. And I couldn't exactly figure out who I am without knowing where I'd come from.

"Someday, I would like to, yes. I added it on there, even though that one is really more bucket-list than fuck-it-list material. Not exactly something I can bang out in a day, nor is it necessarily one of the more enjoyable items for me."

"Well, I think it's brave. Whoever they are . . . they would be amazed to see how you turned out."

"Thank you. And here I was thinking you just thought I was nuts."

"You *are* nuts . . . but you have a lot of endearing qualities, too."

"Thank you."

A few moments of silence passed before he asked, "How much do you know about the day you were found?"

"You can Google 'Saint Andrew's Church Baby Poughkeepsie.' You'll find all the information in old news reports. And that's about as much as I know. It was quite newsworthy at the time. But to this day, no one knows who left me there."

"That's fascinating."

"I guess."

Reed could sense that I didn't really want to talk about it and changed the subject. It was probably the only thing in my life that I wasn't eager to discuss. Deep down, I knew I had abandonment issues. But living in denial was always easier than addressing them.

"So, where do you do your sculpting?"

I grabbed my crutches and angled my head for him to follow me. "Come on, I'll show you."

"You shouldn't be moving around," he scolded.

"It's fine."

I led him to what technically used to be my bedroom. Reed looked stunned to find that it wasn't really a bedroom anymore at all.

A sheet lay over the floor. A pottery wheel sat in the center of the room. My bed, which was covered with junk, was pushed against the wall. Surrounding shelves held both painted and unpainted pieces.

"Where do you sleep?"

"The sofa in the living room turns into a very nice bed. Recently, I've turned my room into an art space. Someday I'll get to have a bedroom and a pottery room, but for now this is how it has to be."

He wandered around, gazing at my pieces. "You obviously made all of these?"

"Yup."

"You mentioned once you went to college for art?"

"I went to Rhode Island School of Design in Providence for a year. But I ended up dropping out."

"Why?"

"I realized that part of the beauty of being an artist is not having pressure put on you to create. And when that pressure was put on me, that was where my creativity basically ended. I sort of like to just throw raw clay on the wheel and see what happens. A bowl often unexpectedly transforms into a vase and vice versa. Sometimes my work turns into a useless piece of junk, and other times, something beautiful."

"Like the one I caused you to break that you made for Iris. That was one of the nice ones, wasn't it?"

"Unfortunately, yes."

"That figures." He smiled. Reed's smile was like a gift. It was rare, but when it happened, it totally consumed me for as many seconds as it lasted. "Do you have a favorite piece?" he asked.

"You'd be surprised." I moved slowly over to the corner of the room to pick up a small bowl. "This one, actually. It doesn't seem like much at first, but if you look closely and become familiar with it, you see it's perfectly balanced. Small, not flashy but colorful. Really exquisite."

"Yes," he said, looking deeply into my eyes. The temperature in the room felt like it was rising. "I honestly had no idea that you were this skilled. It's very impressive."

"Wow, I've impressed Reed Eastwood."

"It's not easy to do."

"It's not."

Reed's normally hardened expression had gone totally soft. His eyes were searching mine, and I felt something indescribable yet very strong between us in that moment. His body was close, and it felt like he could've easily leaned in and kissed me. Maybe that was just because I *wanted* him to kiss me so badly. Tonight we'd reached a level of intimacy that hadn't existed before. Perhaps that made the physical need even more intense.

I could feel his breath a little when he said, "You'd better go sit down and get off your foot."

CHAPTER 22

REED

I felt sick.

I think it might have been a reaction to Charlotte's pixie dust or whatever spell she was casting on me.

I'd driven her to the office for the past few days. My problem was not that I didn't want to do it; it was the opposite. I looked forward to the longer morning commute while ingesting her scent. I looked forward to her laugh and her ridiculous need to go to two different breakfast spots, one for the coffee, the other for the special kind of muffin.

This feeling had followed me around since the night of her little accident. At her apartment, when we were talking about her birth mystery, I'd seen a vulnerability in her eyes that I'd never noticed before. And when she took me into her art room, I'd been truly blown away by her talent.

When I got home that night, I couldn't stop thinking about her and spent an hour googling "Saint Andrew's Church Baby Poughkeepsie."

There was probably only one thing cuter than present-day Charlotte Darling, and that was the red-faced cherublike version of herself from twenty-seven years ago. I might have printed the photo and tucked it away. And I'd take that fact with me to the grave.

The story was pretty much exactly the way she'd described it—a total mystery. A baby was found bundled up in a basket and left in front of the church rectory. The person rang the doorbell and ran, leaving Baby Charlotte in the hands of the church, then the state, before she eventually ended up in the hands of her adoptive parents.

Maybe it was because of the beauty of the little girl, but the news story stayed in the headlines for some time, following Charlotte's plight from the very beginning up until she was adopted six months later.

As I sat in my office pondering Charlotte, she happened to walk by, carrying a few packages. I noticed that she was walking perfectly fine—with no limp. Just this morning, that wasn't the case.

Hmm.

It made me wonder if she was playing some kind of game with me. I decided to message her.

Reed: Judging from how you just waltzed by my office, your ankle seems to be a lot better. I'm guessing you won't need a ride tomorrow.

Charlotte: LOL. I thought you were supposed to be at a lunch meeting on the Upper West Side.

Reed: Cancelled.

Charlotte: Ah, well, yes, I am doing much better. The rides into the office have been very helpful. While I've enjoyed your charming morning personality, you're right. I think I can fend for myself now. The recovery time has far exceeded my expectations.

Reed: It's far exceeded mine as well, so much so that it seems totally unbelievable. In any case, glad to see you're feeling better. I guess now you can fetch my dry cleaning. I have some shirts that need picking up from Union Street Cleaners.

Even though menial tasks like getting coffee were part of Charlotte's technical job description, we rarely asked her to do things like that anymore. Most of her responsibilities kept her in the office or at showings. Her role in the company was expanding. So I was totally messing with her in asking her to pick up my dry cleaning.

Charlotte: I'd be happy to pick up your shirts. Are they ready?

Reed: I was just kidding. I can pick up my own dry cleaning. You don't need to do that.

Charlotte: Oh.

A few moments later, she appeared at my door. Her face was flushed, and she seemed like she had something major on her mind. "Can I come in?"

"You don't have to ask." I could see that Charlotte was definitely nervous. I took off my glasses and placed them on the desk. "What's up?"

She closed the door, and her heels clicked as she slowly approached my desk.

"Is everything alright, Charlotte?"

"Yes." She rubbed her palms on her skirt. "I'm just nervous to ask you something. But I told myself that I was going to do it anyway."

"Okay . . ."

"I was wondering . . . if you would like to . . . well . . ."

"Just say it."

Charlotte looked down at her feet. "Lately, I've been telling myself that I'm going to make more of an effort to go after what I want in life, take the bull by the horns, if you will. And, well . . . I really like your company. I was wondering if you would want to go out with me some-time outside of work?" She let out a long breath. "On a date."

It felt like all my breath left my body.

I. Was. Not. Expecting. That.

Charlotte was asking me out on a date.

She was insane. And ballsy. And so fucking adorable.

And I wanted to say yes. God, how I wanted to say yes more than anything I'd wanted in a very long time.

But I knew that I couldn't lead her on, as much as I enjoyed spend-ing time with her. As much as being around her made me happy. As goddamn beautiful as I thought she was.

My lack of response caused her to backtrack. "Oh my God, Reed. Forget I said anything. It was just an impulsive thing. I really enjoyed our time together this week, and I find you . . . very attractive . . . and you sometimes look at me like you might feel the same and that whole thong experience in my office that one night . . . it was weird yet sexy . . . and I just thought that maybe—"

"I can't, Charlotte. I'm sorry. I just can't date anyone right now. The reasons are too complicated to get into. But my saying no has every-thing to do with me and absolutely nothing to do with you. I think you're remarkable. You need to know that."

"Okay." She just kept nodding repeatedly. "Okay. Can we forget I asked this, then?"

"Totally forgotten."

She turned around and basically fled.

After she left my office, my heart felt like it had been ripped out of my chest. What she'd just done took a hell of a lot of guts. I knew that no matter what I said, she would somehow take it personally, and that killed me. I felt awful. She couldn't possibly know how badly I wished I could've said yes.

And her boldness . . . that was so damn hot. Knowing she wanted me made it even harder to accept that I wasn't going to be able to have her.

As the afternoon wore on, I couldn't stop obsessing about having hurt Charlotte in some way. I wondered if there was a work-around, if there were a way I could spend time with her outside of work but where it wouldn't be perceived as a date.

Deep down, I knew I was bullshitting myself. But if I never put myself in a position where I was alone with her, what would be the harm in spending some time with her?

Again, deep down, I *knew* this was bullshit, but yet I proceeded to walk down to her office anyway.

"Charlotte, can I speak to you for a moment?"

She seemed especially guarded. "Okay . . ."

Pulling up a chair in front of her desk, I said, "I was thinking about what you asked me earlier, and I was wondering if . . . maybe rather than a date, if you would be interested in spending time with me in another capacity—more as friends."

"What do you mean?"

Making Charlotte feel better after my rejection earlier was my number one priority. I knew on some level this proposition was complicating the situation even further. But I wanted to reward her brutal honesty with something, even if meant tempting fate.

"I'd love your assistance in tackling a couple of the items on my bucket list, namely rock climbing to start—since you're an expert and all now. I'm talking about outdoor climbing. There's this place in the Adirondacks with guided instruction. I can send you the info. We could go up this Saturday. It would be one overnight. Separate rooms, of course. Would you be interested?"

◆　◆　◆

My cell phone buzzed as I pulled my door closed Friday night. It was after seven, and the office was quiet. Even Charlotte had left on time today for a change. Although that wouldn't stop me from taking my indirect route out just so I could pass her office.

I locked my door and dug my vibrating phone from my pocket. Josh Decker's name flashed on the screen. Josh was a retired NYPD detective turned private investigator who ran background checks on all our employees. Unfortunately, we'd gotten burned years ago when we hired a real estate agent without a sufficient check, and he basically used Eastwood Properties as a front to gain access to our wealthy clients' apartments and steal. Our backgrounds were now so extensive it sometimes felt like we were crossing a line and intruding on a potential employee's privacy.

"Hey, Josh. What's going on?"

"Same ole, same ole. Working late so I have an excuse not to eat Beverly's tuna casserole."

"What if she saves you the leftovers?"

"Oh, she always does. And I toss it in the dumpster outside my building before I come in. I tried to feed it to the strays outside my office once, but even starving cats wouldn't eat Beverly's tuna casserole."

I chuckled. "How did the Erickson investigation go?" I'd had Josh run a potential new leasing agent.

"He's pretty clean. Got one arrest for smoking a joint in college that was expunged."

"Expunged, huh? Doesn't that mean it's wiped clean from his record? Yet here you are, telling me about it."

"There ain't no such thing as wiped clean. There's always finger-prints, son."

I turned left and walked down the hall on my way to the office exit, slowing as I approached a certain closed door. **CHARLOTTE DARLING**. I stopped and read the gold nameplate on her door. Which made me wonder about what she'd added to her Fuck-It List lately.

"Josh . . . let me ask you . . . do you think you could find someone's birth parents?"

"Found a woman her father a few months back. He'd sold his sperm during college twenty years ago and was homeless today, living under a trestle in Brooklyn."

Wow. I stared at Charlotte's name while debating it for a minute. "I have a job for you. I need to find someone. It's personal—outside of Eastwood Properties. So I would want it kept discreet. No mention to my grandmother or anyone. Especially not our administrative staff. Is that a problem?"

"Discreet is my middle name. Email me from your personal account and give me the details."

"Will do. Thanks, Josh." I hung up and ran my finger over the nameplate. "Looks like we might find out who you really are, Charlotte Darling."

CHAPTER 23

CHARLOTTE

All my clothes were in a giant heap on the couch when Reed buzzed to pick me up on Saturday at five thirty in the morning. I pressed the intercom before hitting the buzzer to unlock the door downstairs. "Running a little late. Come up and have some coffee."

I cracked open the front door to my apartment and went back to frantically searching for the right thing to wear. I wanted to look nice—maybe even a little sexy—but I didn't want it to *look* like I was *trying* to look sexy. Then there was the added complication of the outfit needing to be appropriate for climbing a damn mountain.

Reed rapped on the door before entering. I brushed past him in the kitchen wearing a frantic face and headed to the bathroom to get hair ties. He must've read my mood because his words were said with caution. "Morning, sunshine."

"I have nothing to wear."

Reed looked at the floor and shook his head. "Wear anything, as long as it's comfortable."

I growled at him and went back to ripping apart my closet. He fixed himself a cup of coffee and came to stand in the doorway and watch me struggle to finish packing.

Tilting his mug toward my already full suitcase, he said, "You know we're only going to be gone one night, right?"

I glared at him. It was so easy for guys. He had on a pair of sweats and a fitted T-shirt. Which, by the way, fit *really nice*. "I don't know what to pack."

He smirked. "The little shorts you wore to climb the rock wall were a hit."

My hands went to my hips. "I thought you said those were too revealing?"

Reed scratched at the scruff on his chin, which—by the way—I really freaking loved. "Let me ask you something. It's Saturday, so I'm not technically your boss, correct?"

"No, the weekends aren't part of my workweek. What are you getting at?"

"And we're friends, right? Friends are protective of each other. That's normal, right?"

"Spit it out, Eastwood . . ."

"Well, your hot pants were revealing because of the way your ass looked in them. Not necessarily because you shouldn't wear shorts to climb. In fact, if you asked a professional climber, they'd tell you to wear tight clothes and even tight little shorts like you wore. But as *your friend*, not a man, I should tell you that you have a great ass, so if you don't want men that are underneath you checking it out, you might want to wear something a little baggier."

My brows arched. "So you didn't notice my ass as a man. Only as a friend, then?"

He folded his arms across his chest. "That's right."

"Will you be climbing behind me today?"

"That's the way it works, yes. The more experienced climber generally takes the rear. That way I can look forward and still guide you on where to grab. And if I fall, I won't be hitting into you."

It was difficult to contain my smirk. He'd just helped me decide what to wear. "That's helpful. Be right back. Going to change."

In the bottom drawer of my dresser was a bright-purple yoga outfit that I'd bought last year but never worn. I'd loved it in the dimly lit store, but when I got home, I realized it not only fit like a second skin but also had a shimmery sheen to it. Not to mention that it exposed my entire midriff and showed off a lot of cleavage for workout gear. I'd deemed it too sexy to wear to work out and tucked it away. But since Reed was only *a friend* and not a man this weekend, I was certain he wouldn't notice. I stifled a giggle after I put it on and checked myself out in the mirror. The hot-pink shorts from my rock-wall climb looked demure compared with this getup.

Walking back to the living room, I did my best to act nonchalant. Reed was sipping his coffee and checking out the framed pictures on my wall. He did a double take when he got a load of my outfit.

"You're wearing *that*?"

"Yes. Do you like it?" I did a girly twirl to show off that it was just as tight from the back as the front. "It's a little tight, but you said that's what the experts would recommend. And since you'll be behind me all day, I figured it's only *my friend* looking up at my ass in tight pants all day—not a man."

I hadn't given any real thought to what Reed's day would be like, rock climbing with a first-timer. I guess I just pictured us both climbing Mount Everest today, rather than the reality of learning to climb outdoors. Since the group he'd signed us up for were all beginners, we'd spent all morning learning basic climbing techniques such as rappelling and belaying. We broke for lunch without anyone scaling more than five feet up during practice.

"I feel terrible. You're stuck listening to all this training when you could be doing actual climbing." The tour company we were with had brought bag lunches for everyone, and Reed and I went to sit on a big flat rock away from the group to eat.

"That's okay. I haven't climbed in a while. It's a sport in which you definitely want to err on the side of caution, so the refresher course can't hurt."

I unwrapped a ham-and-cheese sandwich. Reed had picked turkey, and his looked really good, too. "Do you like ham? Wanna go half-half?"

"Sure."

I took the biggest bite. "Oh my God. Is this the most delicious thing you've ever tasted, or am I just famished?"

Reed smiled. "Outdoor climbing makes you really hungry. I can be inside climbing a rock wall for hours and never get hungry. Yet if I do one climb out here, I'm starving. Must be the fresh air and added exhilaration of not having bolted synthetic rocks to grab on to."

He was right. I had barely climbed a few feet during the morning training session, and it was already completely exhilarating. "How long has it been since you climbed?"

"Close to about two years, maybe."

"What made you take a break?"

Something in Reed's face changed. He'd gone from carefree and open to tense and shut down from one simple question. "It was time," he said.

Since he had nowhere to run today, I pushed. "That's vague. How about a more specific answer?"

He shoved a giant piece of his sandwich into his mouth. *Definitely buying time to answer.* I kept my eyes trained on him, letting him know I'd wait for his response. Plus, the way his Adam's apple bobbed up and down when he swallowed was really damn sexy to watch.

"There's been a lot of change in my life over the last year, so I guess climbing has sort of taken a back seat."

"You mean because of Allison?"

"Among other things, yes."

"What other things?"

"Charlotte . . ." Reed hit me with that warning tone.

"Don't 'Charlotte' me. We're supposed to be *friends*, remember? This is what *friends* do. They talk. They share."

"A guy and a girl don't sit around and talk about their lives and tell each other secrets unless they're a couple."

I straightened my spine. "So pretend I'm a guy friend."

Reed's eyes dropped to my cleavage, then returned to mine. "That's not possible."

I sighed loudly. "You know what happens when people open up to each other?"

Reed didn't answer, so I continued via a demonstration. I cupped my hands together tight as if I was holding a ball inside them. "This is someone who is closed off. No one can get in. But nothing can get out, either." I opened my hands and held them cupped side by side as if I were waiting for someone to place something in them. "See. This is open . . . you might have to let someone in that you weren't expecting, but . . . it also allows the people that you had stuck inside—to leave."

Reed stared at me for a long time, then abruptly got up. "I'm gonna take a walk. I'll be back before the afternoon session begins at one."

◆ ◆ ◆

Reed returned just as we all gathered together again as a group. Which I assumed was the point. I couldn't prod him in front of a dozen other people. Well, *I could* . . . but he was reasonably sure I wouldn't.

He stood right behind me as the instructor spoke about the first climb we were going to do. My skin prickled, and it had nothing to do with the temperature outside. The man had a major effect on me. And I was certain that I wasn't alone. I knew there were times when his body reacted to me, too. The only difference was, I didn't want to fight it. I'd been burned by someone I cared about just like he'd been; yet I still wanted to explore what was going on between us.

I felt his warm breath tickle the back of my neck, and something dawned on me. I'd been going about things with Reed the wrong way. I'd been trying to get closer to him by making him talk to me, open up to me. But he was buttoned up so tight that he shut me down at every attempt. Maybe the way to get to him wasn't through talking after all. Even a diamond has a vulnerable spot where the precious stone could be split open. Reed's soft spot wasn't in verbal communication—it was in his physical attraction to me. I wasn't above working with the limited tools I had.

I took a step back so that my ass brushed against his front and turned my head to whisper—a seemingly innocent gesture. "I'm sorry I was so nosy before."

Reed cleared his throat and whispered back. "It's fine."

I didn't take a step away after our short exchange. And Reed definitely didn't back up. Something told me that when I worked on penetrating this man's soft spot, *soft* would be the last thing I'd find.

◆ ◆ ◆

"Oh my God! I did it!" After pulling myself up and over the top of the wall we had to climb, I stood and jumped up and down.

Reed was right behind me and flashed a genuine smile. "You did good."

Even though the wall was probably only thirty feet to get to the plateau we stopped at, I felt like I'd climbed a full mountain. I raised both my hands into the air and screamed. "I'm a gecko!"

Reed laughed. "A what?"

"A gecko. You know." I darted my tongue in and out fast a few times. "The lizardy thing from the Geico commercials—a gecko. They scale walls, right?"

Reed shook his head. "Well, you looked more like Spider-Woman than a gecko, but I can understand the feeling. It's been a while for me, too. I forgot how alive it makes you feel."

"Does the office have a Halloween party? I'm totally dressing up as Spider-Woman. And you need to dress up as Spider-Man!" I couldn't control my random rambling. "Oh my God. That was so much fun!"

"I'm glad we take a half-hour break before climbing to the next plateau. You look like you might run up the wall, stepping on the backs of all the people ahead of you, you're so full of energy."

"I can totally see how this can become addicting. Something physical happens. I was terrified the minute my feet left the ground, even though I knew I was only two feet up and I wouldn't get hurt if I jumped down. The blood started pumping in my veins and my chest started to pound, but then I forced myself to climb one more leg up, and an incredible feeling came over me. It was like I was drawn to the top of the mountain and *had* to climb it. The farther up I went, the more dangerous it became, yet the less I cared about the consequences of falling. I just craved reaching the top and couldn't stop myself if I wanted to. Did you feel like that?"

Reed stared at me, his face less amused and more serious now. "Yes."

I'd been wearing a light sweatshirt over my cropped yoga top, but the climb had made the heat accumulate in my muscles and my body temperature rise. Now that I'd stopped, the sweat began to pour out of me. It happened when I exercised, too. I would suddenly start to sweat profusely after I stopped moving. I unzipped my sweatshirt, slipped it off, and tied it around my waist as I spoke. "I can totally imagine being unable to think about anything else but this feeling for days to come. It must be tough to walk away from this and not obsess about it, huh?"

"You have no fucking idea." Reed's voice sounded funny, and when I looked up, I realized why. His eyes were glued to my sweaty cleavage. Finding that made my breathing almost as labored as it had been a few minutes ago, scaling rock. It also reminded me of Reed's weakness. I took a step closer to him and leaned up on my tippy toes to plant a kiss on his cheek.

"Thank you for sharing this with me, Reed."

He cleared his throat and blinked a few times. "You're welcome."

After another invigorating climb, our instructor called it a day. Reed and I had only signed up for today, but when the instructor said there was an early-morning intermediate climb tomorrow, I encouraged Reed to do it.

"You should go. I'll sleep in, or maybe even splurge for a massage in the morning. I've used muscles I didn't even realize I had today. I'm sure I'll be sore anyway. But you've spent the entire day taking care of me. Go do the intermediate climb in the morning. You've earned it." Before he could say no, I walked over to the instructor, who was packing up his gear, and told him I wanted to sign up my friend for the morning climb.

"Has your friend climbed before?"

Reed finished packing his own bag and walked up midconversation.

"Yes. He was an avid climber, but took a break for a while."

"Okay. Tell him to meet us at the west hiking trail entrance."

I grinned and turned to Reed. "Meet them at the west hiking entrance."

The instructor looked back and forth between us. "Oh. You meant Reed?"

"Yes."

"You said a friend. I assumed you two were a couple." He looked at Reed. "Seven a.m. start. I'm not the guide for the morning climb. Heath is. You met him earlier today when he dropped off the equipment we used."

Reed nodded and turned to me. "You sure you don't mind?"

"Not at all. I'll find something to occupy myself. Don't worry about me."

The instructor hesitated for a moment but then said, "I hike on Sunday mornings. Not a tour or anything. Just me and nature, for fun. Why don't you join me while your friend is on his climb."

"Umm." I glanced over at Reed and caught a vein bulging from his neck. "Thanks for the invite. But I think I'll be too tired to hike."

Oblivious of Reed's death scowl, the instructor reached into his back pocket and pulled out his wallet. He fished out a business card and extended it to me with a flirty smile. "Cell phone is on the card. We could make it a short hike and have some breakfast after? Think about it."

"Umm. Okay. Thanks."

Reed was quiet as we walked to the car. As always, he walked around to the passenger side first to open my door. Only he didn't shut it like he normally did. He *slammed* the damn thing. The awkwardness continued to grow as he drove to the hotel in silence. I knew what he was pissed at—it wasn't like he could hide his obvious jealousy. But I was curious what he'd do with it. So I didn't try to make any conversation, either. I let the discomfort continue to stew.

He parked at the hotel and finally spoke. Well, growl might be a more appropriate description. "Be careful on your *hike* tomorrow."

Did he actually think I would do that? "Did you hear me say I was going?"

"You took his card."

"I was *being polite*."

"I didn't realize that politeness entailed flirting and leading men on."

My eyes bulged. "Flirting? Leading men on? You say I'm nuts; I think you have a few screws loose of your own, Eastwood. I asked him about a climb *for you*. I didn't flirt at all. And I certainly didn't have any intention of calling him."

"I don't think he got that message."

Frustrated, I flailed my arms in the air and slapped them down against my legs. "You know what? *Screw you.*" I opened the car door but then turned back. "Maybe I will call him. I haven't *gotten laid* in a really long time. And God knows, you shot me down when I asked you out. So I might as well move on and find someone else who can get my rocks off." I stepped out of the car door and slammed it shut with as much ferocity as Reed had earlier.

He called after me as I stormed toward the elevator. "Charlotte!"

I answered without turning around, raising my middle finger over my shoulder as I walked. *Screw you, Reed Eastwood. I'm done.*

CHAPTER 24

REED

Once again, I'd fucked up.

It seemed to be a regular occurrence when it came to Charlotte Darling. I'd say or do something that would upset her because I was pissed, and then hours later I regretted it and hated myself for the way I'd acted. Normally, she was good about it. We'd established a routine of sorts—I'd either get jealous of her having contact with another man or get frustrated because I couldn't push her up against a wall and show her how she made me feel. Then I'd lash out and she'd get angry. Her anger would simmer and turn to upset, and my guilt would eat at me. I'd apologize, and we'd go back to being friends. *Wash. Rinse. Repeat.*

Only this time, she wasn't letting me apologize. Even though her hotel room was right next door to mine and I'd heard her moving around, she pretended she wasn't inside when I knocked. I also sent a text that showed as read, but no damn response from that, either. Now it was my second call to her room, and the phone just rang and rang.

I showered, answered a few work emails, and then decided I needed a drink. On my way down to the lobby bar, I knocked on Charlotte's door one last time. Not surprisingly, she didn't respond. After a minute of standing at her door in silence, I heard the sound of movement inside, so I took a chance and spoke with my forehead pressed up against the door. "I'm going to go get something to eat downstairs. I know I'm an asshole. If you'd like to join me to yell at me over a steak and glass of wine, you know where to find me." I took a few steps away from her door and then walked back. "I hope you join me, Charlotte."

The first Scotch went down smooth, so I decided to order a second and eat handfuls of peanuts from the bar rather than order a steak. I'd positioned myself in a corner, facing the entrance, so I could watch who came in. Each time someone approached, my pathetic heart sped up. Then I'd realize it wasn't her, and I'd chase down my sorrow with another gulp of amber liquid. After the third glass in an hour and a half, I decided to skip dinner and get some sleep.

I practically stumbled out of the elevator and onto our floor. Outside of Charlotte's door was a room-service tray. I picked up the metal cover to her dinner to see what she'd had and found a full, untouched cheeseburger. There was a piece of cheesecake with one spoonful taken out of it and . . . a cork. *Guess we had the same meal.*

I took a deep breath and knocked one more time on the off chance that she'd listen to my apology—never expecting her to answer. But she did. And when the door swung open, offering her an apology was the furthest thing from my mind.

Charlotte was standing there in nothing but a black lace bra and panties.

◆　◆　◆

"You liked it so much in the bag, I thought maybe you'd like to see it on."

My eyes had already zeroed in on the little red rose sewn onto the top of the waistband of her thong. After that day in the office when I told her to show me the lingerie she'd purchased, I'd spent weeks imagining her wearing it for me at night. I'd use my teeth to grab that rose and tear the lacy fabric down her gorgeous legs. But anything I'd imagined couldn't hold a candle to the vision before me.

Charlotte was simply stunning. Taking her in, the air rushed out of my lungs. All that creamy, toned skin, those gorgeous killer curves covered in only a few pieces of skimpy black lace. *Fuck me.* Her full breasts were aching for release from that little low-cut bra and . . . I could see her nipples protruding through the sheer fabric. Lush, hard, beautiful, pink nipples that begged to be sucked.

I knew she was watching me but couldn't take my eyes off her body long enough to look up at her face. "What do you think?" she whispered. Charlotte did a slow, seductive turn, stopping so I could get a good, long look at her ass on full display, except for the string that ran up her crack. I imagined what my handprint might look like on the two creamy globes of her ass cheeks.

When she circled back around to face me, our gazes locked. I had no willpower left. I wanted to suck on her skin more than anything I'd ever wanted in my life. I wanted to suck hard and leave marks, hear her cry out my name when my teeth sank into her. This was not going to be gentle, not even close.

"Charlotte—you're so fucking beautiful. Everything . . . your body, your face. You—inside and out." My gravelly voice strained to speak. It wasn't easy with the massive rush of blood heading south.

"It's your turn to get naked," she said. "I've shown you mine; it's your turn to show me mine." I smiled, at first thinking it was cute that she'd messed up what she was trying to say. Then . . . she hiccupped. Followed by a giggle.

I tried to ignore my conscience, even with the warning bells going on around me. I wanted her so fucking bad. But . . . *A cork on her room service tray. Messed-up speech. Hiccups and giggling.*

Looking over her shoulder, I caught the empty wine bottle on the dresser. "You drank that full bottle of wine yourself?"

"I didn't save any"—*hiccup*—"for you, bossman."

Fuck.

Fuck.

I almost did it. I had almost reached for her and taken what I'd wanted from the moment she entered my life. That is, until I realized exactly how inebriated she was. That brought me back to reality. I seemed to have forgotten that I couldn't have her anyway.

Charlotte just kept looking at me with those glassy eyes. I was half-sauced myself with very little desire to move from my spot long enough to head back to my room. I just kept staring at her beautiful body.

"Sometimes you look at me, Reed, and I could swear you want to smack my ass."

"'Want' isn't strong enough of a word to describe what I want to do to your ass."

Fuck. What was I saying? I was losing it.

Charlotte was looking down. My dick had completely betrayed me as it stretched through the crotch of my trousers, displaying a more-than-obvious erection. I was hard as hell, and there was nothing I could do about it.

"Looks like someone is happy to see me, even if you're trying to convince yourself otherwise. Maybe I can help clear up some confusion?"

Charlotte reached behind her back.

What was she doing?

She unsnapped her bra and let it drop to the ground.

No. No. No.

Her gorgeous tits were now on full display. I swallowed, hardly able to contain the need to lick them. Her nipples were erect, and the skin around them prickled in little goosebumps. My eyes then landed on a tiny cluster of freckles in the middle of her cleavage. Charlotte's breasts were beautiful, round, and hung naturally, unlike Allison's stiff silicone.

Jump up and down for me, Charlotte. I want to see them bounce.

"Touch me," she panted.

I literally put my hands behind my back. "I can't touch you as it is, Charlotte. But I most certainly can't touch you when you're drunk."

"What is it about me that stops you every time? You clearly want me. You gave your whole heart to someone like Allison, but you refuse to explore things even a little with me, to see where this could go. Just tell me what's wrong with me. I can take it."

God, I hated to let her think that my hesitancy had anything to do with Allison. Well, it did, but not in the way she thought at all.

She took two steps closer and seemed to lose her balance. Charlotte then wrapped her arms around my neck. Before I could process that, her lips were on mine.

A noise that I couldn't identify came out of me. It felt like all the oxygen in my body escaped into Charlotte's mouth as I surrendered to the need to kiss her. My hands were gripping her hair for dear life. I enveloped her lips with mine. Charlotte's taste was sweet and intoxicating with a hint of white wine. I let my tongue slip inside her mouth for a few seconds, and the pleasure was too much to bear.

I ripped myself away from her in one last-ditch effort to stop from making a huge mistake that I'd never recover from.

With the back of my hand, I wiped her saliva off my lips, not because I didn't want it there. Just the opposite. My hand was shaking.

Covering her breasts and looking humiliated, Charlotte bent down to pick up her bra, then put it back on. She looked more upset than I'd probably ever seen her. I couldn't blame her. I was sure none of this made any sense to her.

Her eyes were glistening as she shouted, "Go!"

"I can't."

"What?"

"I can't leave you when you're upset like this."

"Fuck you, Eastwood," she huffed before making her way over to the bed. Charlotte buried her face in her pillow. I couldn't tell if she was crying or simply in the midst of passing out. It was likely that she might not even remember this exchange tomorrow. At least, I hoped she didn't.

Standing there like a dumbass with my hands in my pockets, I watched her lying on her stomach.

After a few minutes, I moved and sat on the edge of her bed, then eventually kicked my feet up. The room was spinning a little. Turning to her, I watched as she continued to lie there, her face buried in her pillow, her breathing still heavy.

Speaking softly, I said, "Charlotte. What am I gonna do with you?"

My eyes fell to her half-naked ass, my dick still perpetually hard. My balls ached.

"I know none of this makes any sense." I started to open up, knowing she likely wasn't going to process it. "I'm so sorry to have hurt you. I don't know how to be around you anymore. Don't mistake my apprehension for lack of interest. In fact, it's exactly the opposite, a constant battle. The truth is, I've been fighting my feelings for you for a very long time. And it's the hardest thing I've ever had to do. But I know with one hundred percent certainty that I am not the right man for you. You're a dreamer, Charlotte. The biggest dreamer of them all. And you deserve to be with someone who won't ever hold you back in life."

Closing my eyes, I let out a deep breath. "I'm trying so hard to do the right thing here. If I slip and let myself have you, I'm never going to want to let you go. And that wouldn't be fair. I dream of what it would be like to get fully lost in you, to not have any cares in the world. God, you'd probably want to have me arrested if you knew all the things I've done to you in my head. I want to do crazy fucking things to you. It's all so close that I can taste it, but in reality, it's so far away. Anyway, I'm sorry. I'm sorry I hurt you tonight. You deserve better. You deserve the world. And you're gonna make some lucky bastard the happiest man on the planet someday." My chest constricted at the thought. The idea of Charlotte with another man made me feel physically ill. But I couldn't have her, and I needed to learn how to let her go.

Her breathing had slowed. I was pretty sure she was out. I wanted nothing more than to nestle my face in her hair, to breathe her in until I lost consciousness. Instead, I compromised. Fluffing my pillow, I inched in closer so that I could at least smell her without touching.

I closed my eyes and let myself drift away.

It was as close to bliss as I was going to get.

CHAPTER 25

CHARLOTTE

Blinking my eyes open, I looked over at the opposite side of my bed. I couldn't remember when Reed left last night. I couldn't remember much of anything.

The time shown on the clock caused me to gasp. I'd slept till noon? What the hell? Why hadn't Reed called to wake me up?

A vague recollection of his talking low in my ear and apologizing to me last night registered, but I couldn't figure out if I'd dreamed it all. Also . . . did we kiss? I thought we had, but I couldn't be sure if I'd imagined that as well.

An empty feeling came over me as my head pounded. My cell phone rang. It was a number I didn't recognize.

"Hello?"

"Hey, Charlotte. This is John."

John was the instructor from yesterday who'd tried to get me to go out with him.

"How did you get my number?"

"It was on your registration paperwork."

"Oh. How can I help you?"

"Your friend Reed was just taken to the hospital. His instructor drove him. He's okay, though."

My heartbeat accelerated. "What?"

I then remembered that Reed had scheduled an early-morning climb.

"Yeah. He was climbing this morning and fell. His legs gave way from under him. It's company policy to take the client into the hospital for observation if anything happens on our watch."

"You said he's alright, though?"

"Yeah. He was coherent . . . walking and everything. Just with a slight limp. Again, it's just procedure."

"Which hospital?"

"Newton Memorial."

"Can you take me there?"

He hesitated. "Um . . . sure. Yeah."

John met me outside of the resort and drove me the couple of miles to the hospital. I insisted that he drop me off, figuring that Reed and I would call an Uber back to the hotel whenever he was cleared to leave.

After much searching, I spotted Reed inside one of the examination rooms. He was talking to a doctor. Unsure of whether to make my presence known, I instead opted to stand outside of the door. I couldn't help listening to their conversation.

"The thing is . . . I'd really been feeling great as of late. I wouldn't have planned this trip if I thought the muscle spasms were going to return."

"So you have experienced symptoms . . ."

"Yes, but they're fleeting. I'm still in the very early stages."

"Well, multiple sclerosis can be sneaky that way. And the truth is, you may have several weeks or months at a time when you're asymptomatic, only to have the symptoms return. Have you experienced anything else in recent weeks?"

"Aside from some mild vertigo, no."

"Did you come to the Adirondacks alone?"

"No, I'm here with a friend. She doesn't know I'm at the hospital and doesn't know anything about the MS."

MS?

Reed . . . has MS?

Reed has MS.

What?

It seemed like the hospital vestibule was spinning. My heart felt like it was ready to explode as I ran down the hall and to the elevator. I needed air.

Once outside, I knelt down with my head between my legs on the front grass of the hospital grounds.

Breathe.

Everything was suddenly making sense. The cancelled wedding. Everyone saying that Reed had his reasons for the way he was. Why he wouldn't let himself be with me. The bucket list. *Oh my God! The bucket list.*

My shoulders shook as I cried into my hands. Never in my life had I felt so much pain for another human being. At the same time, something else was bursting through me as every moment I'd ever had with Reed seemed to flash before my eyes.

I was hesitant to call my feelings for Reed love. All I knew was that I'd never experienced what I was feeling before. I'd known for a long time that my feelings for Reed transcended normal infatuation. Now that I truly understood why he was preventing us from taking that next step, I could allow myself to really experience those feelings for him for the first time. I went from understanding nothing to understanding everything. *Everything.*

Reed thought he was protecting me.

"You deserve to be with someone who won't ever hold you back in life."

Where had that come from? Had he said that to me? It was buried somewhere in my mind. Had he said that last night?

Then I thought about the dress and the blue note. He hadn't known what lay ahead when he wrote that note to Allison. Reed's hopes and dreams were likely shattered sometime after. But why did they have to be? Surely he couldn't just give up because Allison left him? She was a coward who never really loved him.

What Allison had done to him was really starting to hit me. *She left him because of his MS.* Had she never heard of *in sickness and in health*? To think that I believed that blue note sewn inside her dress represented unconditional love. The fairy tale was an illusion. The fact was, Allison wouldn't know the meaning of unconditional love if it smacked her in the face.

An overwhelming need for information overtook me. Tonight, I vowed to read everything there was to know about MS on the internet until my brain bled. I needed to find every bit of information there was to give him hope.

I remember watching that talk-show host Montel Williams on TV. He had MS and was lifting weights and looked healthier than most people. There had to be a way around this. I *needed* there to be hope. Reed could not let this rule his life.

There were the tears again. How the hell was I supposed to hold myself together today if I didn't tell him I knew? He clearly never intended for me to know about his diagnosis. He was *never* going to tell me. I just knew it.

I had to think long and hard about this, because I didn't want to upset him. He deserved the right to be able to tell me on his own terms. My finding out the way I had was an unintentional violation of his privacy.

My heart. It felt so heavy, like it was weighing my entire body down.

I called John back to come pick me up, asking him not to mention to Reed that I'd ever gone to the hospital at all.

Returning to the resort, I went back to my room and immediately pulled up WebMD on my phone. Scrolling through article after article,

I was doing my best to learn more about MS in the short time I had before Reed came back.

Needing to figure out how I was going to approach it, I decided that I wasn't going to tell him I knew. At least, not yet. When my phone rang, I picked up.

"Reed. Where are you?"

"How are you feeling today?"

"A little hungover, but I'm fine. How come you didn't wake me this morning?"

"Trust me, you needed to sleep." He paused. "Listen, you should know . . . I slipped during this morning's climb. They made me go to the hospital just as a precaution. A few scrapes and bruises, but I'm fine. I'm already back in my room."

Trying to act surprised, I said, "Are you sure you're okay?"

"Yes. I'll be good to drive back to the city."

"When are we heading back?"

"Whenever you're ready."

"I'd like to go soon," I said.

"Okay. How about I swing by your room in about twenty minutes? We can grab some lunch then hit the road."

"Sounds good."

◆ ◆ ◆

The ride back to Manhattan was tranquil. I was afraid if I opened my mouth, I wouldn't be able to hide my feelings. So I chose to say nothing at all.

Reed turned to me as the sun was starting to set over the interstate. "You okay?"

I finally looked at him. "Yeah, I'm fine."

He seemed preoccupied. More silence passed before he asked, "Do you remember anything about last night?"

Last night.

Even if I did remember the details of our drunken encounter in my room, anything beyond the bombshell from this afternoon was a total blur.

"Bits and pieces."

His voice was low. "Do you remember . . . the kiss?"

So it was real.

"Vaguely."

He sucked in his jaw. "Nothing else happened. In case you were wondering."

"I wasn't." That was the least of my worries.

"You passed out. I stayed for a while. Fell asleep. Then I left early in the morning."

"Why did you stay?"

"I didn't feel right leaving you. You were upset."

"Well, thank you . . . for staying."

"I take full responsibility for coming to your room, but we can't get carried away like that anymore."

I just kept nodding. And I could feel tears forming in my eyes. *Shit.* This was why I couldn't talk to him. Turning my head to look out the window, I was hoping he didn't notice my total loss of control.

Reed turned up the volume on the radio when Bonnie Raitt's "I Can't Make You Love Me" came on. The words reminded me so much of my situation with Reed because you only had so much control over another person's feelings. I couldn't make Reed see his future the way I did. He had to come to that realization himself. The song wasn't helping my predicament.

"Charlotte, look at me." When I turned to him, he could see my tears. "What the fuck? Don't cry. Why are you crying?"

Because you have MS.

And because you believe that would matter to me.

Holding out my hand, I said, "It's not about anything you said. I'm just feeling emotional. This Bonnie Raitt song that's on . . . 'I Can't Make You Love Me.' It's depressing," I lied, "and it's also my time of the month."

Reed simply nodded in understanding. He seemed to accept that explanation without questioning me any further.

Keeping everything in was taking a toll on me, and it hadn't even been a couple of hours since finding out. Not even a full day, and I couldn't hold it together.

The rest of the ride home was quiet.

After Reed dropped me off at my apartment, I immediately called an Uber to take me to Iris's house.

Her doorman knew me and let me go right upstairs.

The moment she opened the door, the words fell from my mouth. "Do you know?" Brushing past her shoulder, I let myself in.

Her eyes filled with concern. "What are you referring to, Charlotte?"

Out of breath, I said, "The MS."

Iris closed her eyes and walked toward the couch. "Come sit."

I sat down and placed my head in my hands. "Iris, my heart is breaking. Tell me what to do."

She placed her hand on my knee. "He told you?"

"No. I'm not supposed to know anything. I accidentally found out."

She looked shocked. "How?"

"Long story short, we went rock climbing in the Adirondacks. Reed is okay, but he fell and needed to get checked out. We weren't together when it happened. I followed him to the hospital. I overheard a conversation between him and his doctor. He doesn't know I was ever there or that I know." Placing my head in my hands, I was on the verge of tears yet again. "I don't know how to handle this. I can't just pretend like I don't know. But I'm afraid he'll be irate if he finds out."

Iris nodded in understanding. "Give it some time. The right answer will come to you."

I looked up at her. "You were right. You always said that he had his reasons for being so closed off, but I never imagined this."

She let out a deep breath. "Charlotte . . . you know . . . MS is not a death sentence. Reed was actually cautiously optimistic when he was first diagnosed. He's seen all of the best specialists in Manhattan, and they all reassured him that many people can live perfectly normal lives with it; it's just that there are some who aren't so lucky. There's really no way to know which category Reed will fall into. Only time will tell. But when Allison determined that she couldn't handle the thought of the worst-case scenario, Reed was blindsided. That gave him a different perspective, one none of us have been able to snap him out of. He started to focus on the negative . . . the what-ifs. He lost a lot of faith that he hasn't been able to get back."

"He really loved her . . ." That was the one thing I'd known from the very beginning.

"He did. But clearly, she's not the one. He's determined not to let love in, Charlotte. I can't say with absolute certainty that he will ever change his mind on that. But the thought of my grandson living his life without experiencing the joys of true love and a family of his own makes my heart hurt immensely."

Tears stung my eyes. To imagine that there was a chance Reed might never be able to experience love again hurt my heart immensely, too.

CHAPTER 26

REED

There was no doubt that something was seriously off with Charlotte since we'd returned from the Adirondacks.

For the past couple of days, she'd been avoiding me, and while I knew that was really for the best, my curiosity got to me. I scheduled her to come help me at the showing of one of the more spectacular properties of my entire career. She'd insisted on getting a car service and not driving out to the Hamptons with me, making up some sorry excuse about her schedule. But I knew it was because she was avoiding being alone with me. That should have made me happy. But I was perplexed. Was this about my rejecting her advances? I couldn't be sure.

The Easthampton house was so close to the water it was practically sitting in the ocean. The twenty-million-dollar, European-style estate was designed with the finest imported materials from floor to ceiling and wasn't going to stay on the market long. We had three appointments in a row, and I fully expected to be closing a deal by tomorrow once the three parties had time to mull over their competitive offers.

When the showings were over, Charlotte and I had a chance to really talk for the first time all day. She'd taken off her shoes as we strolled along in the sandy water.

"Let me ask you something, Reed."

"Alright . . ."

"I got the sense from your enthusiasm in showing this property, from the light in your eyes when you talked about its Gatsby-like, stately elegance . . . that you're very fond of it. But would you actually live here, in this house?"

That was a no-brainer. "I absolutely would, yes."

"What if I told you I wouldn't live here because it's so close to the water that I'd be afraid of what might happen if there were ever a major hurricane?"

"I'd say you were seriously crazy."

She tilted her head. "Really? Why?"

Where was she going with this?

"Because this house is the most amazing property I've ever had the privilege to represent. To not want to live in it, to not experience all of its splendor on a daily basis because you're worried about the potential of a storm, is ludicrous."

"You don't think that my fear should stop me from enjoying this beautiful house to its fullest—"

"No, I don't."

She added, "Because the storm may never come."

"That's right."

"So, if this house represented life . . . then you don't believe you should live your life based on fear."

The serious look on her face gave me pause. I stopped walking. The ocean breeze was blowing her hair around. The way she was staring into my eyes . . . something was not right. Charlotte was asking me that question for a reason.

We weren't really talking about the house.

Suddenly, a rush of adrenaline ran through me. Had she figured it out? Had she somehow gotten access to my medical records? Could she possibly know about my diagnosis? No. That's impossible. I'd done everything in my power to keep all that information private.

196

But this was Charlotte Darling we were talking about. Anything was possible.

I had to know.

"What are you really talking about here, Charlotte?"

She wouldn't answer me immediately. Then she simply said, "I know, Reed."

"You know . . . what?"

"I know you have MS."

My heart felt like it fell to my stomach. Her words were like a sucker punch to the gut. I felt simply . . . naked.

"Tell me how you found out," I demanded.

Her face was turning crimson. "It was an accident. Please don't be mad. I'd gone to the hospital to check on you. I was standing outside the door when you were talking to your doctor. I can't help what I heard."

While my instinct was to blow up at her, that wouldn't be fair. She hadn't pried. She hadn't done anything wrong. And the concern in her eyes was genuine.

I placed my hand on her cheek. "Come sit with me."

Charlotte followed me over to a large rock that overlooked the ocean.

"You're not mad?"

Letting out a long breath, I silently shook my head no.

"Thank God. I thought you would be."

"A part of me is relieved that you know. But I need you to understand that this doesn't change anything, Charlotte."

"Listen. I've been doing lots of research and—"

"Let me finish," I interrupted.

"Alright."

"I know you've probably scoured the internet for information that will make you feel better about this. I know you probably have a million positive spins on it. But the truth is . . . I can't ignore what's *there*. The moments where I have difficulty with mobility, the moments where my vision blurs or my legs feel numb. The times where I feel like I'm losing my mind. They're fleeting, but they are *there*."

I inhaled some of the ocean air to compose myself. "It's all whispering to me right now, but the truth is . . . this *will* catch up with me someday. It's enough as it is without having to worry about being a burden on someone. I can't live knowing that might happen, Charlotte. The one favor Allison ever did for me was to leave me before it got to that point."

She raised her voice. "Allison made a huge mistake in thinking a life with you wouldn't be worth it. I will never see things the way you do, Reed. I will never understand how someone wouldn't accept even limited quality time with the person they love over none at all. Then again, it's not love if you could walk away from someone. Life's not perfect. I could get hit by a bus tomorrow. In fact, I almost did this morning!"

I wasn't supposed to laugh at that. It wasn't funny at all, but somehow the way she'd said it made me chuckle.

Charlotte continued, "That said, I understand your fears. The one thing I can't do is force you to see things the way I do. If this is how you truly feel, then I want you to know you'll always have a friend in me at the very least." She then looked down at her phone and stood up suddenly.

"I have to leave."

"Where are you going?"

"My ride is here."

I stood up. "I assumed you were heading back to the city with me."

"No. I called the car service."

My eyes moved back and forth in confusion. "Alright."

Even though she had insisted on leaving, Charlotte was *not* okay.

She looked like she was on the verge of tears when she said, "Bonnie Raitt was right." Then she just walked away, leaving me standing there by the ocean.

Bonnie Raitt was right.

Bonnie Raitt was right.

What did that mean? Then it hit me. The song.

"I Can't Make You Love Me."

I stayed at the beach for a while, pondering Charlotte's words. Not to mention that damn song was now in my head. I was determined not to let her sway me. Things were the way they had to be. Charlotte couldn't consider the long-term implications of being with me because she only saw the world through rose-colored glasses. I had to be the sensible one in this equation. I was sure she was imagining the best possible outcome, not seeing me potentially restricted to a bed or confined to a wheelchair, unable to communicate or effectively eat. But the fact remained that the worst-case scenario wasn't out of the realm of possibility.

Allison had made the decision she thought was best for herself and assumed the least risk as a result. She wouldn't have a husband with a debilitating illness interfering with her freedom. That was what I wanted for Charlotte, to be able to live out all her fuck-it dreams without anything holding her back.

My phone rang, interrupting my thoughts. Checking the caller ID, I could see it was Josh, the private investigator.

I picked up. "This is Reed."

"Eastwood . . . I'm checking on that Charlotte Darling investigation you gave me up in Poughkeepsie. I think I found something."

CHAPTER 27

REED

I was always good at keeping secrets.

Yet for some reason, I could barely look at Charlotte over the last week since Josh had called with information on her birth mother. Of course, I knew withholding was the right thing to do until Josh could verify everything he'd dug up. Especially since a lot of it was word of mouth. There was no way in the world I was delivering that kind of unverified intel to Charlotte.

Then there was also the fact that I had no idea how Charlotte was going to react to what I'd done. The two of us weren't strangers to invading each other's privacy. Oddly, it seemed to be our thing. I'd stalk her social media and open her Fuck-It List. And in turn she'd buy me a Christmas mug featuring my most personal childhood dream that I'd never shared with her. But digging up her mother, finding out her true identity and history, that took things to a whole new level of "fucked up." It didn't help that what I'd turned up wasn't good.

Earlier this afternoon, I'd messaged Charlotte to find out what time she planned to leave the office tonight. She'd responded with six, so I waited until six thirty to drop off the files at her office that I needed her to work on tomorrow. I used my master key to unlock her door, expecting no one to be inside.

Only, Charlotte was definitely still there.

"*Shit.* Don't you knock?" She yanked the dress that was at her waist up, covering her bra.

I stood frozen and staring, rather than doing the polite thing and turning away. "Sorry. You said you were leaving at six, and your door was locked."

"I locked it so I could change."

I blinked a few times, finally managing to snap myself out of it. "Sorry." I backed out and began to pull the door shut, but Charlotte called after me.

"Wait!"

I kept the door partially closed so I couldn't see her. "What's up?"

"Can you . . . help me with this zipper? It always sticks."

I looked up at the sky and counted to ten in my head. "Are you covered now?"

"Yes."

I opened the door and got a look at what Charlotte was wearing for the first time. I'd been so distracted by the contrast of her lacy black bra against her creamy skin that she could've been pulling on a clown suit and I wouldn't have noticed.

I tried to keep my eyes on her face but failed. The little black dress she wore—one with a low neckline that showed off a good amount of cleavage—was just too irresistible to pass up. It cut a few inches above her knees, which made her toned legs look endless as they slipped into a pair of spiky, high-heeled shoes. I'd have given my right arm to feel them digging into my back.

I swallowed. "Going somewhere?"

She turned, giving me her back, and pulled her hair to the side. Charlotte's dress was half-zipped, stopping at the black lace of her bra. "Can you zip me? I'm already running late."

I walked over and stood behind her, taking in a big, deep breath of her scent. "You look beautiful. But where are you going?"

"I'm meeting a friend for drinks."

My hand at her zipper froze. She was wearing a little black dress and smelled fucking amazing, and yet somehow I was shocked at her response. "A *friend?*" It felt like a Mack truck had just hit me.

"Yes. And I'm late. So if you wouldn't mind . . ."

Miraculously, I managed to pull up her zipper even though all I wanted to do was rip the fucking dress off and tell her she wasn't going out with *a friend.*

She turned around and smoothed out her dress. "How do I look?"

How do you look? You look like you're mine.

I made a conscious effort to un-ball my fists. "I told you. You look beautiful."

I felt her staring at me but couldn't meet her eyes. After a minute, I turned to walk away. "Have a good night, Charlotte."

◆ ◆ ◆

I should've gone home. But I didn't. Like an idiot, I went to the bar that my buddies and I used to go to before I met Allison. I have no idea what I was thinking, but whatever it was, it was a stupid fucking thought.

I guzzled the third drink; it was watered down enough to taste like shit but still did the trick. Digging in my pocket, I tossed a hundred-dollar bill on the bar and spoke to the bartender. "I'll take another."

"You sure? You're downing 'em pretty fast there, buddy."

"The woman I'm fucking crazy about asked me to help her zip up the sexy little dress she wore on her date tonight."

The bartender nodded. "I'll keep 'em coming."

While I was drowning my sorrows, a woman slipped onto the stool next to me. "Reed? I thought that was you."

I squinted, trying to figure out where I knew her from. Her face was familiar, but I couldn't place it.

"You don't remember me?" She pouted. "Maya—Allison's friend. Well . . . ex-friend, I guess it would be, technically."

My eyes dropped to her rack. I should've started there. She was pretty enough, but it was her massive tits that no one could forget. I remembered Allison used to talk shit about her all the time—how they had to be fake, how she should be a stripper—yet she was always nice to her face. That should've been my first sign that the woman I was dating lacked integrity. I'd been so fucking blind.

I was halfway to drunk and all the way to a depressing emotional wreck, so I couldn't even properly cover up what had caught my attention. Maya didn't seem to mind. She thrust her breasts forward proudly and flirted. "I see you remember me now?"

I ignored her comment and gulped back the contents of my glass. "Ex-friend?"

"Yep. We had a fight a few months back. Haven't spoken since."

I nodded. The last thing I wanted to do was talk about Allison.

The bartender came back over and spoke to Maya. "What can I get you?"

"I'll have a Long Island iced tea. And whatever he's having." She pointed to my glass. "His next one is on me."

"That's not necessary."

"Maybe not. But we're celebrating."

I looked over at her. "What are we celebrating?"

"Both of us being rid of that bitch Allison."

◆ ◆ ◆

Maya stumbled getting off the stool. We'd definitely had too much to drink. "I have to go to the little girl's room." She giggled. "Save my seat."

"Sure thing." Last call had been almost a half hour ago. The bar was nearly empty. It wouldn't take much effort to reserve her stool.

I finished off my drink. We'd been sitting in these same spots for a long time. Maya had actually turned out to be pretty nice. While I had no desire to discuss Allison, she'd filled me in on their fight. Apparently my ex went out with a guy Maya had dated a few times, even though she knew they were seeing each other.

Alcohol usually made thoughts fuzzy. But for some reason, it made mine clearer tonight. The more I reflected on the woman I'd asked to marry me, the more I realized she'd actually done me a favor by dumping my ass. The woman I thought I'd known was loyal and sweet. They say love is blind, but apparently in my case, it was deaf, dumb, *and* blind.

I waved at the bartender to get his attention. *Screw last call.* I needed another drink.

Everyone was fucking dating—Maya, my ex-fiancée, *Charlotte* . . . I was the only celibate asshole these days. Maybe that's what I needed—to get laid. Make me forget all about the blue-eyed optimist wearing a sexy little black dress while she's out with some asshole tonight.

Maya returned from the bathroom. She really was pretty, even without looking south of her face. She smiled from under her thick lashes—big brown eyes batted what was unsaid. Instead of planting herself back on the stool, she sidled up to me, pushing those massive tits up against my arm.

"I always thought you were too good for Allison."

I looked at her lips. "Oh yeah?"

"You know what else I think?"

"What's that?"

Her hand went to my thigh. "That there's no better revenge than your coming home with me."

She was absolutely right. Allison would flip out if she found out I'd slept with Maya. The problem was—I didn't give a fuck about Allison or getting revenge. And while my dick really wanted to go home with her anyway, I just didn't have it in me.

I covered her hand with mine. "You're beautiful, and you have no idea how tempting that offer is. But there's someone else."

"You're seeing someone?"

I shook my head. "No. But I'd still feel like I was cheating."

Maya stared at me for a moment, then pushed up on her toes and kissed my cheek. "I hope she knows what a lucky bitch she is. Because Allison sure didn't."

◆ ◆ ◆

I felt like absolute shit the next morning. After cancelling my eight o'clock meeting at the last minute and going back to sleep for an hour, I dragged my sorry ass to the office.

A delivery guy was at the front desk just as I walked in. The acid in my sour stomach burned my throat as he spoke. "Delivery for Miss Charlotte Darling."

The receptionist signed for it and took a tip from the petty cash box as I stared at a dozen yellow roses.

I'm such a fucking idiot.

Such an idiot.

A celibate fucking idiot.

I'd turned down a night of revenge sex when Charlotte was out doing *something* to earn a few hundred bucks in roses. *My ass*, she went out with *a friend*. I'd known she had been lying. Steam should've been coming out my nose and ears for how hot I suddenly felt.

The receptionist picked up the phone. I assumed it was to call Charlotte. "Don't call. I'll deliver them to Ms. Darling's office for her."

I thought about shoving the vase in the garbage and passing right by but couldn't resist seeing Charlotte's face when I delivered them. She was on the phone when I barged in. "Delivery for you." I plucked the card that was stapled to the cellophane wrapping. Sarcasm dripped from my tone. "Here, let me read you the card since you're so hard at work." I ripped the tiny envelope open as she tried to rush the person off the phone. Clearing my throat, I read, "'Great catching up. Hope to see you again soon. Blake.'"

Blake? Sounds like a total douchebag.

Charlotte hung up the phone and leaned over her desk to swat at the card in my hand. "Give me that."

I pulled it out of reach and held it up over my head. "I didn't take you for an easy lay, Charlotte. Guess I was wrong."

Her face turned crimson. "What I do during my personal time is none of your business."

"That's where you're wrong. If your personal life interferes with your work, it's most certainly my business."

Her hands shot to her hips. "My personal life has not interfered with my work."

"Getting these flowers delivered today is an interference. You're distracted and that affects your work."

"I think you're the one who's distracted."

Charlotte marched from behind her desk and climbed up on the guest chair next to where I stood. She ripped the card from my hand and leaned her face down to mine. Our noses were almost touching. "Jealousy isn't flattering on you, Eastwood."

"I'm not jealous," I gritted through my teeth.

A slow, evil smile spread across her face. "Really? So you wouldn't mind if I told you how handsome Blake is?"

I wanted to wipe that smirk right off her face—by jamming my tongue into her mouth. "Charlotte, don't screw with me . . ."

"Screw?" She leaned in closer, our noses actually touching now. "So you *do* want to talk about Blake?"

"For heaven's sake!" Grandmother's voice interrupted our screaming match. She slammed the door behind her so the three of us were shut inside Charlotte's office. "What is wrong with the two of you? The entire office can hear you yelling at each other."

Fuck. I raked my hands through my hair. This woman made me crazy. I'm the guy telling people to pipe down when they start getting too loud in the office—not the guy who has to be told to shut up. By my *grandmother*, no less. The last time she'd had to reprimand me was probably when Max and I fought over a toy as kids.

Charlotte spoke first. "Iris. I'm so sorry. I didn't realize we were so loud."

"Get down off that chair," Grandmother snapped. *She was pissed.*

Charlotte climbed down and stood beside me. We both waited with bowed heads for the wrath we knew was coming.

"The two of you need to grow up." She turned her attention to me first. "Reed, you're my grandson, and I love you very much. Although you're a horse's ass sometimes. Life dealt you a shitty hand, yes. But that doesn't mean you fold. That means you take a deep breath and pull all the crappy cards you're holding, toss them in the center of the pile, and grab four new ones. Have some balls, son. Don't fold like a wimp." She turned her attention to Charlotte and her voice softened. "And, sweetheart, we live in New York City. There are two things we don't have to chase after: trains and men. Because there'll always be another one ready to pick us up right behind the first."

Grandmother turned on her heel and reached for the doorknob. Glancing back over her shoulder, she continued. "I'm going to leave now, and I'm going to shut the door behind me and give you two a minute. Then I expect you both to be back at work as usual."

After Iris left, we looked at each other. I took a deep breath. "I'm sorry for the way I acted."

"Apology accepted. And I'm sorry for calling you a narcissistic bastard."

My brows drew down. "You didn't."

She smiled. "Oh. Well, I thought it, then."

I couldn't help but chuckle. "You're nuts, Darling." I extended my hand. "Friends?"

She put her little one in mine. "Friends."

I walked to the door and opened it, but Charlotte stopped me. "Reed?"

I turned back.

"I'm not easy. Nothing happened between me and Blake."

She was trying to make me feel better, but it only made me feel worse. Because I heard the unspoken word missing from her sentence.

"Nothing happened between me and Blake—yet."

CHAPTER 28

CHARLOTTE

"Here are the expense-report summaries on the Hudson property that you asked for." I placed a file on the corner of Iris's desk. She had papers strewn all over. Even though it was almost seven in the evening, it didn't look like she was leaving anytime soon.

"Thank you, sweetheart."

I nodded and turned to walk out but had to say something. "Iris?"

She looked up. "Hmm?"

"I'm really sorry about this morning. It was totally unprofessional, and it won't happen again. I promise." Unexpectedly, tears welled in my eyes.

Iris took off her glasses. "Shut the door, Charlotte. Let's talk."

She walked from behind her desk and sat on one of the four over-size upholstered chairs that faced each other on the far end of her office. "Have a seat."

I'd never been nervous around Iris before. This was the woman I'd spilled my guts to within the first three minutes of meeting her in the ladies' room. Yet my palms were sweaty, and I had to fight the urge to wring my hands.

"Do you want to talk about it? You know that anything you tell me is between me and you, right?"

"I do."

"Tell me about the man who sent you those beautiful flowers. Is your heart torn? Maybe you want to move on but you're struggling? I know you care about Reed."

"Yes. No. Yes."

Iris smiled. "Clear as mud."

I took a deep breath and exhaled loudly. "I'm not struggling or torn. Blake is a guy that I knew in college. I went out with my friend last night and ran into him. We talked for a little while. He asked me out, but I said no. The flowers were nothing more than him trying to get me to change my mind. But I didn't exactly explain that to Reed when he saw the flowers. He got the wrong impression, got jealous, and I liked the way that felt."

"I see."

"Every time we start to get close, he puts up this wall." I began picking imaginary lint off the arm of the chair I was sitting in. "I've tried to get him to cross the line by . . . well, he's your grandson so I don't want to freak you out. But let's just say that he's rebuffed every advance that I've attempted, even the half-naked ones. I've even gone as far as telling him I was going to go out with Max."

"Because you thought making him jealous might get him to react?"

I shook my head while staring at the floor.

"Well, normally I'd say that a man who doesn't show his interest without games is a player and not worth your time. But we know my grandson's struggle isn't about being a bachelor who doesn't want to settle down. He's afraid to burden someone he loves with his condition."

"That's the thing. Reed thinks *he's* a burden. But the truth is, he *has* a burden, and it's easier to handle when it's shared."

Iris stared at me. "You've really fallen for him, haven't you?"

A warm tear slipped down my face as I nodded. "I know he cares about me, too. I can see it."

"You're right. He does. The two of you fight like an old married couple, flirt like you're in high school, and confide in each other like you're lifelong best friends. My grandson isn't pushing you away because he's afraid to fall for you. He's pushing you away because he already has."

"What do I do?"

"Keep pushing back. However you need to. He'll come around. I just hope it's not too late when he does." Iris reached out and took my hand. "You've been hurt before, and with Reed you're fighting another uphill battle. Don't forget to put yourself first. Push Reed, but keep pushing yourself, too, Charlotte."

◆　◆　◆

The more I thought about my conversation with Iris, the more I realized she was right. I needed to push myself, keep working on the things that I'd let slip over the years. So I vowed to at least make progress on my Fuck-It List each and every week, no matter how small that might be. Digging out the list I'd printed and tucked away in my drawer, I poured myself a glass of wine and sat at my kitchen table, ruminating over which item I should work on first.

Sculpt a Nude Man.

Dance with a Stranger in the Rain.

Learn French.

Ride an Elephant.

Go Skinny-Dipping in a Lake at Night.

Well, that one I can cross off, can't I?

Find my Birth Parents.

Make Love to a Man for the First Time in a Sleeper Cabin on a Train Ride Through Italy.

I'd added a new entry to my list last week while sitting in the back of an Uber on the highway and watching the big rigs glide down the road.

Learn How to Drive an 18-Wheeler.

I chewed on my pen cap while deciding what to tackle first. There was one that I kept coming back to. Honestly, it was time.

211

Find my Birth Parents.

I'd been curious about my biological parents my entire life. My mom and dad had always been open about the fact that I was adopted, and they'd encouraged me to talk about it. Yet I was always afraid that if I did, I'd make my parents feel like they weren't enough, when in fact they were more than enough. They were everything a child could have wanted. Somehow, though, that still didn't plug the hole I had from not knowing anything about my family history. I wanted to know my birth parents' story. Had they been young? Had they loved each other? I also wanted to let them know that I was okay—that the decision they'd made was the best one for me, and that I'd turned out pretty good.

Finishing the glass of wine, I took a deep breath and picked up the phone.

It rang once.

Then a second time.

My mother answered on the third ring.

"Hi, Mom."

"Charlotte? Is everything okay?" I heard the panic in her voice. I called every Sunday afternoon like clockwork, but it was Friday night now.

"Yes. Everything is great."

"Oh. Okay. Well, that's good. What are you up to this evening?"

"Umm . . ." I thought about chickening out. But then I thought about what Iris had said—*"keep pushing yourself."* "I'm actually making a list of things I want to do. Sort of like a bucket list but not, since I'm not sick or old."

"Are you sure everything's okay, sweetheart?"

I'd called off-schedule and started talking about making a bucket list. I should've realized that she'd be alarmed. I needed to explain myself better, or she'd be worried. "Yes, everything is really good, Mom. I just . . . I kind of forgot who I was when Todd and I were together. I sort of merged into his life and put things that I wanted out of life on the back burner. So I made a list of things I wanted to do, to remind myself to live my life for me. If that makes any sense?"

"It does. And it sounds like you've done a lot of soul-searching. I'm happy to hear you say you're going to focus on yourself. I hope none of the things are too dangerous, though."

"They're not."

Mom stayed quiet for a long time. She *knew* me. "Is there anything on your list that I might be able to help with?"

I took another deep breath. "Yeah, Mom . . . there is."

"I've been thinking about taking a trip into the city. Why don't I come in on Sunday, so we can talk in person?"

"I'd like that."

"Okay. How about around noon, then?"

"That's perfect."

We talked for a little while longer, skirting around the issue we both knew was on the horizon. She asked the usual—about my job, friends, finances. Right before we hung up, she said, "Charlotte—you have nothing to feel guilty about. I know you love me."

My shoulders relaxed. "Thanks, Mom."

◆　◆　◆

On Monday morning, I arrived at the office earlier than usual. I'd planned on getting a head start on my day so that I could leave on time and go over to the Centre for Arts to sign up for a sculpting class.

But I'd gotten so distracted reading on my phone while I waited for the coffee to finish brewing that I hadn't even realized the sensor had beeped, indicating it was done, and that someone had walked up behind me. "Baseball? I didn't realize you were a fan."

Startled, I bobbled the phone, and it fell to the ground. "You scared the hell out of me."

Reed bent over and picked up my cell. "You're extra jumpy this morning, even for you." He glanced at the screen. "Are you going to the game tonight?"

"What game?"

He smirked. "Guess that answers that question." He handed me my phone, pulled our mugs down from the cabinet, and began to pour coffee. "I saw the Houston Astros logo on your phone when I walked in. You were reading stats, weren't you?"

"Oh. Yes."

He arched a brow. "Baseball fan?"

"Not really."

"Gambling?"

"Huh?"

"Why else would someone be reading baseball stats if they weren't going to a game, a fan of baseball, or gambling?"

"I just . . . I find statistics fascinating."

Reed gave me a face that said *bullshit*.

"What? I do."

He finished making our coffees and handed me my mug. Sipping his, he looked straight into my eyes. "What's the real reason, Charlotte?"

I sighed. I had no reason to lie to him. Yet talking about wanting to find my birth parents out loud always made me feel like I was betraying my adopted mother. I struggled, even though she'd assured me that wasn't the case last night. Reed had already seen my Fuck-It List, so he'd understand. "I spoke to my mother about my adoption yesterday. I pretty much knew almost everything she told me already. The only real new information I found out was that when they found me at the hospital, I was wrapped in a Houston Astros blanket."

Something flickered across Reed's face. "A Houston Astros blanket?"

I nodded. "I didn't know what the logo looked like, so I searched for it on the internet, and I wound up on the team's site. I guess I got sucked into reading all the statistics while my mind wandered."

He stared at me, yet his eyes seemed to lose focus. Reed was definitely acting strange. I joked, "Are you a Yankees fan, and we can't be friends or something? Since I was swaddled in an Astros blanket?"

"I gotta go," he said abruptly. "I have an appointment I'm late for."

CHAPTER 29

REED

The Texas lead was huge.

Josh ended up spending two weeks in Houston on my dime. I needed more time to figure out how to handle telling Charlotte what was going on, and how to get her mind off finding her birth parents until I could be absolutely sure how I was going to approach this.

So I decided to create a distraction—one that I probably needed my head examined for. I'd noticed that Charlotte had recently added *Learn How to Drive an 18-Wheeler* to her Fuck-It List on the server. *Only Charlotte.*

I'd decided that the ultimate distraction on a Friday afternoon was to somehow make that happen, managing to rent an actual 18-wheeler from a distribution company. They parked it for me in an empty lot in Hoboken.

We didn't have much daylight left as we pulled in. Charlotte had no idea why we were there.

"I thought you said we were going to see a new property. Why are we here in this empty lot?"

Turning off the car, I said, "You've really worked hard for the company these past couple of months. As complicated as our personal relationship is, I'm also your boss. I feel like I don't really tell you enough—as your boss—how appreciated you are."

"You had to take me to a desolate parking lot in Hoboken to do that? If we're in Jersey, a diner would have been better."

"Look over there."

Charlotte's eyes landed on the big rig. "It's a truck."

"Not just any truck. An 18-wheeler."

She finally saw what I was getting at. "You've been spying on me."

"Did you not recently add driving one of those bad boys to your Fuck-It List?"

Realization set in and her face lit up. "Are you serious? I'm here to drive one?"

"Well, we can't take it on the road. Especially because you don't even have a *car* driver's license. I don't think either one of us is ready to die tonight. But you can have your fun on this lot." Noticing who I assumed was the instructor I'd hired arriving, I nudged my head for her to follow me out of the car. "Come on."

Charlotte walked alongside me over to the vehicle, which had the words **JB LEMMON DISTRIBUTION** painted on the side. A scruffy man with a long, white beard got out of an older Ford Taurus.

"Good afternoon, folks." He looked Charlotte up and down. "You must be Charlotte."

"Yes, sir."

"I'm Ed. Ready to drive?"

She looked at me and smiled, then bounced back on the heels of her feet. "I am!"

Charlotte took the driver's seat while the instructor, whose name was Ed, sat on the passenger's side. I crouched down behind them in what looked like the driver's sleeper cabin.

"The very first thing you need to do is check your fluids."

"Oh, I'm okay. I drank a lot of water today."

He laughed. "Fluids are at the front of the truck, darlin'. I'll show you."

I whispered in her ear, "'Darlin'.' Should I say it like that from now on?"

Charlotte quickly followed him outside before they returned.

"Now, you need to adjust your seat with these switches here. You're gonna need to come way up to have the best view over the hood."

He was definitely taking full advantage of the situation as he leaned into her from the passenger side. This whole experience was pissing me off.

"Now, you can start your diesel, but before you do, you're gonna push in your clutch and make sure you're in second gear."

Charlotte started the engine. The roaring diesel sound resonated throughout the space, and the fumes infiltrated the air.

"Now, pretend you're looking out to see if other vehicles are coming. If it's clear, you're gonna slowly let out your clutch."

Charlotte continued to carefully follow his instructions.

"Now give it some gas. Bring the RPMs up to about 1200. Then clutch out, clutch in."

She was asking questions as if she was seriously planning to drive one of these someday. My eyes just kept fixating on his hands over hers as they switched gears. Pebbles of sweat were forming on my forehead as the big rig started to move. I was a lost cause.

"Woo-hoo!" Charlotte screamed as she made her first turn around the lot.

After a half-hour drive, she put the truck in "Park."

Ed took off, leaving Charlotte and me alone in the big rig.

"That was seriously amazing, Reed."

"I'm glad you enjoyed it."

What had started as a stalling mechanism had turned into an experience I was happy to share with her. Charlotte's joy was always contagious. It also made me feel good to help her knock another item off her list.

It was quiet inside the truck. The only noise was faint traffic from the highway in the distance.

Charlotte decided to climb in the back, where I was sitting, and lie down on the bed that was located just behind the driver's seat in the cab. I swiftly moved up front to the passenger's seat.

She kicked her feet up. "So this is how truckers live, huh? I think that would be kind of a cool job, traveling the country, stopping and sleeping in different places."

"Aside from the risk of falling asleep and killing oneself . . . I suppose it could be . . . fun," I said sarcastically.

She playfully threw a pillow at me, then said, "Of course, they do it alone. I wouldn't want to travel alone."

As she curled into the bed to make herself more comfortable, it was evident that Charlotte had no intention of leaving the truck anytime soon. God, how I wanted to lie next to her. If I'd known I was taking her to a sex den on wheels, I most certainly would have rethought this truck adventure. It had never occurred to me that there would be a bed.

I stayed glued to the passenger's seat, determined not to get sucked into the vortex.

"Can we hang out in here for a while?" she asked.

"I don't think that's a good idea."

"Why not? It's so peaceful."

"I just think it's better if we go back to the city."

"Because you don't trust yourself with me?"

I refused to answer that, instead deciding to turn the tables. "Don't you have somewhere to be, like a date with . . . Blake?" His name rolled off my tongue like an obscenity.

"No . . . I'm not going out with Blake. But why do you ask . . . would you be jealous if I did?"

Not wanting to lie to her, I just chose to remain silent. My jealousy had already been made pretty clear a couple of weeks ago, anyway.

"Why should you be jealous when you know you could have me, Reed?"

"I can't have you," I snapped.

219

"Oh, but you can. You're just scared."

"Stop," I said through gritted teeth, even though all I really wanted was to hear her tell me some of the things she would let me do to her. I shook my head and sighed. "Where did you come from, Charlotte?"

"You always ask me that. While I can't answer where I originated from, I know exactly how I came into your life. There's . . . something you don't know. Something I never told you."

What was she getting at?

"I'm not following . . ."

"Can I tell you the story of how we met?"

"I know how we met."

"You think you do but you don't. You always thought that I was playing some kind of game when I went to the Millennium Tower showing. There's way more to the story."

I'd always wondered how that whole thing happened, how she came to show up there in the first place. It never quite made sense. There'd been something missing.

"Why don't you enlighten me, then. How did you come into my life, Charlotte Darling?"

She patted the spot on the bed next to her. "Will you come here? Sit next to me?"

"I'd rather not."

"Please?"

Reluctantly, I moved to the spot on the bed next to her. Our shoulders were side by side when I turned my face to meet hers. "Okay, Charlotte. Tell me how we met."

"It was fate," she said matter-of-factly.

I chuckled. "Fate . . ."

"Yes."

"How do you know that?"

"I'd taken my wedding dress to a consignment store to sell it. While there, I fell in love with a beautiful blush, feathered dress."

220

Feathered dress.

Suddenly, this wasn't amusing anymore. I swallowed, knowing *exactly* the dress she was talking about. Even though it was supposedly bad luck to see the bride's gown before a wedding, Allison had insisted that I approve of her choice. While unconventional, the dress she'd chosen was spectacularly beautiful.

"I know the dress," I whispered.

"So you'd seen it? She'd shown you?"

"Yes."

"I found the blue note you'd written on your personalized notepad. It was sewn inside. That was how I got your name. I actually took the dress home because they would only give me a credit for mine. So it was an even exchange. I still have it. It's hanging in my closet. I was curious about the man who penned the note, because it was simple yet so beautiful."

I couldn't believe what I was hearing. Biting my lip, I stayed silent as she continued to tell the story.

"When I looked you up on Facebook, there were some clues that maybe the wedding had never happened. Anyway, you already know everything that took place after I made the appointment. I obviously never expected everything to turn out the way it has. But that dress called to me. And now I know it was much more than just a dress. Not to mention my running into Iris in the bathroom. I'll always believe that I was meant to find you."

Holy shit.

I couldn't help reaching for her hand in that moment. I'd joked about Charlotte Darling and her pixie dust. There *was* always something magical about her, the way she'd just appeared in my life and turned it upside down. I had to admit that this story freaked me out a little. But at the same time, it made so much sense.

I cleared my throat. "I don't know what to say."

"You're not mad at me?"

"Why would I be mad at you for that?"

"Because I violated your privacy?"

"I can't be mad at you. Despite how you got here . . . you came into my world and breathed life into it when I really needed it."

"And now you're pushing me away."

"Charlotte . . . we've been through this."

She went quiet, then said, "You know, despite being hurt, I don't regret how everything started. That note really helped me. I read it, and it gave me hope that love and romance do exist . . . at a time when I was down on life and love. Even if it was an illusion, it still helped me turn over a new leaf."

She was being so candid. Why couldn't I give her a little of that back? I wanted her to know that it wasn't *all* an illusion.

"You weren't that off base about me, Charlotte," I spit out. "The note was sincere. It's only in hindsight that I'm able to see the situation for what it was, that Allison's love for me didn't match mine for her. So the love I had for her was based on a false ideal. But the man you thought you knew from that note . . . he did exist to a certain extent." I blew out a deep, ragged breath. "It's funny. That note stood for something to you. I hung on to a note myself. One that Allison had written, but for an entirely different reason. When she broke off the engagement, it wasn't exactly a heartfelt moment. She showed up at my office a week before our wedding, sat down in a guest chair across from me, and said that when she agreed to marry me she'd thought I was going to take care of her for the rest of her life, not the other way around. I think I was in shock while she spoke for a few minutes after that. It was all very cold and businesslike. But before she left, she took a piece of my stationery from my desk and wrote her new telephone number on it. She'd apparently already gotten a new phone since she was on my cell plan. I kept that piece of stationery in my top drawer for the longest time. Not because I ever thought about calling her, but to remind me of how that moment made me feel." I shook my head and looked down. "Every day when I saw that note, it felt like pouring salt on a wound. Then two days ago, I opened the drawer, looked at it one last time, wadded it into a ball, and tossed it in the garbage. I'm not even sure what made me finally do it. I guess it was just time."

Charlotte stared at me as silence filled the truck. With each second that passed, I felt more and more like being in this truck alone with her, given all the emotions lingering in the air, was dangerous.

"Every time I wear it, I think of you. I'm wearing it right now," she said.

It took me a few seconds to figure out what she was talking about. It wasn't the dress. *She's wearing it right now.*

Oh.

"Want to see it on me?"

Yes.

Yes.

Fuck, yes.

"No."

She chose not to listen when she hiked up her skirt and opened her legs, displaying my favorite black thong with the red rose accent. Clearly, she was trying to kill me.

"I think about your hands caressing the lace every time I put this on."

My voice was gruff. "Close your legs."

"Why? Do you think this makes me a slut because I want to show you? Because I'm really not—a slut. I haven't had sex in ages, and even though I wish I could move on, there's only one man I want to be intimate with."

My body was heating up fast. "Put your skirt down."

"Do you really want me to? Because you don't look like you do. You're sweating, and you haven't taken your eyes off it. I don't really think that's what you want. I think your mind is telling you one thing, and your body is pulling you in another direction. But okay, I'll close my legs."

Just when my pulse started to slow the tiniest bit, I realized while she *had* closed her legs, she was now slipping off her thong.

Charlotte lifted it to my line of sight. "You want it?"

Yes.

Yes.

Fuck, yes.

"No."

"Here." She opened my hand, placing the thong inside before closing my fingers over it.

I was shocked to feel wetness in my palm. Not only had she given me her panties, she'd given me her *wet* panties. My dick stirred.

Charlotte wrapped her arms around her knees and watched me start to unravel.

Unable to resist, I buried my nose in the lacy fabric and deeply inhaled the sweet, feminine scent of her arousal. And that was it. That was what finally undid me, like a drug evaporating my inhibitions.

I needed more.

Turning my body toward her, I laid my head on her stomach, trying to salvage any trace of sanity. There was none. I closed my eyes as I lowered my head to her legs, spreading her knees apart. Charlotte let out a slight, nervous giggle.

"You think this is funny?" I said as I voraciously kissed her inner thighs.

"I do. I—" She stopped talking the moment my mouth landed hard on her pussy, which was completely bare. I couldn't get enough of her soft skin as my tongue swirled over her swollen flesh. My scruff might have been scratching her, but she didn't seem to mind. Her throbbing clit was evidence of that.

Just this once, I kept telling myself. Never in my life had I wanted to weep into a vagina until now. Because the thought of never having this again was torture. This taste, this pussy, this woman . . . would be the end of me. In my bones, in my heart, I knew that Charlotte was made for me. And giving her up would be like a slap in the face of the very universe who'd sent her to me.

I had no idea how I was going to let her go.

"You taste better than I could have ever imagined."

With her hands wrapped around my head, Charlotte pushed me deeper into her. This woman whom I'd lusted after for so long was suddenly coming against my mouth. It felt surreal. I hadn't expected her to climax so soon. My dick was ready to explode.

"I'm sorry," she said.

"Don't you apologize. That was the most beautiful thing I've ever experienced."

"Well, then we *do* agree on some things," Charlotte said as she got up and began to straddle me. "Your turn."

"No." Even though I was protesting, I gripped her hips and pushed her bare pussy over my rock-hard erection that was straining through my pants.

My mouth enveloped hers. Closing my eyes, I relished the feel of her heat as she ground over me. Kissing her harder, I threaded my fingers through her silky hair. Fuck if I knew how to stop this.

I spoke over her lips. "My dick stays in my pants. We can't do anything more than this. Do you understand? This moment of vulnerability doesn't change a goddamn thing."

My words may have been defiant, but my actions were weak. I lifted her shirt over her head and pushed her bra up over her breasts. There were those beautiful tits I'd dreamed about since the Adirondacks. I wasted no time placing my mouth over her breast and sucking so hard one would have thought I was trying to expel nectar.

Who was I kidding? This wasn't going to end in my favor.

My phone rang, but I ignored it.

"Do you need to get that?" she asked.

"No. Fuck it," I growled, sucking on her breast harder.

When it continued to ring, despite several attempts to ignore it, I reluctantly pried myself away from Charlotte just long enough to check the caller ID to make sure it wasn't an emergency.

It was Josh, the private investigator. *Why would he be calling me repeatedly—unless something big was happening?* That snapped me back to reality. Charlotte remained seated on my crotch as I picked up.

"Hello?"

His tone was serious. "Eastwood . . . you might want to pack your bags and head down here as soon as possible."

CHAPTER 30

CHARLOTTE

Reed looked troubled as he listened to what the caller on the other end of the line was saying. His dick was still throbbing under me through his pants. I was still on cloud nine, despite the seemingly urgent nature of his phone call.

My heart started to pound rapidly once I began to really sense that something was wrong.

"What's going on?" I interrupted.

He held his index finger up as he continued to concentrate hard on the information he was being given.

"You need to email me all of this information as soon as possible." He paused. "Alright. Good work, Josh. Thank you."

He tossed his phone aside and ran his fingers through his hair. "Get dressed, Charlotte. We need to talk."

"What's happening?"

Reed was flustered. "Please. Just get dressed."

"Okay."

After I put my clothes back on, he said, "I have to tell you something, and it's going to upset you. But I want you to know I had the best of intentions."

"Alright . . ."

"Charlotte, no matter what happens between us, I consider you one of the most important people in my life. I want you to have closure and peace when it comes to where you came from. I wanted to help you find your birth parents. I knew that if it were left up to you alone, it might take you years, if ever, to find them. I have a private investigator at my disposal, and I put him on the case full-time."

"Oh my God. You what?"

"Josh has been on it for several weeks. He's spent an extensive amount of time in both Poughkeepsie and Houston."

"Houston?"

"Yes."

"What did he find?"

"It seems that a week before you were born, there was a girl who gave birth to a baby that was never assigned a social security number. The teenage girl left the hospital before she applied for it. Josh got ahold of the girl's medical intake form. She'd given a bogus name for herself, but she'd listed her nearest relative as a Brad Spears, and that name checked out. He located Brad, who told him the real name of his friend who had disappeared years earlier. Her name is Lydia Van der Kamp. She was from Texas and had apparently been hiding her pregnancy from her parents."

My heartbeat began to accelerate. "Lydia is my mother?"

Reed nodded. "It looks like it. This guy Brad and Lydia were pen pals when she ran away from her religious family and came to New York. He wasn't the baby's father, but Brad had a thing for her. The plan was that she'd stay, have the baby, and then they'd run away together. That's the part where things get a little fuzzy. For some reason, Lydia had a change of heart. She disappeared from the hospital and took the baby without telling Brad, and that's as much as he knows. Shortly after, you were discovered at the church. Josh located a Lydia Van der Kamp in Houston. She was the only person with that name in the area. Around that time, you told me you were found wearing an Astros blanket. That corroborated the Texas connection."

I covered my mouth. "Oh my God."

"Since then, Josh has been in Texas and has spoken to Lydia's children."

"Children?"

I have siblings?

Reed half smiled. "Yeah. She has two sons. They confirmed that their mother recently confessed that she'd abandoned a child in a New York church as a teenager. We don't have a blood test to confirm anything, but I think it's safe to say we found your mother."

I wanted to know what she looked like. "Do you have a photo of her?"

"No, unfortunately, I don't. But I can get that for you."

Nodding my head repeatedly to absorb all of this, I said, "Okay . . ."

I got the sense that he was hesitant to tell me something else. "Is there more?"

Taking a deep breath, he closed his eyes. "She's dying, Charlotte."

My heart felt like it was disintegrating. "What?"

"That phone call I just received brought some unsettling news. Apparently Lydia has been suffering from complications of Crohn's disease, which hit her very hard and young. She got something called sclerosing cholangitis, which resulted in liver failure. She's on life support at the moment and is not expected to survive."

My mother is dying? She's so young.

"Oh my God. What does this mean?"

He paused. "It means you and I are heading to Texas."

CHAPTER 31

REED

I hated having put her in this situation, but what was the alternative? She'd have regretted it for the rest of her life if she hadn't come to Texas.

As we stood in front of the hospital in the sweltering heat, an overcast sky was a fitting addition to this ominous day.

Charlotte stopped short of the entrance. "I'm not ready to go in yet."

"We can stay out here as long as you need." Placing my hand on her shoulder, I said, "Can I get you anything?"

"I need some water, I think."

"Let's go to the cafeteria."

"No. I want to stay out here. Can you just get me a drink and bring it back here?"

"Of course."

Charlotte definitely wasn't in her right mind today. Who could blame her? That was further evidenced by what I witnessed upon returning outside.

The skies had opened up and it was pouring rain. I was walking back with two bottles of water when I noticed that Charlotte was dancing with the man who had been smoking a cigarette outside when I'd left her. They were smiling and laughing as they rocked back and forth with their hands intertwined.

What the fuck?

Then it hit me.

Dance with a Stranger in the Rain.

She'd decided to take this opportunity to knock an item off her Fuck-It List. Kind of an odd moment to choose to do that, but if you knew Charlotte, you knew to expect anything. She'd likely needed the distraction from the stress right at this moment and had taken it.

I was trying not to let my jealousy creep in.

Charlotte stopped dancing when she saw me approach. "This man was nice enough to humor me. I explained the Fuck-It List."

"Don't worry." He smiled. "I'm happily married. Didn't mean to offend."

The look on my face must have been obvious. "No offense taken."

She turned to him. "Thank you. I really needed that."

"My pleasure."

As we walked away, I spoke in her ear. "What's his name?"

"I have no idea. That would have defeated the purpose."

I shook my head and chuckled. "Here's your water."

"Thanks." Charlotte opened the bottle and drank half of it down in one long gulp.

We lingered for a few minutes just outside the door and then I turned to her. "Ready?"

Expelling a long breath, she held on to her stomach. "As ready as I'll ever be."

After we wrung out our clothes, we were given easy access to Lydia Van der Kamp's room just by saying we were family. No one bothered to question anything. We weren't sure if we were going to run into her children, but when we got to the room, she was alone with a nurse.

The woman flashed a friendly smile. "Hello."

"Hi," Charlotte said, her gaze fixed on the comatose woman with tubes sticking out of her mouth.

"Are you here to see Miss Lydia?"

"Yes."

"You must be her daughter. You two look alike. I'm just changing out her bedsheets."

"Can she hear what we say?" Charlotte asked.

"Well, she's heavily sedated. It's not really clear what she can and cannot hear."

After the nurse left, I lingered in the corner of the room to give Charlotte space. She made her way over to Lydia's bedside.

The woman looked old beyond her years, likely from the stress of her illness. She was connected to a bunch of tubes, looking like the life had been drained out of her. Despite everything, I could see a trace of resemblance to her daughter.

It took Charlotte a while to conjure up the courage to speak.

"Hi, Lydia . . . I don't know if you can hear me. My name is Charlotte, and I'm . . . your daughter. I just found out about you, actually. I rushed here as soon as I found out you were sick. I've dreamed about meeting you under different circumstances. I'm sorry that this happened to you. You're too young. It's not fair. I can see how much we look like each other. Now I know where my icy-blonde hair came from."

Charlotte looked over at me. Her eyes were glistening, and I took that as my cue to go stand next to her, figuring she needed me for comfort. I held her hand as she continued to speak to Lydia.

"Anyway, I'm here to tell you something. Whatever guilt you might have about leaving me at the church, let it go. Everything turned out the way it was supposed to. I have two wonderful parents whom I adore. So don't feel like you did a bad thing. You were young, and you made the decision you thought was best. Thank you for choosing a church . . . and not like . . . I don't know . . . a gas station or some other random place. They took good care of me there. I hope you can hear me. Everyone deserves peace, and I'm hoping to give that to you. Thank you for choosing to have me. I'll always be grateful to you for that. And I'll always love you for giving me life."

Charlotte rested her head gently at the edge of the bed near Lydia's nearly lifeless body. She took Lydia's hand and held it.

A few moments later, Charlotte jumped. "Did you see that?"

"What?"

"She just squeezed my hand!"

"I didn't see it. But if you felt it, that's amazing."

"I hope that means she heard me."

I placed both hands on her shoulders. I hoped so, too. I really felt for Charlotte. I couldn't imagine meeting my mother for the first time under these circumstances. She was being so strong, and I was really proud of her.

The smoker from outside who'd danced with Charlotte in the rain suddenly appeared in the doorway. Why was he here?

"Can I help you?" I asked.

"Depends. Can you make my mother come back to life?" he said as he entered the room.

Charlotte froze.

"I just figured out who you are, Charlotte. We've been talking about you every day since that investigator left. I thought you looked familiar outside, but now I realize it was just because you look like a younger version of Mama. We've already met . . . but I'm Jason . . . your brother."

Tears filled Charlotte's eyes as she hugged him. "Oh my God. Hi."

Jason's hands were trembling a little as he wrapped them around Charlotte's back. He smelled like a chimney, but on first impression, he seemed like a decent person.

This was pretty damn surreal. He must have looked like his father, because I would've never guessed that this dark-haired guy was Charlotte's brother.

"How long has she been this bad?" she asked him.

"About a month."

"Is there any hope?"

He frowned. "I'm afraid not. She's dependent on the machines at this point. We're in the midst of some tough decisions."

Charlotte returned to her spot next to Lydia, then looked up at Jason. "I'm so sorry."

"She loved you, Charlotte. She'd only recently told us about you. Mama was afraid to look for you because she thought maybe you'd hate her. But she carried you in her heart."

The tears that had been threatening started to stream down Charlotte's face as she stared at her newfound brother. "Can I stay? Until . . . I . . . I want to spend time with her. And with you. And my other brother. If that's okay?"

He smiled. "Mama'd like that. In fact, I can't think of anything else in this world that might bring her more peace than having you here today."

"How long does she have?"

Jason walked to the other side of his mother's—their mother's—bed and covered the woman's other hand with his. "Not long. Weeks . . . days . . . maybe even hours. We've been struggling to take her off life support. We all had this feeling that it wasn't time yet." He looked up at Charlotte. "Now it makes sense. We were all waiting for you. *She* was waiting for you."

◆ ◆ ◆

"Hey," Charlotte whispered, blinking sleep from her eyes as she looked up at me. A few hours ago, she'd curled up in a ball on the chair next to her mother and fallen asleep. It was almost two in the morning, Texas time. She stretched her arms over her head and let out a big yawn. "How long did I sleep for?"

"Not long enough. A couple of hours."

"Did Jason leave?"

My first impression of Jason had been right. He turned out to be a pretty decent guy. We'd spent the hours while Charlotte slept getting to know each other. At only twenty-two, he'd already served four years in the military and married his high school sweetheart. He'd also been the sole caregiver to Lydia the last few months since she'd taken a steep turn for the worse, and his mother clearly meant the world to him. I shook my head. "He went downstairs to get us some coffee. I didn't want to go far in case you woke up and were confused."

She gave me a sad smile. "Confused as to how I could be an only child pouring my boss coffee in New York yesterday, and tonight I'm halfway across the country and my brother is getting my boss coffee?"

I reached over and squeezed her knee. "Yeah, that, wiseass."

"Did you get any sleep?"

"Not yet. But I booked us a hotel room nearby while you were snoring."

Charlotte arched a brow. "A hotel *room*? As in one, not plural?"

"I booked a suite with two beds. I don't want you to be alone."

She leaned to me and whispered in my ear. "Or . . . maybe you were hoping I'd lift my dress for you again?"

Jason walked back into the room, saving me from having to answer that. I'd actually debated over how many rooms to book for an hour and a half. In the end, I figured I'd already seen her naked, tasted her pussy, and lost my mind over this woman. I'd crossed the line by a mile—comforting her and staying by her side as she struggled through this difficult time couldn't dig me any deeper. Her brother handed me a coffee from the cardboard carrying container, then turned to Charlotte. "Got one with cream and sugar for you. Wasn't sure how you took it. Me and Ma take it light and sweet, so I figured maybe the taste is hereditary or something."

She smiled. "That's perfect. Thank you."

Jason took a seat on the other side of the bed. "Don't know how long you're planning on staying, but you should probably get some shut-eye. I don't have much room in my little apartment. I live in a studio with my wife. But you're welcome to stay at Ma's place if you want. I have her keys, and it's not too far from here. Maybe fifteen minutes up the road."

"Thanks. But Reed booked us a hotel nearby already."

"You have a good husband." He looked at me. "Though I think he could use some sleep. He was watching you like a hawk while you slept and looked as stressed as you were when you were awake."

It hadn't occurred to me that we'd never labeled our relationship. Considering I'd been next to Charlotte the entire time, his conclusion was logical.

"Oh. Reed's not my husband. He's my"—Charlotte struggled—"boss."

Jason raised a brow and sipped his coffee. "Boss?"

"Yes, he's my boss back in New York. I work at his company."

"From the way he looked like he might murder me when he found us dancing outside, and the way he watched you sleep . . . I just assumed."

Charlotte glanced at me and then back to her brother. "It's . . . complicated."

He smirked. "I'd imagine it is."

After we finished our coffees, Jason again suggested we go get some sleep. Even though Charlotte seemed hesitant, she agreed when he said that we should come back around ten in the morning, since that was when they did rounds.

The hotel I'd booked on my phone was walking distance from the hospital, and check-in was smooth and quick. It wasn't until the two of us were alone in the quiet room that I began to question if I'd done the smart thing by setting us up in a place with two giant beds.

"I'm going to take a quick shower," Charlotte said.

"Are you hungry? The hotel has a twenty-four-hour room-service menu. Why don't I order us something? You haven't eaten anything since before we left New York."

"Okay. Yeah. I guess we should eat. Thank you."

"What would you like?"

"Whatever you're having." Charlotte's drooping shoulders and the sadness in her voice were killing me.

"So two orders of double cheeseburgers, large fries, a milkshake, and dessert?"

"Sure."

I'd been teasing—although I didn't think she really wanted all that food. So I tested if she was paying attention. "Okay. I'll also order a double of pigs' knuckles and roasted squirrel."

When I looked over at her, she responded, "That sounds good." She'd had no idea what I'd just said.

Room service came just as Charlotte emerged from the bathroom. I wasn't sure if it had been really quick or her shower had been really long. I lifted the silver cover from the first plate. "Chicken Caesar salad?" Setting it down, I lifted the second cover. "Or penne alla vodka?"

"I'm sorry. I'm not really hungry." She sighed. Charlotte had on a thick white hotel robe, and her wet hair was wrapped in a towel on top of her head. She wasn't big to begin with, but buried underneath all that, she looked downright tiny in the moment. I rubbed at a spot on my chest, even though the pain was inside.

"Come here." I opened my arms, and she didn't hesitate to walk into them. She closed her eyes and let out another loud breath as I wrapped her in a tight embrace. I stroked her back. "It's been a long day. Or two days. You should get some sleep."

She made no attempt to move but nodded. "Will you hold me? Lie with me, I mean."

"Of course."

Together, we went into the bedroom. I slipped off my shoes and took off my dress shirt, stopping short of removing my pants and white undershirt. Charlotte needed my support, not an erection prodding at her ass. Pulling back the covers, I slipped into the bed and held my arms out for her. She unwrapped the towel from her head and snuggled into me, her wet head resting on my chest right over my heart.

I wanted to say something—to offer some sort of verbal support. But it felt like the words were trapped in my throat. Instead, I did what felt natural and stroked her head with one hand and her back with the other.

After about ten minutes, I thought she'd fallen asleep, but she whispered, "Thank you for this gift, Reed. Even though my heart is broken into a thousand little pieces because she's slipping away and I'll never get to know her, in a weird way, I feel like it's the first time that I have all my pieces. I've always felt like a few were missing."

I kissed the top of her head and firmed up my grip around her. "It's my pleasure, Charlotte. I just wish that things with her health could be different."

A few minutes later, she drifted off to sleep. I chose to stay awake and enjoy the feeling of her sleeping peacefully in my arms. It felt so right. So amazing to do nothing but lie with the woman I'd fallen for on my chest and pretend that this was my life.

I *wanted* it to be my life more than anything.

But seeing the emotional distress Charlotte felt watching a woman she'd really just met dying was a glaring reminder that it couldn't be my life.

This woman finally had all her pieces, and I wasn't about to take one that I might never be able to give back.

CHAPTER 32

CHARLOTTE

"Will she suffer?"

Reed stood behind me squeezing my shoulders as we spoke to the doctors outside of Lydia's room. Jason had said they were facing some tough decisions, but hearing the team of doctors recommend turning off life support this morning made it real. *Really real.*

"We're giving her a sedative and pain medication to keep her calm and relaxed," Dr. Cohen said. "We would increase the dosage before we remove the ventilator so that she wouldn't feel any pain."

"How long would she . . . is she even capable of breathing on her own?" Jason asked.

"It's hard to tell. There're always exceptions, but in general, with a patient in your mother's medical state, we wouldn't expect her to make it more than a few days. Likely less."

Jason swallowed. I could see he was trying to hold back tears. Reed and I had been standing on the left side of the three doctors that had come for rounds, my brother on the right side alone. I walked over and stood next to Jason, taking his hand. He looked at me, nodded, and cleared his throat. "We have another brother that goes to college out in California. He's flying in tomorrow. I'd like to wait to discuss it with him and also give him a chance to see her."

"Of course," Dr. Cohen said. "You take your time and get your family together. We're not rushing you. Your mother is comfortable. She just has no reasonable prospect of a meaningful recovery at this point. So it's a matter of time, and the time needs to be right for you and your family. If I felt that she was suffering, I'd push harder. But take a day or two and give it some thought." He dug in the breast pocket of his white coat and took out a business card and a pen. Jotting something on the back, he offered it to Jason. "My cell phone is on the back. If you or your family has any questions, just give me a call. Anytime. I'll be back tomorrow morning to check in on everything."

"Thank you," we all said, one after the other.

After taking a few minutes in the hall to talk without the doctors, the three of us went back into Lydia's room. I sensed that Jason needed some time alone, so I asked Reed to take a walk with me and told my brother that I'd pick us up some lunch.

The Texas heat was thick outside of the hospital. Both of us seemed lost in thought as we walked side by side on the path around the building. "I need to call Iris," I said. "I feel terrible taking time off when I've only been there a few months, but I can't leave."

"Of course. And no need to call her unless you want to talk. I've kept in touch with her, and she knows what's going on. We had a long-term temp before Iris hired you, so I contacted the agency she was with to see if she's available for a thirty-day assignment. I figured you would need some time here"—he looked at me—"and after."

"Thank you." I shook my head. "I honestly don't know how to thank you for everything, Reed. For finding her, for taking me here, for staying with me, for holding me while I sleep. None of this would be possible without you."

"Stop thanking me, Charlotte. If the roles were reversed, you would've done the same for me. I'm sure of it."

We walked in comfortable silence twice around the hospital. But I couldn't stop thinking about all that Reed had done for me. He was absolutely right that if the roles were reversed and I could help him, I would. Which made me think about the value of my previous relationship.

After four years with my ex-fiancé, I was lucky if Todd brought me chicken soup from the Chinese restaurant when I was sick. And he had to pass the restaurant on his way over to my place. Reed had put his life on hold because I needed him in mine. I wasn't even sure when he'd made hotel arrangements or spoken to Iris—he must've been doing things while I slept so he could give me his full attention while I was awake. I'd noticed that he didn't spend his time scrolling through his phone when we were together. Another thing Todd wasn't capable of doing for me. *God, that Allison is a moron.* Reed gave fully and unconditionally—even to me, whom he wasn't planning on promising his heart to, for better and for worse.

Unfortunately, the more I thought about how generous he was, the more I realized I'd monopolized enough of his time already. Reed worked ten to twelve hours a day, normally. Our little trip would have him backed up for weeks. "You should be getting back to New York. I'll be okay on my own."

"I'm not leaving you here alone, Charlotte."

"Really . . . I'm fine."

Reed flashed a face that said *bullshit.* "I hate to tell you, but you're not fine on a normal day, Darling."

I laughed. "That's true. But you can't stay here and hold my hand forever. We have no idea how long it will be. It could be weeks."

Reed stopped. It took me a few paces to realize I was walking alone. When I turned back, he said, "Do you want me here with you?"

"Of course. But you have to work. You've already done so much."

"I can handle a lot of my work remotely."

"Not showings, you can't."

"I have staff that can fill in for me. I'm here as long as you need me." He held out his hand. "And I rather enjoy holding your hand, if you want the truth."

I placed my hand in his and walked the two steps to close the distance between us. Pushing up on my tippy-toes, I kissed his cheek, then whispered in his ear, "That Allison . . . total fucking moron."

◆ ◆ ◆

Nine days after we'd arrived in Houston, Lydia Van der Kamp died at 11:03 p.m. on a Sunday. Reed, Jason, my youngest brother, Justin, and I were all at her bedside when she simply took her last breath. It had been less than twenty-four hours since they'd removed her from the ventilator.

Nothing could have prepared me for that moment. After the doctor pronounced her legally gone, a priest came in and said a few words. Then we took turns saying our goodbyes. Reed offered to stay with me while I said mine, but I felt like it was something I needed to do on my own.

She was gone, but I hoped her spirit could hear me as I spoke.

"Hi, Mom. I'm so glad I got to know you. You're probably thinking I'm a little crazy for saying 'I got to know you' when you weren't awake the entire time I've been here. But I did get to know you, because I got to meet my two brothers, who you raised. They're loving and kind and the type of men who are a living testament to good parenting. So while we might not have had the opportunity to chat, I got to know you through them. And you're really pretty great." I wiped a few tears from my cheek. "I know it mustn't have been easy for you to give me up. My brothers said you always felt like I took a piece of your heart the day you left me at that church. Well, I feel the same way right now. A piece of my heart that I'd just recently found is missing again. It disappeared when you took your last breath. Someday, we'll meet again and make each other whole." I leaned down and kissed her cheek one last time. "Until then, I'll have an angel watching over me."

I didn't even remember walking out of her room that last time, or even saying goodbye to my brothers before we left the hospital. On the ride back to the hotel, Reed kept asking me if I was okay. I thought I was. Thought I'd made peace with finding her and losing her all in barely a week's time. I wasn't crying anymore and didn't feel distraught, oddly. But there's a difference between finding peace and going numb. It wasn't until we were back in our room and I went into the shower that everything hit me. I'd stepped under the water fully dressed.

Hot water sluiced over my back, making my clothes droop from weight. I squeezed my eyes shut and started to cry. My shoulders shook and sobs racked my body, yet for the first twenty or thirty seconds no sound came out. But then the cork popped off the bottle, and it all started to pour out. I cried hard. *Really hard.* A sickening, howling wail gurgled from my throat. It didn't even sound like it came from me. I leaned against the tile to keep myself up.

I vaguely heard the bathroom door click open, but Reed's presence didn't register until he was right behind me standing in the tub. He wrapped his arms around my waist from behind. "It's okay. Let it out. I got you."

I leaned back, shifting my weight from the wall to the man standing behind me, and pressed my head to his chest. I cried for so many things—Lydia dying so young, my brothers being without a mother, never being able to hear her voice or see her eyes, my mother—my amazing adopted mother—who did everything right, yet I could only give her 99 percent of my heart because the other 1 percent belonged to a woman I'd never known.

Reed just stood there, one hand holding me up and the other stroking my sopping-wet hair. We stayed like that for a long time, until the water turned cold. Eventually when my tears ran dry, he reached around me and twisted the knob to shut off the water. It squeaked as he wound it. "Let me get you out of these clothes."

Shivering, I nodded.

He knelt down in front of me and unbuttoned my jeans. Peeling the soaked denim down my legs, he looked up at me and spoke softly. "Hold my shoulders. Step out."

Doing as I was told, I pulled one foot from my jeans, then the other.

"I'm going to take off all your clothes, so I can get you into something dry. Okay?"

I nodded again.

Reed slid my wet underwear down my legs, and I stepped out—this time at least without needing to be instructed to.

"Lift your arms."

He pulled my soaked T-shirt over my head and unfastened my bra, letting the heavy clothes fall to the tub floor with a loud *thunk*. I still hadn't moved an inch as he stepped out of the tub, grabbed a towel, and shook it open before wrapping it around me.

"You okay?" he asked again.

More nodding.

"Come on. Let's get you dressed in something warm and into bed under the covers."

I finally spoke. "But you're soaked, too."

"I'll get out of my clothes after we get you settled."

I shook my head. "No. I'll wait."

Reed's eyes lifted to mine, and he seemed to mull over what I asked. Although hesitant, he wouldn't deny me anything in the moment. He closed his eyes and nodded.

The air conditioning was frigid, making wearing wet clothes unbearably cold. Even wrapped in a dry towel, I still trembled. Reed had to be freezing, yet he didn't show it. He unbuttoned his drenched shirt and let it fall to the pile on the floor of the tub. His thin undershirt followed next. He hesitated at the button of his jeans, looking up at me one more time before opening them. I stared, waiting, until he continued. He peeled one pant leg down his long leg and then the other before bending to step out.

When he stood back up, I realized why he'd been so hesitant.

The thick bulge in his boxers made my heart pound.

Reed looked down at the erection protruding from the wet fabric. A frown marred his beautiful face. "I'm sorry. I . . . I can't help it."

"Don't be," I whispered. "I'd be disappointed if you weren't."

He searched my face, swallowed, and reached up to hook his thumbs into the waistband of his boxer briefs.

I held my breath while he stripped out of his underwear. His rock-hard cock bobbed against his lower belly as it sprang free. It didn't matter that the room was freezing and we stood among a pile of soaked clothes, a sudden warmth spread all over my body.

Reed watched my eyes while they roamed all over his gorgeous skin. I'd never seen a body so perfect—defined abs, broad shoulders, a narrow waist, but it was his undeniable arousal that my eyes kept coming back to. When I unconsciously licked my lips, Reed groaned. "*Fuck*, Charlotte. Don't look at me like that."

My eyes jumped to his. "Like what?"

"Like if I told you to drop to your knees and suck me off, that it would make you feel better. Like it would make that smile that I miss so much return to your sweet face."

I looked down and then back up under my lashes. "What else do you think would make me smile?"

"*Charlotte . . . ,*" he warned.

The mood shifted. We both felt it. Tension crackled in the air. It was pretty insane how my emotions could jump from needing him to hold me while I wept to needing him inside of me in such a short period of time. While I was reasonably certain I was currently unstable, I was also absolutely positive that I wouldn't regret anything that happened between the two of us. Whatever incited the spark to flame didn't matter; I wanted to feel the burn.

I took a tentative step closer to him. He might never give me his heart, but I wanted to at least pretend he was mine for one day. The closeness between us the last week, the way he'd kept me standing when I was ready to fall, it was easy to feel like we were really a couple. I needed to feel the rest. My heart thumped against the walls of my rib cage. "I want you, Reed. I just want to feel something that isn't painful tonight." My gaze dropped to his wide crown before I looked back up and our eyes met. "Well, that thing might be painful, but it's a different kind of pain."

Reed's nostrils flared. He was a bull watching the red cape swing around from behind a latched gate. I wanted to swing the fence wide open and see him charge. Reaching up to the knot in the towel he'd wrapped around me, I loosened it and it tumbled to the ground.

The muscle in Reed's jaw flexed as his eyes traveled all over me. His voice was strained. "You don't want this, Charlotte. You don't understand."

"That's where you're wrong, Reed. I *do* understand. After the last week, I understand better than anyone. Because I would rather have had these last nine days with my mother that ended in pain than never have known her at all. I don't care if our time is shorter or more difficult—I just want whatever it is we can have."

His chest heaved up and down. "You're destroyed from nine days. Think of what it would be like after nine years if I'm not lucky."

I closed the remaining distance between us so that our skin touched and looked up at him defiantly. "Think of what we could have for those nine years."

He bowed his head. "I can't hurt you, Charlotte. I just can't."

I felt him slipping away again. The window began to close at the mention of anything long-term. Reed wouldn't promise me anything that involved commitment because he didn't think he could fulfill it the way I needed him to. But tonight I needed him, no matter what. In any way, shape, or form. I'd take whatever part of him he was able to give, even if it wasn't his heart. "Then just give me tonight. I *need* you, Reed. Help me forget." I wasn't above begging. *"Just one night."*

He stared at me. I could see the internal debate being waged within him. Deciding more than words might be necessary to tilt the scale in my favor, I reached down between us and slowly ran the pad of my thumb gently over the crown of his glistening, swollen cock. Then I brought my thumb to my lips and sucked the pre-cum off. Reed's eyes blazed. His head dropped back and he roared, *"Fuuucck."*

Suddenly my back hit the wall of the shower. Reed pressed his hands into the tile on either side of me, and I couldn't seem to control my breathing. "Is this what you want?" His head dipped and he sucked in a nipple.

Hard.

My lips parted and a whimper answered his question.

He bit down and tugged my aching nipple between his teeth. "Is this what you want? *Answer me.*"

"I . . . I want to feel you."

A wicked grin spread across his face as his head rose to meet mine. We were nose to nose. "You want to feel me for one night? I'll make you feel me *for days.*"

Reed crushed his mouth to mine, swallowing a gasp of shock. He wound my hair around his fists and used it to tilt my head and deepen the kiss. Skin against skin, caged against the wall, my hair in his tight hold—it still wasn't enough. I needed to be one with this man more than anything in the world. It felt like the only thing that was right.

Hooking both arms around his neck, I lifted my legs and wrapped them around his waist. He ground his cock hard against me, the friction against my clit making me almost lose my mind. My eyes rolled into the back of my head as he sucked on my tongue in tandem with rubbing his shaft up and down. I'd never been so turned on in all my life, never needed anyone so badly. I was drenched between my legs, and it had nothing to do with the shower.

Reed muttered against my mouth, "No condom. I want you bare."

"God, yes."

He detached his lips from mine and pulled back enough so that he could look into my eyes. Panting, his face was hazy with lust as he reined himself in and studied me. He seemed to be making sure that I was really okay with what he'd said.

I offered reassurance. "I'm on the pill."

For a few painful seconds, he closed his eyes, and I thought that he might be reconsidering. But I couldn't have been more wrong. He shook his head.

"I've fantasized about being inside of you since the first time we met. You were in that little black dress, walking around the penthouse I was showing, acting all innocent. I wanted to bend you over and spank your ass for wasting my time." It was impossible to contain my smirk. That was *exactly* what it had felt like he wanted to do to me that day. I remembered vividly the feeling that he'd had a dangerous energy about him that conflicted with his custom suit and proper bow tie. I'd thought I was imagining it at the time.

"You should've. I didn't realize that was an option with all the luxurious amenities that place had offered."

"That day you had those flowers delivered from *Blake*." He spat the name like a curse. "I went home and jerked off to the thought of fucking you from behind while that asshole watched from a window. You were bent over and facing the glass so he could see you, but I covered your face with both of my hands so he couldn't even watch you come with *my dick* inside of you. That's how much I *fucking hate* the thought of you with another man."

His confession made my mouth hang open. I'd known he was attracted to me, had feelings for me even, but I never thought I'd hear him admit that he was as obsessed with me as I was with him. It fueled my boldness.

I moved my hands from his shoulders to his hair, tangling my fingers into the wet strands. "We could do that if you want. I could call him and . . ."

Reed cut me off. "*Don't*. Don't talk about calling another man. Not tonight."

He reached down and fisted his cock, leading it to my opening. Catching my gaze again, he spoke with our lips touching. "Tonight . . . tonight you're fucking mine."

He drove his hips forward and gently but firmly pushed inside. Unconsciously, my eyes fluttered closed.

"Open, Charlotte." His voice was gruff.

I opened and our eyes locked.

"Keep them open. Let me see you. I want to watch your beautiful face as you take my cock. The only thing better than dreaming about it is seeing it in real life." He slid in and out a few times. "*Fuck.* You feel so good."

It had been forever since I'd had sex, and Reed was thick and long. My body squeezed him like a glove. I smiled. "You feel . . . *big.*"

Reed smiled back. The sight was breathtaking. Him inside of me, and for one moment in time, he looked like he didn't have a care in the world.

His hands slid down to cup my ass and he lifted to adjust us. The small tilt of my hips allowed him to sink in even deeper. His smile faded into deep concentration. *"Fuck."*

I whimpered when he reached down and began to rub my clit with two fingers. Neither of us was going to last long. My body tingled, and my legs began to shake. Reed began to thrust harder and harder. "I want to fill you. Pump my cum so deep that you'll always have a piece of me inside you."

God. So dirty, yet at the same time, so beautiful.

I moaned his name as my orgasm took hold. My nails dug into his back, my body began to shudder and jerk, and I lost any awareness of the world around me. We were in a tunnel, just the two of us, secluded from the rest of the world. Reed looked into my eyes and allowed himself to give so much more than his body. We were connected on a level that I'd never experienced before; our minds, bodies, and spirits were in perfect harmony.

When my body began to go slack, Reed stopped holding back. He pumped into me harder and harder until his body went rigid as his hot climax filled me.

Simply spectacular. Better than fireworks on the Fourth of July.

He kept moving in and out for a long time afterward, kissing me and telling me over and over how beautiful I was. Feeling spineless, I held on for dear life as I caught my breath. Reed kissed my neck, my collarbone, my cheeks—even my eyelids. The moment felt so intimate, as if we lived in a little bubble protected from the outside world.

Eventually, though, he pulled out and set me down on my feet. He brushed his lips to mine. "Thank you for tonight, Charlotte."

It was a seemingly innocuous thing to say—sweet, even. Yet it burst that little bubble wide-open. Reed was thanking me for tonight, because things wouldn't be the same tomorrow.

CHAPTER 33

REED

What the fuck did I do?

I didn't want to regret what had just happened. Regretting it would mean it was a mistake, that we'd done something wrong. And what happened between Charlotte and me . . . felt the opposite of wrong. Nothing had felt that right in longer than I could remember. But that didn't mean it wasn't stupid.

One night.

Charlotte was *not* a one-night type of woman, and even though that's what we'd said, I'd only be hurting her more in the end. Now that the blood had left my engorged cock and returned to my brain, I was painfully aware of that.

For the last nine nights, since the first night I'd held her until she'd fallen asleep, I'd made a point of going to bed after Charlotte. No matter how exhausted I'd been, I'd waited until she was out cold and then pretended to fall asleep on the couch. It was the least I could do to keep the small distance between us. But picking up my laptop and pretending to work after what we'd just done felt like a shitty thing to do. Awkwardness hit after we both finished changing for bed.

Stalling, I took a towel to my wet head as Charlotte climbed into one of the two queens in the bedroom. When I started rummaging through my suitcase to buy more time, she sighed loudly.

"Are you going to take all your clothes out and refold them in order to avoid coming to bed with me?"

Of course, she knew.

I chuckled and grabbed a T-shirt before going to sit on the edge of the bed.

"I don't know where I should sleep."

She grinned. "You don't say . . ."

"Wiseass."

"Get into bed, Reed." She pulled back the covers. "And in case there's any doubt . . . I mean *this one.*"

There was actually no place else that I would rather have been in the world. And screw it—one night was more than an hour in the bathroom. She didn't have to ask a second time. I walked over to the light switch and flicked it off before joining her in bed. Positioning ourselves felt as natural as touching her always did. I lay on my back, and Charlotte snuggled into the crook of my shoulder. My arm wrapped around her, and my hand stroked the top of her hair.

After a few minutes she said, "Do you believe in God, Reed?"

For months after my diagnosis, I'd contemplated that exact question. I wasn't sure I did. But then I'd realized I was afraid to *not* believe, which meant that I actually *did* believe there was something to be afraid of.

"I do."

"Do you believe in heaven?"

"I think so."

"Do you think dogs are there?"

I smiled in the dark. *Typical Charlotte.* I'd figured we were entering into a philosophical discussion about the existence of heaven and hell, and she was worried about where dogs go. "I do. Is there a particular one that you're worried about?"

"Richard Stamps."

"Who?"

"My old dog. He died when I was seventeen. His name was Richard Stamps."

"Was he named after someone?"

"Sort of . . ."

From her reluctance, I knew there was a story there. One that would be uniquely Charlotte. "Spit it out, Darling. Where did he get his name?"

"Would that be a capital *D* or a small *d*?"

"After the bathroom, we're not going to mention anything involving *small d*."

She giggled. *God, I love that sound.*

"Promise you won't laugh?" she said.

"Absolutely not."

She swatted at my chest. "When I was in kindergarten, we learned the Pledge of Allegiance. Since we were just starting to read and a lot of the words were big, the teacher taught it to us one line at a time. I was really proud that I'd memorized it. So one night, I unscrewed the flag my parents had in a flagpole on the porch and stood after dinner to show off how smart I was."

"Go on . . ."

She sat up in bed. It was dark, but I could see her hand go to her chest. "I pledge allegiance to the flag of the United States of America, and to the republic for *Richard Stamps*, one nation under God, indivisible, with liberty and justice for all."

I cracked up. "You thought *for which it stands* was Richard Stamps?"

"My parents thought it was amusing, too. It sort of became our little inside joke. Whenever my dad would say to my mom, 'What was that guy's name we met at the party the other night?' my mother would say, 'Richard Stamps.' So when my parents surprised me for my seventh birthday with a puppy, his name was obviously meant to be Richard Stamps."

"*Obviously.*"

"Are you mocking me?"

I laughed. "Richard Stamps is in heaven, Charlotte. I'm pretty sure all the other dogs with names like Spot and Lady are jealous of his cool name, too."

Charlotte lay back down. This time she rested her head over my heart. "I hope he's with Mom."

"He is, beautiful. He is."

She was quiet for a long time after that. I'd started to think she'd fallen asleep. But she'd apparently been thinking about more than Richard Stamps. "Why would God let someone so young die?"

"I've spent a lot of time thinking about that very question. And the answer is, I have no idea. I'm not sure anyone really has that answer. But I like to think that maybe heaven is a better place than here and death isn't always a punishment, but sometimes it's a reward to put people out of their pain."

Charlotte tilted her head up to look at me. "Wow. That's a beautiful way to think about it."

I cupped her cheek with my hand. "Lydia is in a good place. It's harder for the people who are left behind."

"I can't even imagine what my brothers are going through. I feel like there's a hole in my heart, and I didn't even get to make memories with her."

Her sentiment lingered in the air.

I kissed the top of her head and squeezed her. "Get some sleep. Tomorrow we'll make arrangements, and it'll be a long day."

She yawned. "Okay."

Right as I started to doze, she whispered, "Reed? Are you asleep?"

"I was . . ."

"I just want to say one more thing." She paused. "I think it's better to spend years treasuring a memory that might hurt sometimes than to never make one at all."

◆ ◆ ◆

People loved her. Men, women, young, old, it didn't matter.

I watched from the back of the reception room as Charlotte spoke to an older couple. The only people she'd met before the wake began had been her two brothers. Yet today, as people came to offer their respects at the funeral parlor, everyone knew her and walked away with a smile after a couple of minutes of small talk.

I'd started the day standing by her side, wanting to be near her if she needed my support. But after a while, I wandered off to give her privacy with her newfound family. Charlotte's adoptive mother had flown in last night to support her daughter. We'd had a late dinner and then dessert at a different restaurant that her mother had read about in a magazine on her flight, which was enough time to realize that Charlotte's quirkiness came from *nurture* in the *nature versus nurture* battle.

Nancy Darling walked over to the row that I sat in. She slipped an untied silky scarf from around her neck and used it to wipe off the clean, empty seat next to me before sitting—something I'd noticed she'd done before she took any seat.

I pointed my chin at Charlotte. "She seems to be doing well. How are you holding up?"

"It's odd to be here, but I'm fine. I'm glad that I got a moment alone with Lydia before it got too busy. I had a lot to thank her for."

I nodded. "I wasn't sure how Charlotte was going to handle today. She had a tough week. But she seems good, too."

"Ah. Rookie mistake. You'll learn," Nancy teased, only she wasn't really kidding. "Don't let the smile on my daughter's face fool you. It's not the emotion she shows during a trying time that makes me worry about her."

I squinted at Charlotte, watching her smile yet again. It *looked* like she was okay. "What do you mean?"

Nancy hesitated. "You two seem close, and since you work together, you'll be around her a lot more than I will. So perhaps you can keep an eye on her for me."

"Okay . . ."

"I'm not sure you're aware, but Charlotte has some latent abandonment issues. It's not uncommon in adopted children. But how each person's anxieties manifest can be very different. Abandonment is a trauma and causes post-traumatic stress disorder—most people don't realize that."

"I didn't realize she suffered from any long-term issues," I said.

"Everyone has issues. Charlotte just has a tendency to bury hers and then act impulsively to avoid feeling what she's really feeling."

Fuck. Impulsively. Like going from crying to wanting to have sex in the shower.

"The hardest time for people who suffer a loss is usually after everything is over," Nancy said. "No more hospital vigils or family bonding together. Everything gets buried—literally and figuratively. Then everyone around you goes back to normal, and you're not ready yet. That's when I'll worry most about Charlotte."

"What can I do to help?"

Nancy patted my leg. "Just be there for her. When the person who is supposed to be there most for you in life leaves you behind, you tend to be a little skittish. Her relationship with that jackass, Todd, didn't help reassure her that people stick around, either. The best thing we can offer Charlotte is continuity—be reliable when she needs us most, in whatever form that may be."

CHAPTER 34

REED

We were back in New York, but nothing resembled the way things were before we'd gone to Texas. It felt like everything had changed.

Charlotte was taking a much-needed break from work, some time to clear her head after everything she'd endured in Houston. The office was completely lackluster without her around. She'd decided to stay with her parents up in Poughkeepsie for a while, and I fully supported that idea. It was a reluctant but much-needed break, one I intended to use to figure out what I was going to do when it came to her.

It pleased me that she was choosing to lean on her parents and not me. It wasn't that I didn't want to be there for her. I ached to be able to comfort her. But being physically around her after what we'd done in that hotel room in Texas would have been too much. My rational brain was useless whenever she was around. And I had big decisions to make that I needed my brain for.

Alone in my office, I kept hearing Charlotte's mother's words repeating in my head.

"The best thing we can offer Charlotte is continuity—be reliable when she needs us most."

Nancy Darling likely had no clue that while I could offer her daughter short-term continuity and reliability, my being there for her now would be to Charlotte's detriment later in life. Charlotte thought she knew what was best for herself. She was young, bright-eyed, and naive. The situation with me wasn't as simple as she was making it out to be. She'd said she'd rather have a limited amount of time with someone than none at all. She couldn't possibly make that decision for herself now. It's easy to say something like that when everyone is in good health. Would she feel the same if I weren't healthy and if my slow deterioration went on for years of her life?

I had to be careful. We'd crossed a very big line when we had sex.

Incredible, mind-blowing, raw sex that I would never forget for as long as I lived.

I'd told her it would only be one night, and I had the opportunity to stick to my word and not fuck everything up for good.

Unless I was going to be with Charlotte long-term, it was imperative that I never have sex with her again. Once we broke the one-time rule . . . that would be it. It would be extremely difficult to go back from that. Not to mention, she would become even more attached to me.

But I want her attached to me, don't I?

That was the fucked-up thing. I was so incredibly torn between the selfish desire to give in to my need for Charlotte and the smart choice of letting her go.

I hated to say it. I really hated to say it, but I needed my brother. Max's head was in the clouds half the time. He was self-absorbed and not necessarily in the loop with my life. That was partly my choice for not opening up to him when it came to Charlotte. But when the shit really hit the fan, he was always the one I turned to for advice at the eleventh hour.

Since Charlotte was taking some time off, it was the perfect opportunity to ask Max to meet me at the office for an impromptu meeting to catch up. Even though it wasn't the usual day of the week that he normally decided to grace us with his presence, Max made a special trip in to see me after I left him an urgent voice mail.

He sauntered into my office with a box of doughnuts and two coffees, because urgent matters apparently warranted doughnuts. Max was the only person I knew who could consume endless amounts of crap and still maintain a toned, rock-hard body.

He took a bite of his cruller and spoke with his mouth full. "Dude . . . you dying or something? I can't remember the last time you called me in just to talk."

I could remember. It had been after I'd found out I had MS. That was literally the last time I'd asked Max to meet me for an emergency powwow.

"Sit down, brother," I said.

"What is this about?"

"It's about Charlotte."

"You got it bad for her. Grandmother told me you helped her find her birth mother out in Texas, that the mother died. That's crazy. How's Charlotte doing?"

"She's with her parents upstate, taking some time off. The Texas trip sort of did me in, too, in more ways than one."

He squinted. "You fucked her, didn't you?" My lack of denial was enough for him to add, "You lucky bastard."

Letting out a long breath, I said, "I need you to figure this out for me, Max."

"What's there to figure out?"

"You know what. I never wanted to get involved with her, never wanted to take things this far, because of my diagnosis. I fucked up royally."

"You fucked *her* royally. I don't see the problem with that at all." He picked up another doughnut and waved it at me. "You want me to tell you how to get rid of the best thing that's ever happened to you and not have it hurt like hell? You think I'm some kind of fucking magician? There is no easy answer to this because you're in love with the girl, am I right?"

Taking a deep breath in and out, I conceded, "Ass over head in love with her."

"Then *be* with her. She knows everything about you. She's accepted it. Be with her, Reed."

"What if I can't? What if the guilt is too much? How do I leave her? Tell me how to leave her."

"There's no happy medium. Either you be with her, or you stop. You just stop cold turkey. You don't lead her on anymore, and you don't try to be her friend, or be her fucking hero, because we both know that's a bunch of bullshit. You're beyond that point. And I hate to say it, but you really can't work together if you decide to walk away from this. That shit won't work. You'll continue to slip, and you'll end up in the same situation, and that's not fair. So either shit or get off the pot. And you'd better find her a new job if you decide to walk away. She'll be okay. Believe me, there are plenty of men who would love to lick her wounds."

I knew he added that last part to test me. He knew that would make me crazy. His words were harsh, but I knew they were the goddamn truth. There was no middle ground with Charlotte. Either I was all in or all out.

"Max, you're nothing if not a straight shooter. Thank you. I needed the slap in the face."

That night, alone in my apartment, I stared out at the skyline, no more certain of what I should do. The only thing I was certain of was that Charlotte and I really couldn't ever just be friends. It would be too painful to watch her moving on with her life. There would never be a time when I didn't want Charlotte Darling more than my next breath.

When my cell phone rang past midnight, I'd almost ignored it until I saw it was her.

I picked up. "What are you doing up so late?"

"I couldn't sleep."

My body stirred at the mere sound of her voice, a testament to exactly how weak I was when it came to her. It was much easier to consider a hard break from Charlotte when I wasn't looking at her or even hearing her voice. Even without her around, I was perpetually hard just thinking about our night together.

"I'm sorry you're having insomnia."

"Did I wake you?" she asked.

"No. And it wouldn't have mattered if you did. How are things at home?"

"I'm feeling very lost, like I'm here but I'm not. I don't really know how to explain it. So much of my life had been spent wondering where I came from. I feel this weird void now. But it's more than that, more than my mother's passing. I feel like I'm at a turning point in my life, but one where I don't even know what my options are, only that something needs to change. Yet I don't have the energy to think about any of it or figure it out. I haven't even wanted to get out of bed most days."

"That's depression, Charlotte. I know it well, because I went through a long bout of it, especially after I was diagnosed, when my mind would go to the worst-case scenario. You'll be okay. I promise. You just have to ride it out."

"What would you specifically think about during that time?" she asked.

Even though I didn't want to turn this conversation onto me, I began to open up a little.

"I'd just start to picture myself incapacitated, unable to move, stuff like that. And that would make the depression worse."

There was some silence before she said, "You know, if someone really loves you, they would rather have any time with you than none at all, right? When you love someone, even taking care of them when they can't take care of themselves is an honor, not a burden."

The fucked-up thing was, I was starting to actually believe she felt that way. I just couldn't imagine burdening someone I loved, regardless of how they saw the situation. My chest tightened. I needed to get off this subject.

"Let's get back to you. Is this the first time you've ever gone through anything like this?"

"Yeah. This has never happened to me before."

"People will tell you to just get up and do something, take your mind off it, but you can't even pinpoint what *it* is. It's just a feeling of emptiness that follows you around. Sometimes, it just needs to pass on its own. It *will* pass. Your mind will clear, you'll figure out what you want, and you'll get your spark back."

"How are things at the office?"

Fucking miserable without you.

"Uneventful. You're not missing out on anything. Don't worry about that."

"You said you have the temp there for up to thirty days?"

"Longer if need be. Just take all the time you need."

"I might in fact need more time. I'm thinking of doing some traveling."

My stomach dipped. "Where are you going?"

"I haven't decided yet."

"Charlotte, if you need anything—money—anything for your trip, please let me know."

"No. No, I don't need your money. You've done enough for me." There was a pause, then she said, "Anyway, I'd better let you go to sleep."

"I can stay up all night if you need me to."

"It's okay. I need to try to sleep myself."

"Call me again. Please, keep me updated."

"I will. Good night, Reed."

"Charlotte?"

"Yes?"

I didn't even know why I'd called her name out, why I didn't just let her go. It wasn't like I could say the things I wished I could.

It's killing me that you're hurting.

Come home with me. Let me take care of you.

I love you.

I love you, Charlotte.

"Take care of yourself," I simply said.

CHAPTER 35

CHARLOTTE

My email notification showed I'd just received an instant payment of five thousand dollars. That was definitely the most money I'd ever gotten in one lump sum. Allison's designer feathered wedding gown had sold on eBay in less than a day.

That hadn't taken long at all. The dress was worth far more—at least twenty grand—but I needed the money soon to fund my trip to Europe. Well, I'd already bought the tickets, but I needed the cash to pay the hefty credit card bill that would be coming at the end of the month. The only way I could guarantee quick money was to undersell.

I hadn't told Reed I was back in the city. As far as he was concerned, I was still in Poughkeepsie with my parents. I would only be here long enough to ship the dress and pack my things before my flight this weekend anyway.

I'd decided to fly into Paris and would spend a few days roaming the city before taking an overnight train to Rome. I'd booked a sleeper car. It wasn't quite the scenario I'd hoped for on my Fuck-It List, but it was as close as I was going to get.

After carefully clipping Reed's blue note out of the dress, I held the paper in my hand and read the message a few times.

To Allison—
"She said, 'Forgive me for being a dreamer,' and he took
her by the hand and replied, 'Forgive me for not being
here sooner to dream with you.'" —J. Iron Word
    Thank you for making all of my dreams come true.
Your love,
Reed

How I wished to be loved by him. But maybe he wasn't capable of loving the way he had when he'd penned the note. He'd hardened. As much as I wished he would see things the way I did, I just couldn't force him to. His resistance had worn me down. Couple that with my numbness as of late, and I just had no energy to fight anything, least of all Reed Eastwood.

As I carefully packed the dress into a large, flat white box, I hoped that it would bring good luck to Lily Houle of Madison, Wisconsin. Lily would now be the recipient of its magic, which no longer seemed to be working for me.

I thought about how this dress had changed my life. It had brought me Reed, and even if he and I never had anything more than what had already taken place, he'd changed my life. He'd made me feel things I never had before, and he'd given me the closure I needed when it came to my roots.

Taking one last look at the fabric before I closed the box, I was ready to put the fairy tale to bed. Love wasn't about a beautiful dress, a note, or even poignant words. It was about being with someone through thick and thin, about seeing them through not only the best moments of life but also the worst. It was about being there for someone like I would have been there for Reed if he'd let me. I thought of my birth mother. True love was also about forgiveness.

It made me sad that I felt like I was giving up on Reed, especially after the night we'd had in Houston. But if that amazing sex couldn't finally bring us together, what could? I missed his body, the way he felt inside of me, so much. The need kept me up at night lately. We'd become one physically, yet emotionally he was still so guarded, still so far away. How many times could I stand to get rejected by one man? I'd rather be alone than alongside an unattainable Reed, playing this cat-and-mouse game that never ended. I didn't want to quit working at Eastwood, but I was probably going to have to. I had some big decisions to make, and I was hoping the overseas trip would bring clarity.

First day in Paris consisted of bread and cheese, followed by bread and more cheese.

Sitting in front of La Fromagerie, I wondered if I'd accomplish anything more than gaining an extra five pounds while on this trip. I wasn't going to find my solutions in a baguette, that was for sure. Yet eating alone seemed to be what I wanted to do. And this trip was just as much about doing nothing as it was about finding something meaningful.

I was surrounded by smoking Parisians sipping their coffees and speaking in a language that I really couldn't understand despite my best efforts in trying to learn. Staying in my own world, I enjoyed the cheese-and-fruit platter I ordered.

I'd decided I was going to visit as many cafés as I possibly could before I had to board the train to Italy.

As alone as I was here, I didn't feel lonely, mainly because of all the other people around me enjoying solitude. Take, for example, the artist sitting in the corner, sketching something. I was in good company in being alone. And that was comforting.

The sight of the Eiffel Tower in the distance served as a spectacular reminder to look up from my plate once in a while and to not forget the splendor of where I was. Instead of a hotel, I'd opted to stay in an Airbnb in the Quartier Saint-Germain-des-Prés, a small but charming neighborhood not far from the tower. Tomorrow, I would take a break from my culinary tour to visit Notre Dame and the Louvre.

My eyes wandered to a man who looked like he could be Reed from the back—dark hair, dressed in a suit, broad stature. My heart felt like it skipped a beat at the thought of how incredible it would be to have him here with me.

The man was sitting alone, reading a newspaper. Suddenly, it hit me that you could travel across the Atlantic, seek out all the distractions in the world to suppress the pain in your heart . . . but one little reminder was all it took to unravel everything. A few moments later, the man was joined by a woman and two rosy-faced children. He stood up from his chair and bent down to embrace the two little cherubs. Still observing him from the back, the man was basically Reed to me. And the sight I was witnessing was Reed and his children—a life he might have had if it weren't for his fears. A life I might have had if it weren't for his fears.

Tears started streaming down my face. I was a sight to behold between the crying and the chewing.

Just as I was about to get up and head to my next culinary destination, the artist in the corner began to approach me. He said something in French that I couldn't understand, then winked and handed me the portrait he'd been working on. He scooted away—literally—before I had a chance to say anything back.

I looked down and gasped. It was the most hideous picture of myself. Hideous not because it was poorly drawn, but because it was very likely exactly what I looked like today. In the drawing, my mouth was open as I stuffed my face with a piece of bread. My eyes were bugged out, and they looked swollen from tears. Tomorrow, I would be going to see the calm and collected Mona Lisa. This hot mess in my hands was the polar opposite.

As I continued to stare at the portrait of myself, though, it hit me that despite the fact that I felt my life was a mess, this stranger had found something artworthy in me. By simply being and enjoying the present moment, I had inspired him somehow. I stared at the picture some more. The longer I looked at it, the less I saw the lost girl eating bread and the more I saw the independent woman. One who'd just found and lost her mother, yet who persevered anyway—and despite being in love with a man she could never have. She survived anyway. Eating cheese. Maybe this was a lesson that I'm okay just as I am—alone and experiencing whatever life throws my way. Maybe *I* am enough.

I am enough.

In that moment, I realized that while it might take some time, I would really be okay no matter what happened between Reed and me— because I would have *myself*. And I was strong—perfectly imperfect.

◆ ◆ ◆

Later that day, I happened to walk by a boutique on Rue du Commerce that sold vintage wedding dresses.

I couldn't help but stop to gaze at the gown that was on display in the storefront. It was stunning, not in the same way that Allison's blush feathered dress was. This one was trumpet-style, white, and covered in sequins. It was a simple style but had a beautiful waistband that gave it character and tied the look together.

I thought back to my last wedding dress–boutique experience all those months ago, how much had happened since, how much I'd changed. My tastes had matured along with a lot of things about my life.

So much was left uncertain. Would I stay working at Eastwood, or would I go back to school? I had a lot to think about when I got back home. Despite the uncertainties, there were so many more things I *had* become certain about in terms of what I wanted out of life.

I was certain I deserved the kind of man who would love me like Reed might have if he weren't so scared. And I knew I shouldn't give up hope about finding that. Even my mother had gone on to find love and live a happy—albeit short—life after all that she'd been through after giving me up.

I took one last look at the dress in the window. It was the type of dress I might have chosen today—not as ostentatious as the feathered gown, but not plain, either. If the feathered dress represented a false ideal, this one represented . . . me.

Simple yet elegant with lots of sparkle.

CHAPTER 36

REED

It wasn't easy, pretending not to be wondering where she was or what she was doing every moment of the day. I'd vowed to give Charlotte space and to not interfere with her trip. But I couldn't help wondering if she was safe or whether she was still sad and depressed. All I knew was that she'd be visiting France and Italy and planned to be gone a couple of weeks. She'd left her return date up in the air, too. I wondered if she ever planned to come back to Eastwood at all.

It was getting more difficult each day to concentrate at work. I did something I almost never do: I ventured to Central Park at lunch and decided to just sit on a bench and think. The autumn leaves were blowing around me as thoughts of Charlotte consumed me. Even with all that this city had to offer, it was amazing how bland a life could seem when the one person who matters suddenly disappears. I suppose it isn't until that point that you realize just how much the person matters at all—until they leave you.

Suddenly, there was an awareness of a presence in my periphery. When I turned to my left, I noticed a young guy in a wheelchair who'd pulled in next to my bench.

He was probably around eighteen or nineteen and could have been a younger version of myself with dark hair and chiseled features. Good-looking kid.

I nodded. "Hey."

Previously oblivious, he turned to me. "Hey."

Feeling like I needed to say something more, I said, "Nice day, huh?"

"Uh . . . yeah." He half smiled, seeming like he had a dozen better things to be doing than talking to me.

"Just out enjoying the weather?" I asked.

"No . . . uh, actually, I'm waiting for a Tinder date."

Oh?

He must have noticed the look of surprise on my face when he squinted. "What? You think someone in a wheelchair doesn't have game?"

"I didn't say that."

"Yeah, well, the look on your face did."

"I'm sorry if I looked that way." A few moments of silence passed. I looked up at the sky, then turned to him. "So, Tinder, huh? It works for you?"

"Oh yeah. You wouldn't believe the number of chicks who want to play the hero with me. I mean, I hook them with my face initially. We connect, and then they find out I'm in a wheelchair after the fact. You think they'd run? Fuck, no. That's actually what seals the deal. It's like they think they're gonna save me or some shit. Meanwhile, I just want some ass. And I get it. Every single time. So it works out for everyone. So take that sorry look and save it for yourself. I'm the one getting laid today." He leaned in. "Sex on wheels."

Sex on wheels.

I bent my head back in laughter. Something told me I would never forget this kid. So much for preconceived notions. This dude was badass.

A few moments later, an attractive redhead walking a small dog approached.

"You must be Adam."

He wheeled himself toward her. "Ashley . . . you're even more beautiful in person."

She blushed. "Thank you."

He looked over at me with a slight smirk, then said to her, "Shall we get going?"

"Absolutely."

Adam nodded once. "Nice talking to you, man."

"Yeah. Take care." I watched them until they were out of sight.

Here was this guy, living what was basically my worst nightmare, and he was happier than a pig in shit. It proved that attitude is everything in life. He exuded confidence and wasn't missing out on anything because he believed he deserved more, and he chose to live, not hide.

It was funny how sometimes the universe placed something in front of you that was exactly what you needed to see at exactly the right time.

God, I sounded like Charlotte.

Pointing my index finger up at the sky, I said, "Damn, you're good. Almost have me convinced."

◆　◆　◆

Fiddling with my watch in Iris's office, I asked, "Have you heard anything from Charlotte?"

"No, but she sent me a file with her itinerary in case of emergency so that I'd know where she was."

"And?"

"Well, I happened to look at it and noticed that she's going to be taking an overnight train from France to Italy in a couple of days."

"You mean . . . like a sleeper car?"

"Yes." Her expression turned sullen. "Reed, I'm not so sure she's traveling alone."

My pulse sped up. "What makes you say that?"

"Just a feeling I have. I think that Blake man might be with her."

Then it hit me.

The item on her Fuck-It List.

Make Love to a Man for the First Time in a Sleeper Cabin on a Train Ride Through Italy.

Panic started to set in. What if Iris was right? What if Charlotte wasn't alone? She wasn't in her right mind. Charlotte was too vulnerable to make smart decisions. Not to mention, she didn't understand how I really felt about her. What if she was taking this trip with Blake to spite me for sleeping with her and flaking? She'd been distant lately, and she'd never mentioned that things were exactly over with him.

Charlotte had no idea the level of impact she'd had on my life, the depth of my feelings for her, because I'd never told her. Who could blame her for thinking she had nothing to lose at this point? Fuck, if the roles were reversed, I'd be on a sleeper train with Blake, too.

I'd been bullshitting myself and Charlotte for months. She believed the man who wrote the note was mostly gone. But the truth was . . . even if it she wasn't with another man, I wanted to be the one to make love to her on that train.

"Are you okay, Reed?"

I was speed-talking now. "No. No, I'm not. I'm afraid I really screwed up with Charlotte. I thought I could live without her, but I can't. Now it may be too late to fix things. One of the items on her Fuck-It List is to make love to a man for the first time in a sleeper cabin. If she's with this Blake, then she's going to sleep with him on that train." I stood up and paced.

"It's not too late, Reed. Charlotte wants to be with *you*. Even if she's with another man, it's only because you've chased her away. You're the one she wants. You need to go to her and tell her how you feel."

I whipped around. "What if she's with him?"

"Then you do it anyway. You can't let her slip away."

By God, she was right.

"No, I can't. She's the one, Grandmother. She's the one, and that realization has been terrifying . . . but it's undeniable."

"Then go! You don't have much time to catch her before she gets on that train."

◆ ◆ ◆

I wasn't able to get onto a flight that would allow me to board Charlotte's train in Paris. The only chance I had to get onto that train would be to catch it when it stopped in Venice on the way to Rome, which according to the itinerary was her final destination. That meant I could very well arrive and find that Charlotte had already fulfilled her wish of making love in a sleeper cabin with Blake, since by the time the train arrived in Venice it would be morning.

That was a chance I had to take.

When I landed in Venice, I just needed to get to the train station. I'd depended on the fact that I'd have internet on my phone to help me find my way there. But for some reason, I had no service. For the life of me, I couldn't find anyone who spoke English. Even though I had no wireless, I could still text.

Note to self, never trust Max to take me seriously when I ask him to translate something into Italian for me. Instead of finding myself at the nearest train station, I ended up at the nearest whorehouse.

Remind me to wring his neck when I get home.

Even though my service returned, that detour set me back by at least a half hour. *Fucking Max.* I was really cutting it close.

I finally arrived at the Venezia Santa Lucia railway station. There were sixteen platforms, and I had to figure out how to find out which one Charlotte's night train would be stopping at. Apparently Venice was the first stop and also the final destination for some of the passengers. Those who were continuing on to Rome would stay on the train. Not only did I have no clue whether Charlotte was actually on this train, I didn't know if she was with that guy. My nerves were shot. My stomach felt sick.

Finally speaking to someone who understood English, I was able to find out which platform her train would arrive at. I purchased my ticket to Rome, then made my way to the other side of the station to wait by the tracks.

My mind was racing. What was I going to say to her? It felt like I had to prepare two different speeches for two different scenarios. Emotions were flooding my chest, but no words seemed to travel to my brain. I just hoped I could form something coherent if given the opportunity.

Right on time, at 11:05 a.m., the train pulled into the station. With my heart pounding, I watched as a swarm of people exited the front car and retrieved their luggage.

Handing my ticket to the conductor, I stepped onto the train, found a seat, and waited impatiently. I didn't want to do anything that might get me in trouble while the train was parked, figuring they'd be much less likely to kick me out if we were moving.

Once the train took off again, I got up out of my seat to walk down to where the cabins were located. I knocked on every single door. Either there was no answer or I was greeted—in some cases, not so cordially— by people who were not Charlotte Darling.

Was she even on this train?

I was pretty sure at this point I would rather have not found her than discover her with another man in some kind of postcoital situation.

My heart stopped for a moment when I made my way to the final car, the dining room. It was empty, except for a beautiful blonde angel sitting in the corner, eating a croissant and looking out the window—alone.

CHAPTER 37

CHARLOTTE

The overnight train was a mistake. I hadn't been able to sleep all night. The jerking motion combined with my own busy mind had prevented me from getting any quality shut-eye.

Traveling on a sleeper car through Italy was nothing like I'd imagined. It was a lonely, uncomfortable experience.

I missed home.

I miss Reed.

As sad as that made me, it was the truth.

Deciding to head to the dining area to grab some breakfast, I took a seat by the window and had the entire car to myself. Still on my French-food kick, I ordered a croissant and a coffee.

Looking through the glass, I marveled at the scenic Italian landscape. My eyes stayed transfixed on the agriculture outside until a reflection of a man who looked awfully like Reed appeared in the window.

I was hallucinating.

Can too much dairy make you hallucinate?

I blinked. When he was still there, I turned to my left and placed my hand over my chest at the sight of him.

Reed?

Oh my God, Reed!

His mouth was trembling as he stood staring at me. "Are you alone?"

Unable to form words, I simply nodded.

His shoulders were rising and falling. He looked rugged, unshaven, like he'd been backpacking through Europe. He was wearing cargo pants and boots.

Is this a dream?

"You look like you're going to war," I said.

"I thought I was." He expelled a long breath. "I thought you were here with a man."

"You came all this way because you thought I was here with a man?"

"Yes." He closed his eyes. "I mean, no. I don't know. I think I would have come either way. I have so much to say, Charlotte."

"I can't believe you're here."

He finally approached, landing in the seat next to me and into my arms.

Squeezing him tightly, I started to cry. "I missed you so much, Reed."

He breathed into my neck. "Oh, beautiful. I missed you, too." Pulling back to look at me, he said, "Bonnie Raitt *was* right . . ."

"What do you mean?"

He stared into my eyes for several seconds before he said, "You can't make someone love a person. But the opposite is also true. Nothing can make someone *unlove* a person, either. I have tried so hard not to love you, Charlotte. But I love you with all of my heart and soul."

Tears fell harder as I wrapped my arms around his neck. "God, Reed, I love you so much."

Speaking into my ear, he asked, "Can we go to your sleeper car?"

Excitement filled me. "Yes."

We both rushed up out of our seats and headed to my cabin. The second that the door closed behind us, his lips were enveloping mine. I couldn't take it if he told me one more time that we couldn't be together. I loved this man and didn't want to live a second without him ever again.

His erection pressed against my abdomen as he pushed me down onto the bed.

"I have so much to say," he spoke over my lips as he hovered over me. "But I need to be inside of you while I say it. Please."

Panting, I nodded. "Yes."

His hands were fumbling to get my jeans off. I helped slide them off my legs without breaking my lips away from his for even a second.

I was already so wet when his thick crown pushed into my entrance. He was fully inside of me in one hard thrust. He was fucking me as if he'd traveled across the world just to do this. I suppose he had.

My hands raked through his already messy hair. His stubble scratched my skin as he devoured my mouth.

He whispered into my ear as he penetrated me, "I love you, Charlotte. I love you so much, and I'm so sorry that I don't know how to stop. I can't fucking stop. I'm a selfish bastard. And I need you by my side even if it ends up ruining your life. I need you."

"You've *saved* my life, and I don't ever want to live without you."

"As long as I'm breathing, you won't have to."

The talking stopped as he pumped into me harder. The bed beneath us shook. The train was moving, but somehow it still felt like we were rocking it. Our first time in Texas had knocked my socks off, but there were no words for how good it felt this time. My orgasm came without warning. As I screamed out in ecstasy, his body trembled before his hot cum filled me.

Maybe it felt different this time because now I knew for certain that he was mine.

"Is this for real, Reed?"

Still inside of me, he kissed my neck and said, "This is the realest thing I've ever experienced. I want it all, Charlotte. I want to marry you, I want you to have my babies if that's what you want, and I want to give you everything you've ever dreamed of."

His proclamation caused me to really burst into tears.

"Did I say something wrong?" he asked.

"No. I'm so happy, Reed."

We just looked into each other's eyes and smiled. The happiness in his expression mirrored my own.

He slowly pulled out of me and cradled me in his arms, speaking against my skin.

"You know, I never really looked at what happened with Allison as a blessing until you. If she had never left me, I would have never met you. My love for you is beyond anything I've ever felt for anyone, Charlotte. There's no comparison."

"Part of why I was crying was that you mentioned babies. For some reason, I was scared that maybe you would be afraid to have children. Hearing you say you want them with me, it's like a dream come true."

"We never really talked about it, but I always suspected you wanted kids," he said.

"Yes, but not more than I want you."

"Well, I want to give you both. I'll have to put a certain amount of faith in God that I'm making the right decision. You know I worry about my ability to take care of you and them. But there's nothing I want more than to have a little Charlotte."

Tears were filling my eyes again. "I'm so happy, Reed."

"Me, too." He kissed me before saying, "I can't wait to see Rome with you. How about we fly back to Paris for a few days after, too."

My eyes widened. "Really?"

"I want to see it with you. I've never been."

"I can show you so much! There are so many cafés I found. So much good bread and cheese!"

"Cheese, huh? Well, now I'm really excited."

I started to replay the events of the past half hour in my head. "Hey . . . what made you think I was here with a man?"

"Iris. She put the idea in my head that Blake was here with you."

Closing my eyes, I had to laugh. Iris knew full well that I didn't go out with Blake. She'd said that to make Reed jealous. She'd totally tricked him.

I'd have to remember to thank her.

CHAPTER 38

REED

Three months later

Staff meetings when Charlotte was in attendance were always distracting.

It didn't matter that I'd moved her into my apartment and got to sleep with her every night. Whenever she was around, I could focus on nothing else. But today, that feeling was particularly strong, and I knew exactly why.

Iris always wore a permanent smile on her face whenever Charlotte and I were in the same room with her. My grandmother considered Charlotte a part of the family already. At Sunday dinner in Bedford last week, Iris had taken out my old choir recordings. I could have fought it, but I let her play them for Charlotte. That was how confident I was in Charlotte's love for me, that nothing could deter how she saw me, no matter how embarrassing.

The accountant was going on and on about the quarterly reports, and I honestly hadn't heard a word he'd said.

Discreetly opening the folder on my laptop that contained my bucket-list document, I added a line item: *Marry Charlotte Darling.*

She looked over at me, and I immediately closed out of the document, even though she couldn't see what I was writing anyway. It felt like she knew I was up to something, though.

As the meeting wrapped up, I took my pen and scribbled on my notepad.

From the desk of Reed Eastwood

Charlotte,
Take the rest of the afternoon off. Boss's orders.

I slipped her the note as the meeting was dispersing.

She looked down at it and squinted. "What are you up to . . . *boss?*"

"I've cancelled my afternoon meetings. Let's go home and chill."

"Who are you? You've come a long way from the workaholic I used to know."

"Yeah, well, I have better things to do these days. Namely, you."

◆　◆　◆

Back at the apartment, Charlotte had just stepped out of the shower when I decided to let her in on a couple of surprises I'd had up my sleeve.

"Remember our first showing together in Bridgehampton? The owner was an artist who painted portraits depicting how couples met?"

"Yeah, I remember thinking that was so cool."

"Well . . . I looked her up and asked her to make one for us."

Her mouth hung open. "Are you kidding?" Then she seemed to think about it some more. "Wait . . . how we *met?* That wasn't exactly the most romantic experience; quite the opposite. This is going to be interesting."

"Well, I realized that. So let's just say I put a unique spin on it."
I walked to the corner of the room and lifted the portrait, bringing it over to her.

Peeling the bubble wrap off, I slowly opened it. I hadn't seen it yet myself because I wanted to be just as surprised as Charlotte.

"Oh my God!" Charlotte yelled. She covered her mouth with her hand and then began laughing uncontrollably.

I was holding on to my stomach in laughter myself.

The artist had done a phenomenal job depicting Charlotte and me on a surfboard—with a dog in front of us. We were dog surfing. Her interpretation of Charlotte's face was spot on. I'd given the artist actual photos to work with. In the painting, I was on the back of the board, hanging on for dear life and looking terrified while Charlotte was laughing without a care in the world. The dog's tongue was hanging out and his eyes looked possessed. This was classic and would forever be displayed front and center wherever we happened to be living.

She was grinning so hard. "This is seriously . . . the best gift anyone has ever given me."

"I'm not exactly done with the gifts today," I said.

"Oh?"

Rubbing my hands together, I geared up for my next surprise. "So I was thinking . . . as of last check, you only have one more item on your Fuck-It List that you haven't completed."

Her eyeballs flitted back and forth as if she had to think about it. "Sculpt a nude man . . ."

"Yes." I smiled nervously. "Anyway . . . I'd like to be your model."

"Are you serious?"

"Dead."

My spare bedroom was now Charlotte's art space. I had no idea if she even had the right tools to do this today, but I was hoping she'd go along with it.

"This is nuts . . . but in a good way." She was beaming. "I would *love* to sculpt you."

"Well, then I'm your man."

"I can't believe you actually want to do this."

"Why not? It's not like I want you sculpting some other dude naked, right?"

"I guess I can see your point."

"And I'm pretty sure this will somehow end in sex. So I'm looking forward to that."

"You're gonna have to stand there for a while, you know."

"I'm in it for the long haul."

A wide smile spread across her face. "So am I, Reed." I knew she wasn't just referring to today.

"Remember the first night I ever came to your apartment, when I said Allison dodged a bullet?"

"Yeah."

Placing my hands on her shoulders and looking into her eyes, I said, "I was the one who dodged a bullet, Charlotte. I can't imagine having gone on to marry her. I would have never known that my one true love was still out there. What I feel for you is beyond what I've ever felt in my life. Even the MS . . . everything had to happen exactly the way it did for me to be with you. I wouldn't change anything if it still meant finding you. I will always be grateful to Allison for leaving me, because I now know that I have a deeper capacity to love than I ever thought possible. It would've been tragic to never realize that. I just hope I can make you as happy as you make me."

"You've already made me the happiest woman in the world. I don't know if it was the magic of the dress, or fate, or God, but something brought me to you. There was never a moment where I really doubted that I was meant to find you and meant to be yours. I always felt your love for me, even when you were trying to fight it like hell. That was what kept me from giving up on you. I will never give up on you, Reed. I'm in this for the long haul, because I want to be. Do you understand?"

"I understand that now, baby."

"Good."

I smiled. "Shall we get going into the art room?"

"After you."

Charlotte turned the lights on and began gathering her supplies. "Normally, I would just do the torso. But I would love to try to sculpt below the waist."

"You want to mold my cock? Do you have enough clay?" I winked.

"I can make do."

"If you want me hard, take off your shirt. It's only fair if I have to stand here naked for an hour that I get something to look at, too."

To my delight, she obliged, agreeing to sculpt me with her beautiful tits hanging out.

It was fascinating to watch her so focused. She'd placed a big slab of clay onto a metal pole and used what looked like a spatula to smooth around it.

At one point, she said, "I just have to get some water. I'll be right back."

This was it. This was my moment to put my plan into place. I somehow had to stay *hard* for this to work.

Stay hard.

Stay hard.

Without Charlotte and her beautiful tits in the room, it wasn't guaranteed. I reached over to my pants pocket and took out the small velvet pouch, tying the drawstrings to form a loop at the end. I slipped it over my still rigid cock and let the bag hang from my dick as if it were an ornament.

When she returned, I resumed my stoic pose and waited for her to notice.

A few seconds later, she looked down. "What is that?"

"What do you mean?"

"That black thing hanging from your cock."

Stifling my laughter, I said, "I don't know what you're talking about."

She tilted her head. "Reed . . ."

I looked down. "Oh! This . . . yes." I nudged my head. "Why don't you come here and see."

She wiped her hands and slowly approached before carefully sliding the velvet pouch off me.

"What's inside of this, Reed?"

I took it from her. "While sculpting me nude completes your Fuck-It List for now, I happened to add a very important item to mine today, one that my life would not be complete without." I got down on one knee and opened the pouch, taking out the two-carat, pear-shaped halo diamond engagement ring. "Charlotte Darling, will you help me make my ultimate bucket-list wish come true? Will you be my wife?"

My hand trembled as I placed the ring on her finger. It gave her pause. She looked down at me, and I smiled reassuringly, refusing to believe it was a tremor and convincing myself it was just nerves.

Not now. Fuck you.

Tears were streaming down her cheeks. "Yes! Yes, of course, I will!"

Still stark naked, I lifted my topless beauty into the air. "You've just made me the happiest man on earth."

"I can't believe you pulled this off without me knowing."

"It wasn't hard."

She gave me a tug. "I beg to differ."

EPILOGUE

CHARLOTTE

Twenty-six years later

Sparkling chandeliers lit up the rustic villa that was adorned with towering centerpieces of lush flowers. Cascading fabric draped from the ceilings completed the fairy tale–like ambience.

As I gazed out onto the dance floor, I couldn't help wishing that Iris were here to see her great-granddaughter get married.

Overcome with emotion, I reached for Reed's hand as we watched our daughter, Tenley Iris, and her new husband, Jake, dance to "What a Wonderful World" by Louis Armstrong.

Tenley undeniably had her father's genes—darker hair and dark eyes—while our son, Thomas, took after me with blond hair and blue eyes. My focus wandered to the head table. Sitting next to his uncle Max, Thomas was grinning from ear to ear as he watched his big sister dance with her new husband. It was nice to have him home from Brown for the weekend.

In the other corner of the room, my two brothers, Jason and Justin, sat with their families. We'd gotten closer over the years and spent every other holiday out in Texas. I was never able to figure out who my father was. My brothers said my mother told them that it was a boy passing through town who ended up moving away. Even with Reed's investigator on the case, we never found him.

When the dance ended, the DJ announced that it was time for the father-daughter dance. Goosebumps peppered my arms.

I looked down at Reed. "Are you ready?"

"Yes," he said without hesitation.

Tenley approached and offered her hands to her father, who slowly and carefully rose from his wheelchair. While my husband wasn't bound to one, he needed to take frequent breaks when on his feet all day. I knew he'd wanted to save all his energy for this dance. His performance at the church earlier in the day had already taken a lot out of him, emotionally and physically. My beautiful husband had surprised us all when he finally gave that performance he'd always wanted to by singing with the church choir during the wedding ceremony. He'd even had a short solo part.

Over the years, the MS had crept up, but it hadn't taken away Reed's spirit and determination. There were good days, when he felt stronger than others, and overall the good days outweighed the bad. But the MS was no longer something we could ignore—as much as I'd wanted to.

When "Dream a Little Dream" by Cass Elliot started playing, I got chills. Tenley had chosen that song because Reed used to sing it to her when she was a little girl.

With their hands intertwined, they rocked back and forth to the rhythm of the song. He was doing everything in his power to not show that he was struggling. I was so incredibly moved that Reed was able to do this. It meant so much, especially because of the last item he'd added to his bucket list: *Dance with Tenley on Her Wedding Day.*

So this dance was everything.

Tears clouded my vision. The guests cheered especially hard when the dance ended. Tenley and Reed walked hand in hand over to me, and the three of us huddled in an embrace.

Reed then promptly returned to his seat in the wheelchair. I knew he'd used every ounce of energy he had for that dance and needed to rest. He was going to dance with his daughter today if it was the last thing he ever did.

Tenley scurried away, leaving Reed and me alone.

Leaning down to kiss him, I said, "You did great."

He smiled mischievously up at me. "You know what I would love to finish off this day?"

"What?"

"You riding me on this thing."

Some things never change.

"Sex on wheels?" I smiled.

We both broke out into laughter. Reed had told me the story about the guy in Central Park who'd made an impression on him all those years ago. We'd often joke about "sex on wheels" whenever he had to use the chair. And we had indeed had "sex on wheels," plenty of times.

Tenley hung on to the skirt of her gown as she rushed toward me. "Hey, Mom. I don't want to dance around with the note in my dress. Something might happen to it. Can you take it for me?"

"Of course." Lifting up the material, I carefully unpinned the note.

As her something blue, Tenley had wanted to pin the blue note that Reed had given me on our wedding day—the same note I'd worn inside of my own dress.

"Thank you, Mom." She bent down to give her father a kiss before running off.

As Reed fixed his eyes on his daughter across the room, I smiled at the look of pride on his face. Before I put it away in my bejeweled clutch purse, I reminisced as I read the note.

From the desk of Reed Eastwood

To my one true love and soulmate, Charlotte,

I don't need the help of a poet to articulate my love for you. But to try to reduce it to a couple of sentences could never do my feelings justice. Even my wildest dreams could never have conjured up the level of love in my heart today. You're beyond my wildest dreams. My love for you is infinite. You. Are. Everything.

Your love,

Reed

ACKNOWLEDGMENTS

First and foremost, thank you to all the bloggers who enthusiastically spread the news about our books. We are eternally grateful for all that you do. Your hard work is what helps to build excitement and introduces us to readers who may otherwise never have heard of us.

To Julie—Thank you for your friendship, daily support, and encouragement. We can't wait for "moore" of your phenomenal books coming soon!

To Luna—What would we do without you? Thank you for being there for us day in and day out as a friend and so much more, and for blessing us with your incredible creative talent.

To Erika—Thank you for your friendship, love, and support. Your eagle eye is pretty awesome, too.

To our agent, Kimberly Brower—Thank you for working tirelessly to help see this book come to fruition. We are so lucky to call you a friend as well as an agent. We're excited for the year ahead and are grateful that you will be there with us every step of the way.

To our amazing editor at Montlake, Lindsey Faber, and to Lauren Plude and the entire Montlake team—Thank you for working so hard to ensure that *Hate Notes* was the best that it could be. It was an absolute pleasure working with you.

To J. Iron Word—Thank you for allowing us to use your beautiful quote that inspired our story.

Last but not least, to our readers—We keep writing because of your hunger for our stories. We love surprising you and hope you enjoyed this book as much as we did writing it. Thank you as always for your enthusiasm, love, and loyalty. We cherish you!

Much love,

Penelope and Vi

SIGN UP!

Dear Readers,

    We hope you've enjoyed reading *Hate Notes*! Please sign up for our mailing list so that we can keep in touch. We often send exclusive bonus material and stories only to our mailing list members!

https://www.subscribepage.com/MailingListSignup

Much love,

Vi and Penelope

ABOUT THE AUTHORS

Penelope Ward © 2016 Angela Rowlings; Vi Keeland © 2017 Irene Bella Photography

Penelope Ward is a *New York Times, USA Today*, and #1 *Wall Street Journal* bestselling author. She grew up in Boston with five older brothers and spent most of her twenties as a television news anchor. Penelope resides in Rhode Island with her husband, son, and beautiful daughter, who has autism. She is the author of more than twenty novels, including *Stepbrother Dearest, Neighbor Dearest, Drunk Dial,* and the #1 *Wall Street Journal* bestseller *RoomHate*.

Vi Keeland is a #1 *New York Times*, #1 *Wall Street Journal*, and *USA Today* bestselling author. Her titles have appeared on more than ninety bestseller lists and are currently translated into twenty languages. She resides in New York with her husband and their three children, where she is living out her own happily ever after with the boy she met at age six.

Together, Vi and Penelope have written *Cocky Bastard, Stuck-Up Suit, Playboy Pilot, Mister Moneybags, British Bedmate, Rebel Heir,* and *Rebel Heart*. Visit them at www.vikeeland.com and www.penelopewardauthor.com.

Connect with Vi Keeland

Facebook Fan Group: www.facebook.com/groups/ViKeelandFanGroup

Facebook: www.facebook.com/pages/Author-Vi-Keeland/
  435952616513958

Website: www.vikeeland.com

Twitter: @ViKeeland; https://twitter.com/ViKeeland

Instagram: @Vi_Keeland; http://instagram.com/Vi_Keeland

Connect with Penelope Ward

Facebook Private Fan Group: www.facebook.com/groups/
  PenelopesPeeps

Facebook: www.facebook.com/penelopewardauthor

Website: www.penelopewardauthor.com

Twitter: @PenelopeAuthor; https://twitter.com/PenelopeAuthor

Instagram: @penelopewardauthor; http://instagram.com/
  PenelopeWardAuthor

WITHDRAWN
UPPER MERION TOWNSHIP LIBRARY